A FAREWELL TO PRAGUE

A Farewell to Prague

DESMOND HOGAN

faber and faber

LONDON · BOSTON

First published in 1995
by Faber and Faber Limited
3 Queen Square, London, WC1N 3AU

Phototypeset by Intype, London
Printed and bound in Great Britain by
Mackays of Chatham PLC, Chatham, Kent

A CIP record for this book is available from the
British Library

ISBN 0–571–17427–2

Author's acknowledgement:
This book was written with the help of the DAAD

2 4 6 8 10 9 7 5 3 1

In memory of Jonathan Warner, with gratitude.

wie heisst es, dein Land
hinterm Berg, hinterm Jahr?
Ich weiss, wie es heisst.
Wie das Wintermärchen, so heisst es,
es heisst wie das Sommermärchen,
das Dreijahreland deiner Mutter, das war es,
das ists,
es wandert überallhin, wie die Sprache,
wirf sie weg, wirf sie weg,
dann hast du sie wieder, wie ihn,
den Kieselstein aus
der Mährischen Senke,
den dein Gedanke nach Prag trug . . .

                    Paul Celan, 'Es ist alles anders'

what is it called, your country
behind the mountain, behind the year?
I know what it's called.
Like the winter's tale, it is called,
it's called like the summer's tale,
your mother's threeyearland, that's what it was,
what it is,
it wanders off everywhere, like language,
throw it away, throw it away,
then you'll have it again, like that other thing,
the pebble from
the Moravian hollow
which your thought carried to Prague . . .

Translated by Michael Hamburger

'What are you going to do now?'

'Don't know. Go to Africa.'

Robin had his arms about me and behind him I could see the mecca of dirty-black and nebulous South-East London high-rises.

We were on the eleventh floor of a high-rise.

As he held me, I was touching in my mind the great naked statue of David in Florence I'd travelled to once from University College, Dublin, having climbed steps to it, finding it wet from November rain.

I was in the same gesture with Robin as I'd been with a girl two weeks before, in a high-rise in Catford, who'd had the sudden inspiration to try to change my sexuality. A teacher from the polytechnic I had worked in part-time, she had stood, naked from the waist up, for this embrace. I was wearing a white sleeveless vest which had a theatrical ancientness. The woman who held me was from Antrim.

She'd told me that night about a young boy with a tattoo showing a gentian-violet swallow bearing a bunch of pink roses on his right arm. She used to sleep with him on the beaches of North Antrim the previous summer. He'd run around at night in the full regalia of the IRA, come home in the small hours when his mother would be waiting to give him a box on the ears. One night he went out in his regalia to inspect a place where he knew Semtex to be buried and was shot dead by the British Army.

Robin had a semi-troglodyte face that always looked as if it was going to apologize for something, sable curls barely held back from it. His cheeks had a high violet colouring and he had large lips, the lower lip always pulsating a little, which had been sealed by many people, men and women.

His mother had called him Robin because he was born in the year Robin Lee Graham had sailed from South Africa to California and to remind them all there was a photograph over the piano in Pulvensey showing Robin Lee Graham with sun-kissed hair holding up a dorado fish.

The cassette player was playing a Marvin Gaye song:

Has anyone seen my old friend Martin?
Can you tell me where he's gone?
He freed a lot of people but it seems the good die young.
I just looked around and he's gone.

From the corner of my eye, reflected in a mirror, I could see a buff-coloured dole card beside a few tubes of oil paint. The flat belonged to a friend of Robin's. We had spent the night here, sleeping on mattresses a few feet away from one another because Robin was covered in spots he'd gotten from sleeping with a girl on the heath in Pulvensey. She had tried to kill herself when he wouldn't intensify the relationship, slashing her wrists, was put in the mental hospital in Norwich, dyed her hair cowslip-pale and alizarin and haze-blue and escaped in a diseased bituminous fur coat, taking the boat to France.

Robin was teaching English at the moment in Hastings. He'd come to London for Friday night.

'Well, I'm off to Prague in a few weeks,' Robin said.

'I've been to Prague.'

'I know.'

Suddenly I started crying. I broke down crying a lot now. My mind seemed to stop and the world blurred. There were a few weeks when even walking was difficult, walking was walking through torpor and if not it was an intoxicating experience. A pendulum inside propelled me back and forth. There was no way forward, no further lap I could make, and the only thing that seemed possible was to exit, to finalize

2

myself to save others trouble and to preserve intact achieve-
ment, totality.

Words had stopped for me, the ability to speak, the ability to
express. And instead of words came images from childhood.

A drummer in the brass band who'd emigrated to Glasgow,
a collector of cigarette cards showing athletes, always wore
nice suits, sometimes floral waistcoats, became engaged to a
member of the Legion of Mary in Glasgow, and then one day,
inexplicably, in a suit, hankie in his breast pocket.

A boy with a Teddy-boy quiff who'd chalked a billiard cue
in the men's club and played billiards the night his mother
died.

Later he went to South Africa for a few years, then became a
singer in England, turned alcoholic, lived as a tramp. Recently
I had seen a scrawled sign for his singing outside an Irish pub
in London. 'It's the crack here every Saturday night.'

His name had been Guy 'Micko' Delaney. 'Micko' for a
father who had left his mother, gone to fight in the war, lived
with a Russian woman in Crouch End and died – they said of
drugs – in the late nineteen-forties.

> Cocaine Bill and Morphine Sue
> Were walking down the avenue.

He was in Berlin in 1945 and had brought home a girl's Holy
Communion wreath, lilies appliquéd on lace, that he had
found in a wrecked house. Mrs Delaney had buried it with him
when he died.

Micko was the bad element of our town. I was Micko now,
or had become so these past months.

Robin and I said goodbye at Kennington tube station. An
Alsatian, not too big, leapt into a youth's arms in the waste
ground nearby.

'I'll write.'

Flashy-coloured or old technicoloured postcards in my
mind: a boy in mod clothes stealing the scene from a pair of

nuns on Salthill prom; a guard directing traffic under Nelson's Pillar.

I walked home. A baby was crawling around the window of a pawnbroker's in Camberwell. Lampposts were swathed with posters for wrestling, a Mardi Gras incoherence about the way they were pasted over one another, a *bricolage* of names like Kendo Nagazaki and Ravishing Robbie Hagan, of mammal-like breasts and Titan heads in balaclavas.

'I've got more scars on my back than I can count,' a stooped old man was telling another old man outside a bookie's in Peckham.

The Appleby Fair would be beginning just about now, black boxing gloves embossed with red satin roses hanging in the windows of vardos. I'd once known a boy from Derry who lived with an adoptive mother in Appleby for a while.

In Catford, outside a shop which had fluorescent green pens in the window, pictures of reclining nymphs in Scandinavian forests, cups with ferny patterns, Limerick Benny was singing.

He was wearing a black hat and, although it was summer, a black overcoat.

'Tis not for Limerick that I sigh though I love her in my soul.'

Perhaps it was because I'd just left Robin, but I heard the words of an English folk song and the English folk song in turn conjured a landscape in Ireland with an insistent narrative.

Hurrah for the Scarlet and the Blue
Bayonets flashing like lightening to the beat of the military
  drum
No more will we go harvesting
Together in the golden corn.
I took the good king's shilling
And am off tomorrow morn.

The landscape, like the words, was heraldic; the eighty English acres my father's people had come from Tipperary to tend the time the railway station was being built, the coral-red station building against the bog.

In my flat I picked up a tiny photograph of a woman in a crisply fluted black coat and white saucer hat by a porch adorned with traveller's joy, her legs like the legs of malnutrition. On the mantelpiece beside her was a framed photograph of two Teddy boys in the middle of a street, a row of council houses running behind them, a man bending his head into the distance and a row of trees in a conflagration of bloom. Close by was a snapshot of me and my parents in Bray in the early fifties. Behind us, advertisements for Bradmola and Dundyl.

I picked up a letter that was on the mantelpiece, partly for decoration, partly because it had never been resolved.

Hearty congratulations to you both on the arrival of your little son. I was delighted to get the good news, and aren't you the lucky one not to have been kept waiting too long. I just got the news before the pater arrived on the 3 p.m. bus from Trim.

I am sending a wee frock for the baby. You know all the shopping one can do from a bed. I feel middling. The same routine still, from bed to school and back to bed.

A red bus to a house which has a white sifted feel where traveller's joy comes in summer, a runaway bit of white fence in a field behind. There was also another bus in my mind. Eleanor travelling south in California, through a landscape of mustard fields, green mountains, blue skies, red earth, a landscape which had crowd scenes of people from India who had come here because rice and soya beans were grown in the area. It was some months after she had arrived in the States. She'd been living in Sacramento in a hostel mainly for Hawaiian girls and some days she did not have the fare for work. In her mind she was writing to me, telling me of her new life, her new religion.

Birds had gathered on the wires along the road.

I'd passed through Sacramento in the small hours this last Christmas, a woman with pigtails, leading her six little boys,

5

all of them with chinquapin eyes and chipmunk mouths, off the bus.

I knew her to be in Berlin just now, with her second husband, out of reach. But at Summerleaze in Cornwall a few weeks before, where I'd gone with a group of Bangladeshi children, when I'd been pulled out to sea in an undertow, it was her image and the voice of a Bangladeshi child which brought me in.

'Come on, Des. Come on.'

A girl with sculpted face, sculpted olive-yellow hair. I saw her in a café when I was in the sea, a German café whereas once it had been an American café, a red bulb over the upholstery of rich crimson at the door, a little picture of a village with rose roofs by a lake in a mountain valley by her shoulder, a solvent handbag beside her.

I was given a coffee after coming in from the sea, in a miserly-looking sand-dune café of white and teal-blue which had a big sign saying 'Special offer on Tuesdays. Fish and chips £1.55.'

And then we drove away from the sea and visited a church in which there was a picture of a worried king, a gold and black check jerkin on him. Outside, a man in wine socks, fawn trousers sat on a bench, and harkened when he heard my Irish accent. I sat on a bench near him. The names on the graves were Trythall, Stoat, Willis.

After nearly drowning there were flowers I was grateful to see, tucked into the crevices of this town of big masculine buildings, like Clonmel in Ireland, where my father had once worked in the hosiery and shirt department of a shop.

'We will give you a position at a salary of £3.10 per week. (Three pounds, ten shillings.) Please come soon as possible.'

I'd lost my part-time job after my breakdown, and now had to start anew.

By now, Robin would be arriving at the house he was staying in in Hastings, boats piled up under the castle nearby, gulls dropping mussels.

6

On her wedding day my mother had worn a froth of white lace on her head, her eyes frightened.

There was mental illness on both sides of our family. I had often imagined what it was like, but now that I was on the other side, that I'd lost what was most precious to me – flow – I was faced with what seemed an undifferentiated future.

I looked around me, wanting to be held by someone, wanting to be in someone's arms, but there was nobody there, only the ghost of a girl's arms, hopeless conjugality, of Robin's arms, of a young Englishman with a face full of indigo grooves, and I thought of my first embrace, with a teacher of French on a sofa in 1968. In her flat.

There had been oak trees in bloom outside, and she had remarked on the abortion law which had just been passed in England.

Last night, as we walked the streets of Soho, we met a tramp who said he'd been a music teacher until recently in a South London public school. A horde of destitute people passed us, heads bent, most of their rucksacks sooty but one of them bright orange. And before we got a tube from Charing Cross Station we passed a tramp who was sleeping just outside South Australia House, a picture of vineyards in the window above him and two white seals snogging.

I met Carl Witherspoon in a café in Soho.

He lived both in Berlin and London, his mother a rich German woman, his father English.

He'd recently spent a few days in a town on the border of Portugal and Spain. Sunday morning in a café, a boy in holy communion costume, red rosette on his white shirt, watercolour blue eyes, a few men in dove-grey suits, an old man with a bottle of red wine in his satchel staring at him. A mosaic of the Immaculate Conception on the wall, a swish of royal blue sash over her white robe. St Martin de Porres among the vodka and port.

Outside was flat land where white ignited cauliflower shapes bloomed.

Carl had wondered what had brought him here, what he was doing here. He went all over the place, a tickertape of journeys, sometimes losing tickets, sometimes foregoing a journey to one place at the last moment in order to go somewhere else. His life felt wasted, hopeless. He wanted to die.

A woman came into the café and asked in a religious tone, almost bowing her head, for a *religieuse*.

I'd been to Carl's flat in Berlin two years before. In the bathroom, on a cabinet, had been numerous bottles of milk of magnesia tablets from England.

Carl had tributaries of black hair which vaporized over his forehead and he had asparagus-green eyes which could assume a popping effect at will. He got up, took a few steps away from the table, then came back.

I thought of the mental hospital at home, three particular sister buildings, bony windows, high chimneys, a batch of dead elms brushing against the windows, some of the windows savagely latticed, the lattices painted gleaming white.

The young man at the next table was talking more intently, as if to drown us, about the best poem in Bengali about premature ejaculation.

Carl looked at me, and it was as if he realized that I wasn't of his class, that his madness, unlike mine, was immured, and as if to dissolve the sympathy he suddenly said, 'I've been offered a job at £750 a week.'

I walked to the South Bank after we parted and met a beggar boy, one of his shoes pink, the other blue, who told me how he'd run away from home in the Midlands when he was twelve. Recently he had gone back for his sister's wedding in the village he was from, Ashby de la Zouch, disguised in the uniform of the Queen's Own Regiment, posing as boyfriend to a cousin; no one had recognized him.

I recognized the village as being that of a fisherman who

used to come to our town each spring when I was a child and teenager, a place off the route north to Holyhead and Ireland.

Further along the South Bank some men were doing Morris dances against the orange sunset. They were adorned in beads, sashes, and were waving batons. 'The size doesn't matter. It's how you use it,' one little man cried as he threw his baton into the air, a middle-aged woman tramp with silver spikey hair looking on from her array of rags which were dolled up by the sunset.

Limerick Benny sat on a bench in Catford Arcade shouting: 'I believe in the controls of 747s.' He looked up, spreading his arms out. 'All the cunts singing and dancing up there and me on the ground.' An old man limped by, a green plastic flower in his lapel, a green handkerchief in his breast pocket, a pheasant feather in his hat and an earring which looked like a Russian cross hanging from his right ear. Further along the arcade, under the huge papier mâché cat splayed above it, there were four evangelists who looked like the Beatles, crew cuts, polo necks, little bibles unerringly in their hands.

'Latecomers. End of the day people. They hear the call too late. Try to enter by the back door but often find it's jammed.'

I rang up J. M. Tiernan looking for a job on a building site. They had no need of anyone.

I went to Catford Job Centre looking for a job. A honey-haired girl looked at me as if I was crazy.

An evicted family huddled beside a cluster of Tesco bags.

A man worked a glove puppet towards the traffic.

A youth cycled by with a mongrel on the trailer behind his bicycle.

'My life means something since I met Jesus' and 'Love is something you do' billboards said outside a hut of a church on Stanstead Road, which was surrounded by lavender bushes.

Outside the ancient tram man's toilet at the top of Stanstead

Road a dispatch rider paused. He wore a red bandana around his right wrist.

'The worst danger is scatty-brained women. They're suicidal. Rob, he worked as a courier in London, in New York; was killed when he went back to work on the buildings in Rye, walking down the street. It's time to go. The English girls are only alive from the shoulders up. I'll pick up a girl in France and work on the vineyards. It's time to go.'

A postcard came from Prague. Wenceslas Square, a haze of salvia on the front of the museum, trails of cloud having made it half-way across the sky.

I could hear Robin's affected worry.

Went to this café where a really old woman in a long red wig and crazy clothes came up and sat beside me, batted her huge eyelids, and whispered *'Lasst Blumen sprechen.'*

She was wearing a ra-ra dress the first evening she came up to me, blue with white polka dots, a little black cloak with a gold clasp – the lining rose-madder. A little bunch of paper violets on the cloak. Her wig was ginger, reaching down to her waist, tressed in many parts, confluences of tresses in it. Block high heels were sawdust-coloured and harlequin stockings cream. She batted her false, mahogany-coloured eyelashes, some of the pearl around her eyes lit up, bowed, sat down.

As she waited for her drink, her head coyly turned to one side, she hummed *'Ich Kann es nicht Verstehen dass die Rosen Blühen.'* 'I Know Not Why the Roses Bloom.'

Some soldiers in sandy uniforms came through the café, inspecting identity cards, and took off a young bespectacled man, somewhat unshaven, in a vermilion T-shirt.

The band resumed then with 'You Must Have Been a Beautiful Baby.' Behind them was a painting of the Three Graces – one of them elderly, her white hair in a bun – being attended by monkeys, a parrot hovering overhead.

You could still see the red of salvia through the lime trees outside. The neon signs on the opposite side of the street were quiet ones – Diskotek and Machino Export Bulharska.

The old woman's eyelids accelerated every few minutes.

There were huddles of young men at a few tables, many rings on their fingers, striped trousers popular with them, tongues on their shoes. One young man with hair like Goldilocks kept looking over at the old woman.

When the band played 'La Paloma' she said, 'My song,' and sang with it.

Later that evening an accordionist played the same song at the top of Wenceslas Square, under the lime trees, and a couple danced and a man in a white workcoat let himself free from a sausage kiosk and put a lighted cigarette in the accordionist's mouth.

The woman dancing was wearing a daisied navy dress and white bobby socks and I thought of Mrs Delaney who dressed this way when she was working for us. After her husband died she started getting electric shock treatment. She was very proud of it. Being strapped in, electrodes clamped on to her forehead. She used to walk in from the mental hospital, past the two-storey Victorian house beside an Elizabethan ruined castle.

Then one day her bones broke under the electric shock treatment and she died. That was the day her son played billiards.

The ninety-year-old lady who lived a few houses away from me was out sweeping the leaves the morning I left for Prague. 'I was down in Margate yesterday, loafing around.' She was eager to tell me. She wore a long adamantine necklace. Her husband was killed in the war and she still spoke about him as if he were alive. She frequently hummed 'We'll Be Lit Up When the Lights Go Out in London.'

Hedgehogs, owls, starlings lived in this grove.

She reached out her hand and touched my wrist. 'Have a wonderful time wherever you go.'

On the train into London, in the middle of a conversation about work, a woman suddenly leaned towards a man and whispered, 'You've got to suit the horse and the horse suit you.' It was just as we were passing the tinker encampment, roses in pots that were swan-shaped outside modern caravans, and geraniums on ironwork above the doors of little huts.

In the latter part of 1968 there were two photographs in my room. One of Nguyen Thanh Nam, a prophet who lived up a coconut tree in Vietnam, and one of a woman, lamé stole around her neck, kneeling on the front of a tank in Prague, arms outstretched.

There were tanks at Prague airport the first time I arrived. Inside, people from sundry nations were having cocktails and beers. By the exit there were a row of stalls, one of which had matchstick angels with fluted dresses under glass. In a cavernous underground toilet there was a picture pinned to the wall showing a funfair by the azure waters of a Russian port.

I got the bus into the city. A broom stood at the back of the bus. An old couple walked by outside, holding hands, the woman holding a scarlet handbag in her other hand. Viburnum cut the avenue. A little man in a black beret and persimmon shirt kept consulting a little fat brown-covered dictionary he had with him. The high-rises on the way in were like the high-rises of the suburbs of Paris where I'd stayed in 1968.

Wenceslas Square on that first day: lime trees in bloom on a downsloping pavement; flanks of ice-cream awash with viridian syrup in plastic tubs in a window; fat creamy cakes called Budapest with wide-brimmed chocolate papal hats on them; a young man in shorts and white workcoat darting between buffets in a sudden downpour; amber make nude statues over a magazine shop; a man in a buffet cleaning up, a disabled hand outheld, like an unpeeled prawn; a dreamy-eyed woman in the same buffet, her white workcoat stained lemon, like butcher's blobs. There was a young tinker in Lewisham called Foncie who had a pen-pal in Prague and one recent summer, according to legend, he journeyed to Berlin to meet her in Friedrichstrasse.

High-rise buildings, bluish, like another city, on the horizon, the yellow and green fields slightly carmined with poppies. I got off another red bus. There was a gypsy family at the bus stop, a gradation of them, father, mother, two sisters, a brother, tattoos on some of their wrists. It had rained torrentially and suddenly the sun came out, the grey sky with a rust tint like an orange galvanized roof on a shed which was part of the panorama behind our house in County Galway. A boy sat on a stool in the meadow, a plastic bag of orange in his arms. A woman with fungus-like veins on her legs stood by the bus stop, a little away from the gypsy family. And for some reason there were flowers in a glass jar, isolated, in the meadow.

I had to get away from London. I had a brother who'd been a monk in County Waterford. He left and came to London, followed me, surveyed me. You were compounded in *clan*. When he entered the café I frequented one day, looking around, an old lady tramp seated near him over tea, I dashed into the lavatory and locked myself in.

Some people said living in London was an escape from Ireland, but there were more people from County Galway in London than there were in County Galway. While I lived in Dublin I met middle-class people. In London I had to deal with family again.

Every day I saw the images: Irishmen with red faces, chipped noses, tottering along Camberwell Road; a tramp wearing a silver Bridget's cross on a pendant playing at a UN squadron

pinball machine in a café in Kilburn, a girl companion alongside her with a blue ribbon in her hair, her cheeks the red of the
Virgin Mary's cheeks on roadsides in Ireland.

Afterwards, when I had the breakdown, I dreamt of it over and
over again, this place where I came alive after the not so much
death-existence but fretful, shadowy one in London; sweet-
peas, sunflowers, geraniums, hollyhocks in the gardens at the
foot of high-rises; rabbits in pens; old people talking to one
another from deck chairs; tarmacadam tarnished with spill-
ages of coal; groundsel, elder, warts of poppies in the grass;
young Africans wandering around in happy huddles; a
woman in a T-shirt showing a fighter-jet wheeling a child;
a song blasting out from a high-rise, 'I Love Your Daughter, I
Love Your Son'; washing decorating every balcony, pink the
favourite colour; dead lakes in the distance. I lived on the
eighth floor, in a bare room which had plywood walls. One
day I looked out and saw what I had not noticed before – a
field spanned by blue chicory.

I made love in this room to a long-haired boy called Radvj
whom I met on a path in the fields. He was from Bratislava. He
was wearing gooseberry-green bermudas and told me he was
looking for somewhere to stay. He stood proudly in front of
the bed before getting in, showing off his genitals. There was a
tattoo on his left shoulder which depicted a cairn.
    'The quiet sculpture of your body,' I thought.
    'You've got a beautiful body.'
    'Not as beautiful as yours.'
    He told me of his favourite sexual memory, being fucked by
an older boy in a field at night, season of the gathering of the
hay, while he looked into the boy's eyes.
    I wanted to smell his buttocks. I wanted to smell the pink
T-shirt thrown in a heap on the floor. I wanted to return to life.

14

I thought of Foncie, the tinker boy, my nearest connection to life in London. His twin brother, Vincent, had been killed by a car near the encampment when they were six. An uncle was supposed to be minding him. Later, that uncle went to Brighton and drowned himself.

Porridge every morning of his life; at seventeen a job with a cousin's painting business; first sex with a Chinese prostitute on Lee Road; the pubs of the West End marauded in large, flashy groups.

With every wedding there was an essential video. Though born in England they often journeyed to Ireland – the occasion of the erection of a grandmother's headstone, of a wedding. London tinker young mixed with the young of Ireland on hills in Cork city on Sunday nights.

There was a car dump near the encampment. A famous actress had gone there on a supposed errand to buy ginger ale, taken alcohol and pills and been found dead by a tinker dog.

Foncie too had felt the life being dragged out of him by London and, with a crest 'Wild Ireland' on the elbow of his jacket, he'd gone to Berlin and met a Czech girl on Friedrichstrasse. They never corresponded again. She'd been carrying white chrysanthemums. They'd strolled to the temple-like building nearby where two helmeted soldiers stood guard by the flame to the unknown soldier, the lime trees lit up, in the late afternoon August sunshine, in biblical incandescence.

With Radvj I dreamt of tinkers on a cart passing a shield of oak trees just outside our town in County Galway and shouting after them a customary tinker farewell, 'See you in Claremorris.' My eyes consumed then in a colour like the pink T-shirt of my guest, who left abruptly early in the morning.

The Prodigal leaving his father's house, corn being loaded distantly, a glimpse, just as it was in a photograph, of an ancestor in a cloche hat bending over the grave of my mother's youngest sister.

Rest in peace, O dearest Una
Thou art happy
Thou art blest
Earthly cares and sorrows ended.

The headstones are splattered with lichen and meadow barley grows in profusion in the graveyard.

Women bearing baskets of redcurrants across fields that were lime-coloured, poppies on stalks that had seized up in the field, men raking lime hay, an azure tooth of a small mountain above them.

A pudgy, slightly obese Christ child in a see-through gauze dress, the edges of the dress gilded.

Lambeth Palace, the foreign painter having endowed a pearly light to Westminster Bridge, a tiny figure in a red swallow coat supporting himself against a privet hedge, back turned. The main character in the little film I made was dressed like that. An Irish poet in London at the end of the eighteenth century and beginning of the nineteenth. His favourite song had been 'Lillibullero' and he'd drunk himself to death in Catford. On his tombstone in Lewisham you can read 'Let fall a holy tear.'

An uncle of mine, my mother's half-brother, had worked in a jeweller's shop near Lambeth Palace in the mid-nineteen-forties. When he was a teenager he'd joined the army in Mullingar; the Twenty-seventh Infantry Battalion. Then he'd moved to England. Wrote a card home, 'Rotten lonely here.' A grey embankment scene with painted wallflowers on it. Fought in Egypt, wore a hat like a funny-shaped brioche and desert shorts. Returning to England he worked in the jeweller's shop in Lambeth and became engaged to an English girl with lavish ginger-blonde hair. One night, when they were dancing in Forest Hill, just after the compère announced, 'Please take your partners for the last waltz', and the band started up with, 'Who's the lucky man who's going home your way?', the hall was hit by a doodlebug and the place confounded. He'd wandered through all the nearby hospitals looking for her, and eventually heard her screaming in one of them. But it was because she had toothache. He died a few years after the war. No one really knew why.

His sister, my mother's half-sister, the woman who wrote to my mother on my birth, also died young. She died of tuberculosis two weeks after my birth.

An open-air dance in Prague. Two old ladies dancing together, one with white hair, the other black. The black-haired one is the taller, she wears dark glasses and her mouth grins like that of an American tough guy. There are men in suits, and men in white shirts and casual trousers. A gipsy woman, in white bobby socks, black high heels, black dress with a white belt on it, is the proudest dancer. She wears a white braid through her long, flattened black hair. The white-haired woman, who is quite frail, is almost throttled in an embrace by the black-haired woman. There is a wood of lime trees around the dance area. I had a black-haired aunt who wouldn't behave herself when I was a child, dancing at the crossroads, especially with young men. Dances which were periodically interrupted by a ferocious display of Irish dancing by girls in dark emerald dresses and cloaks, in black tights. A few funfair swings near the crossroads.

She married a radio expert from Sligo. They opened a pub, but she drove him off. When my grandmother died my aunt wanted to look after my grandfather, in his little town house with the gipsy vardo in the front window, but my mother took him. My aunt became unruly and she died, in one of her reprieves from mental hospital, in her pub.

My first summer in London I stayed a few days with her husband. Walked down the Uxbridge Road on a Saturday afternoon, past a black people's wedding, hair in cornrows, white roses in lapels, to a flat where there were beds in the kitchen. There was a mass card for my aunt, a camellia in her hair, beside a picture of St Bonaventure.

'We put towels over the mirrors the day she died,' a young man who had his shirt off told me.

The old lady in the ginger wig sat at the table across from me tonight, in sailor trousers, sailor top, sailor cap with gold braid around the peak, platform high heels, and kept nodding to me. The orchestra played 'Hong Kong Blues', 'Jeepers Creepers', 'Two Sleepy People', 'You Must Have Been a Beautiful Baby', 'La Mer', 'We'll Meet Again'. Someone had told me that the old lady had owned a hotel on Wenceslas Square which was confiscated in the early fifties, when high-ranking officials were being thrown downstairs to their deaths in Czechoslovakia, when there had been mass rallies in Wenceslas Square, with people like tornado clouds, when trams ran up and down the square, when there was a rendezvous with Stalin's profile around every corner, alongside posters of faded, aquatic-coloured cherries, for even then the Czechs had a fondness for communicating in pictures on the walls.

There was puce-violet kohlrabi in the little shop windows in Prague that summer, and peppers that looked like snoods. Some of the shop windows were mainly yellow, like a Dutch painting, with a few items in them. There were window displays of red hats with ladybird spots on them, and mauve trilbies. Men with satchels full of vodka beside them throwing bread at swans; old men huddling past alabaster-faced Marys with alabaster-coloured lilies, sequined in gold, in front of them. There was a poster for 'The Mikado' everywhere, a poster for Dvorak's 'Requiem', a girl with one eye on it. There was a poster for a Goya exhibition with a man with a letter in one hand which he seemed to be giving you, the word

'*Expulsis*' on it, his other hand missing. Tram number seventeen brought you to Podolí, where naked men waited in the lemon light of a sauna as if for a ceremony, and where a jubilant body-building life-guard congratulated me on being Irish against the dazzle of a pool.

It was part of a journey East, a journey which had begun in Berlin the previous summer.

From the eighth floor of a high-rise, gauze curtains ruffling, it was a look back. It was a city which grew out of little tales I'd written, not knowing where they'd come from, whence a hotel, a crossroads.

It was a city which grew out of the punitive damp of a little flat in Catford. But in coming out of those things it also showed an alternative truth – that life is humbler than art and more loving.

Sometimes, early in the mornings especially, I spoke to her: Amsterdam, you woke crying. I did not know why you were crying.

She was looking at a painting of a huddle of women with hats like geese on them in the Van Gogh Museum and suddenly she turned to me and smiled.

Later that autumn I journeyed to Italy alone, to Florence. Walked along a street where there were salmon-coloured hearts with lace borders under a statue of Mary. I got accommodation in a dormitory in a monastery. There was a broom hanging on the wall at the end of the row of beds on the opposite side to the door.

She started having an affair in Dublin with a boy who came from the countryside near our town, a house with lily of the valley wallpaper in the sitting-room, a house always visited by the tinkers at the same time in spring. He had rooster-orange hair and the same colour was rumoured to be elsewhere on his body.

The following summer she left for the United States.

I heard Rodrigo's 'Concerto d'Arjuanez' today as I was painting walls and it was a miracle. Afterwards I went to the Pacific at Cissy Field. It was very, very deep blue. There was an old Chinese woman there in red socks and I threw a pebble in for you.

Two years later I found her. She had joined a religious group. We stayed in Carmel, with an old Czech man who wore a black beret with a tongue on it. He gave us pancakes with strawberries. He'd left Prague when he was twenty-six.

Then we stayed with an Indian family near Arcadia, and used to watch the elk come down to the ocean, in the fog.

But when she came back to Dublin the following summer a girl, a supposed comrade, attacked me at a party. 'You're incapable of having full physical relations with women except with Eleanor.' She raised a closed fist to indicate an erect penis.

I couldn't make love to Eleanor any more. She went back to California and I left Ireland, carrying impotence, making stories, doing odd jobs.

Sometimes our cities connected up, and we were in the same place, or near one another. But she was always just that girl in the café now, behind a window.

9 August 1987. I sit in a café near the Vltava. Sunset on the edges of women's hair as if on waves of the sea. Boys in asterisk-splattered bermudas skating across Maje Bridge.

'Do you know Seamus Heaney?' a worried-looking boy from a nearby table, who's heard that I'm Irish, comes up and asks me. There are four boys with shaven heads at the next table. A man with a little bullion of a goatee looks as I answer the boy. A man in a beret with a tongue has his head bowed over an empty plate as if in prayer.

There is a boll of light to the left side of Prague Castle.

The orchestra plays 'La Paloma', 'Melancholy Baby', 'As Time Goes By'.

Pictures of robins, clumps of pansies at their feet, ripple, in my mind, into advertisements for Kincora Plug.

There were dead aunts outside the windows of cafés at sunset, and against the Vltava visions of drownings in my town when I was a child, a chain of swimmers across the river searching for a body.

A woman opened a wallet beside me, and instead of the young Slavonic face inside I saw the face of a drowned Teddy boy.

'I'll be watching to see if you go to the altar tomorrow,' his mother admonished him on the Saturday he was drowned, urging him to go to confession. He was laid out in a brown habit. At his funeral a phalanx of liquorice-haired girl-cousins had carried wreaths of purple-carmine roses.

Years later, his father, a widower, put a memorial in the *Connaught Tribune*, where the photograph looked tragically fashionable and the handsomeness savagely unrequited. 'That we might meet merrily in Heaven.'

At night there were the cafés, the one with the lady in the ginger wig, the one by the river, the same repertoire of songs over and over again.

I was troubled by these songs. I could hear my mother's voice through these songs. 'At Night When I Listen to Late Date I'm in Dreamland.'

She and her boyfriends would go to Dublin and dance to Billy Cotton, Ambrose, Jack Hylton, Oscar Rabin.

Then she got tuberculosis, had her lung punctured, refilled. She broke off an engagement because of it but didn't tell her boyfriend, and so left him broken-hearted and bewildered.

Her doctor was in Mullingar: Dr Keenan, Church View. It

was while she was attending him that she met my father. He recoiled when he heard about the tuberculosis, but after a few months proposed to her and they became engaged. He told her about the funeral of his mother in 1926, how it was one of the biggest for many years in East Galway, the blinds drawn on every private house in town as well as on businesses.

Her friends in his town were three Czech sisters and their brother who ran the jeweller's. They liked sweets a lot and in their honour I gazed at chocolate ducks with marzipan legs in windows. They used to leave gifts of boxes of chocolates in my pram.

They had arrived in Ireland after the First World War, orphans, and after spending a few years in an orphanage in Dublin moved around Ireland, looking after jewellery businesses. The brother was epileptic and had visions by the oak trees just outside town.

I shared his visions this summer: a fresco depicting orange trees on the wall; clouds of gnats under lime trees; a cobbled street, violet and pale blue cobbles, a water-pump with a high tiara of black iron-work around it in the middle of the street; a lock on the Vltava, a huge fan of surf in front of it, hundreds of swans just before the lock; a girl in a flowered bonnet and crimson dress in a painting; grapes by a goblet in an illuminated book; a vase with pink nude swimmers on it.

'I see Czechoslovakia as a free spirit over which the body has no power.'

They thought they'd never grow old, but the epileptic died in County Galway. One of the sisters, in old age, married the driver she'd met on a pilgrim bus to Knock, the other two sisters moving to Dublin. The sister who married the bus driver joined them when her husband died. She died, and the eldest sister died, and a sister who permanently hobbled was left. She crossed Ireland to live in an old people's home, a bungalow on top of a hill in Galway, called Ave Maria. She was visited often by my mother. Then she moved to another old people's home on the sea coast outside Galway. When she died she left £17,000 for masses. The eldest one had left me a tablecloth which had yellow flowers on it and green leaves.

The epileptic with his charcoaled face always veered towards the leaves outside town, to pause and see something. Maybe he was looking back at Czechoslovakia, some memory of childhood, the olive-yellows, the sap-greens, the pistachios, the *rose dorés* of Prague, the acacia trees in blossom, the molten rose of summer roofs above houses of tallow and primrose-yellow.

13 August 1987. The Old Jewish Cemetery in Prague. The graffiti outside said 'Who is my love?' 'John Lennon.' 'AIDS.' The headstones are a monsoon. Some are pink-coloured like the undersides of mushrooms. Some are white and with shapes like clefts of snow. Groups of them hug one another. Pairs of them in intimate proximity are like two men talking. There is a shape on one of the headstones like the palace in *Snow White and the Seven Dwarfs*.

Women look down from the windows of the houses around, leaning on the windowsills. Gargoyles rise out of sun-illuminated webs. Alders protect the borders of these seas of headstones and in some places intrude among the headstones, the sun pocketing its way among the leaves above a density of headstones, turning the leaves to gold. Under a cairn on a headstone is a Munich bus ticket with the words 'May the Jewish people find peace. No more oppression.' Under another cairn is a note: 'Life is short. Do what you can to enlighten the world so your epitaph won't be written: Life lived in vain.'

An Ashkenazi Jew sits on a scarlet bench.

The eldest of the Czech sisters had marigold hair, sashes of it. She fell in love with an Englishman who managed the local pencil factory. He'd played the Baron Minho Zeti in the light opera the year the Pontevedrian Embassy in Paris fell down.

She wore brown alpaca suits. It was a brief romance, a winter one.

23

In Dublin, when the sisters lived there, up the road from Red Spot Laundry, Grace's Pub, Costello's Garage, I dined on that tablecloth, drinking tea from white cups with gold handles, and tried to recall how the romance ended but couldn't. It was just an image, the elderly lovers walking out by the oak trees in the direction of the Railway Hotel, long converted into the local army headquarters.

14 August 1987. When I stayed in Paris in 1968, it was in a high-rise like this one. *The Marriage of Giovanni Arnolfini* by Van Eyck on the wall. Stashes of Wagner and Beethoven records and glossy magazines in their assigned corner of the room. I had held a woman who gave French lessons that spring. A woman who used to go to mass in a harlequin hat. Why did she talk about abortion so much?

She'd been having an affair with another teacher in town. A man who played rugby every Sunday afternoon in the asylum grounds. One Sunday, when she felt he had kept her waiting too long, she went looking for him and saw them showering in their brute, grey place, the rugby players of town. Why hadn't she fled there and then, she asked? Why hadn't she gone to the Prague spring or the Paris revolution? Why hadn't she re-immersed herself in the pastels of Europe, Europe where she'd studied for a while? Why hadn't she admitted to herself there and then that sex is sacred and of God, and that to find salvation we must not fool ourselves, just be adventurous and seek holy union with other people, not the animalistic sex of this small town.

The only thing that stood out for me about that summer in France was my first trip to Chartres, the twin spires rising above the cornfields on a grey afternoon. My first summer at University College, Dublin, I returned to Chartres, boys speeding on mopeds on the summer evenings. On one of those evenings I heard a black American girl sing 'There Is a Balm in Gilead' in the cathedral.

Towards the end of my time at university I visited Chartres again, with Eleanor.

'How long have you been together?' an English girl asked us on the bus from Calais to Paris.

'Let's All Go Search for America' was playing.

Eleanor's hair stood out, very blonde, against the windows of the cathedral. We held hands in front of the black pearwood Virgin who was dressed in gold. Afterwards, in Paris, we had chips in Montmartre, a prostitute with ghosted henna hair seated at the open-air table opposite us. We started kissing on the boat back to England and made love in a house in Barnes, dove-coloured squirrels in the garden outside.

I remembered what the teacher of French had said about sex and it seemed prophetic. In Liverpool three black children, Peter, Peter and Paul, sensed the thrall between us and offered to carry our bags to the boat. For some reason I felt a fear, thinking of what should have been exotic, chocolate over the froth of cream of a cappuccino in our favourite late-night café in Dublin.

I hear that the French teacher married a doctor in Galway, lives in a house in a miasma of white houses by the bay, has four children with deeply nationalistic names. I hear that her hair is still red, that she wears beautiful clothes to art openings, that there's something beautiful and grieving about her face, and that she does charitable work with the tinkers, walking in a red coat down lanes where the tinkers are encamped, red being the tinker colour of mourning.

'I was beautiful in the early days.' From Florence I went on to Rome, a stubble of marigolds and leaf parsley on the black wetness of Campo de' Fiori when I arrived at evening. In Mario's I had a modest meal and got a yellow bill with burgundy stripes on it. Just as I was getting up to leave the table a boy from Dublin with a toothbrush moustache and wearing a Fair Isle jersey sat beside me. He was organizing the first Hare Krishna march in Rome the following day and he invited me to join them, which I did, chanting 'Hare Krishna' with some Italians, a Scots boy with chestnut hair in a ponytail and radically illumined cheeks, American girls with pigtails, all in salmon-coloured robes.

A middle-aged man in a silver suit came up to me in the crowd to say, 'You are beautiful.'

We passed a bridge over the Tiber which the sun had turned into a carmine fog.

Someone told me in Dublin early the following year that the boy from Dublin had died in London from a drug overdose.

Later that year, Eleanor gone, I returned to London. Lived in a squat in West London. The trade of stolen colour televisions was negotiated at the Windsor Castle and Lord Palmerston. A girl who used to walk around barefoot was picked up and jailed for doing a bombing. In the kiosk at the end of the street I would wait for Eleanor's calls. Early in the month of the Birmingham pub bombing she told me that she would not be coming back, that she'd joined a religious group.

25 January 1975. I saw a person in Berkeley recently who walked and looked like you – so much so that I stood in fascination with many emotions turning, thinking it was you.

26 November 1975. I have had many abodes since coming here. And now I am living away from San Francisco. There is a thrift store in the nearby town which is fun. I purchased a little mink for $1.50 and a crocodile handbag for $1. Last week down in San Francisco I accidentally met with some boys from Dublin – they'd met on an Alaskan pipeline. They were joking and laughing. It could have been in a pub in Dublin. One of them had a pet goat when he was growing up in Ballyfermot.

Auntie Dymphna had a goat which had been deported from the garden next door. She used to keep her in the back. Once she nearly sent her to the butcher.

It's autumn now and there's a crispness in the evenings and the swallows are gathered by day and all the sounds are set apart from one another by night. It would be great if you came to America. The places you mention are each wonderful and there are also other things that are wonderful too. I work in a drug rehabilitation centre. It's very nice here, quiet. Northern California greatly resembles Ireland – the land is green and there are many trees and rivers. There are no lambs. This is not sheep country.

I'll light a little candle for you – it is shaped like a mushroom. Blues and yellows and whites.

I think of candles around a golden Virgin in Chartres and a sanctuary lamp suspended in a convent chapel in Mayo.

You talk of Ireland and of England, of endearing landscapes as 'a common country'. But something about being surrounded by my past – by mistakes – weighed me down in Ireland and in England. Each way I turned they would confront me, sometimes mockingly. Though I did not realize it for many years I had to be away from them.

It is an odd place, California.

I'll fly now.

14 August 1987. An old Italian stands to attention in front of the Child Jesus of Prague. There are sea shells and jewels at the feet of the child and yellow irises mixed with gypsophila in front of him; what could be riverine flowers, yellow flag, hornwort, the bogbean flower, which were always a relief for a lone and stellar cormorant.

Messages are sculpted on the wall. Thanks from Michele, Toronto, Canada. Dékuji Adrienne 1944. *Graci a Familia Cacho Sousa.* In a frame a picture of the Church of Minino Jesus de Praga, Rio de Janeiro, palmettos outside it.

Further down the church there are angels with gold brassières and batons under the blue and pink smoke of an Assumption scene. The Czech women had a reproduction of Poussin's *Death of the Virgin* in their home in County Galway. A boy from the North of Ireland I knew in London, a carpenter, had the same reproduction on his wall. He had a row over some repair with his oily Greek-Cypriot landlord who reported him to the Anti-Terrorist Squad. They burst down his door and when they found nothing never bothered to apologize or fix the place.

A sunset over the high-rise. The sun is an isolated boll and a pale blue mist rises to meet it.

'Where I live there's a couple who have just come from Mexico. He's French. She's American. You would like them. The opportunities for going so many places offer themselves here – South America, the Orient, Russia, India.'

There's a song coming from a ghetto blaster: 'Running Away Forever with the Shepherd Boy Angelo.'

A tapestry has been hung from the balcony of one of the flats, showing night in El Salvador: bodies rising from graves, men in cowboy hats being tortured in police stations, devils pulling naked women out of houses, nuns in outlandish wimples kneeling outside confessionals, Indians praying by open coffins in their sitting-rooms, houses, under huge coconut trees, going up in fire.

In one flat I pass a group of young people, some in baseball caps, are huddled on the floor. A boy is playing an accordion. Its borders are tallow and green-coloured and its body is gold. There are bottles of red wine on the floor around. Cervano Vino.

In Paris in 1968 I went to a concert given by a guitar-playing priest in the basement hall of the high-rise in which I was staying and drank wine for the first time, red wine, coughing it up.

Eleanor was in Paris the same summer. She lost her virginity to the father of the children she was minding. She liked sitting in the cigarette smoke of tables on the Boulevard St Michel. When the first chestnuts came to the Luxembourg Gardens we were both preparing to leave. But she was returning to the three-tier trays of cakes in Bewleys and the prospective boy-lovers from Rathmines and Rathgar and Monkstown.

'Remember you told me how that blond solicitor leaned towards you in the toilet in Toners. That French boy looks like him.'

She wore a white blouse the night before I left Prague, silver caterpillar brooch on it, a little black hat, spears of black lace standing up on it, black leaves imprinted on the lace. Her face was nearly that of a skeleton, powdered and pearled. She sat beside me, singing along with 'La Paloma' as usual, head bowed.

There were two lovers seated on a bench on Wenceslas Square, the girl wearing white bobby socks and a skirt of cedar-green with pink roses and ruby crab-apples and pale green leaves on it, her head inclined towards the boy's thighs. Around them the humble blue and red and yellow of Traktoro Export, Machino Export Bulharska Telecom Sofia Bulgaria, Lucerna Bar, Licensintory Moscow USSR, Vinimpex Sofia, Licence Know How Engineering, Hotel Druzhba.

Next morning there were marigolds being sold all over Wenceslas Square before I got the Metro to Leninova.

Tinker boys in white shirts and kipper ties outside St Saviour's Church of John the Evangelist and St John the Baptist in Lewisham as Sunday mass proceeds inside, looking like boys outside churches on Sunday in Ireland.

A plea for the Peru missions near the railings and a sign saying 'Do you want to know more about the Catholic faith?'

One of the women has taken home a collection of pamphlets with saints' faces on them – Blessed Margaret Clitheroe, Blessed Cuthbert, St John Fisher, St Thomas More – I notice on my next visit to them and when I feel uneasy and an intruder, as I often do on these visits, I browse through them.

On the windowsill is a girl dancing with sunflowers at her feet, a scarlet bow on each of her feet; two matchstick caravans; two toby jugs; a lampshade held up by an elephant who has foxgloves at his feet. To the right of the window a photograph of Vincent, the dead boy, beside a picture of Marie Goretti.

'It's all going back to the 1300's,' the youthful and even-voiced father says, and we discuss a recent court case in London where a girl was prosecuted for killing a rat. Now that winter is moving in there'll be no more journeys this year for them. But I'll be leaving Lewisham for a while before the end of the year. I am planning to go to the United States.

All this was a year ago. Now it's summer. I am separated from every country in the world. I hold Robin's card and grasp for seconds the last night on Wenceslas Square, the powdered salvia, the lights. But after having been nearly swept out to sea, and having toyed with the idea of suicide, there's a decision, despite the emptiness I had to fight, to keep trying for a path.

I keep hearing the voices of ancestors which started up in Prague.

'He'd never have become a priest but for your vigilance.'

I see a clutter of young, newly ordained priests cycling into a town, bunting strung up and confetti being thrown at them, a middle-aged priest walking behind them, throwing bon-bons from a biretta to children.

My mother, deep down, had hoped I'd become a priest.

After her marriage, as she walked out the Galway Road wheeling me, her boyfriend passed, the one she forsook because she had tuberculosis, on his way to the Galway races. He stopped his car, admired me and said: 'He'll have to do great things, this child.' When I was three I got a gift of a river boat for Christmas. Ultramarine and white, with yellow wheels on it. A fat little fellow, I was standing at one end of the long dining-room, holding the river boat, my mother standing on the other side, crying.

Last Christmas I went to the land of river boats, the Deep South. I'll go back to Alabama I think, get a job hewing wood. Always, always, there is something keeping you apart in England. The ancient war. Always, always, there is something reducing you as an Irish person to thief, to criminal. They just want you to sweep the roads, to be squalid for them.

'Take care, soldier,' one boy said to another as they parted near the tombstone of Thomas Dermody in Lewisham.

Thomas Dermody was a poet from County Clare who lived in Catford. He met a recruiting party in a pub in Great George's Street on 17 September 1794. Went to England with the 108th Regiment of the Earl of Granard. Fought in the first Napoleonic wars. Journeyed through France, Holland, Germany as second lieutenant in the waggon corps. Saw the graves of Abelard and Heloise in Lombardy and was injured, his face disfigured and his left hand rendered useless. Returned to England. Published verse and drank. His clothes were found by the Ravensbourne river one night and the people of Catford went searching for the body, with candles. But he'd thrown them out of Catford manor, having been given new clothes within. His final friend was an Irish cobbler at Westminster. There were still cattle fields in Westminster at the time of their friendship. He drank himself to death at the age of twenty-seven.

'Degraded genius! o'er the untimely grave / In which the tumults of thy breast were stilled,' Lady Byron wrote. This poem she sent to Lord Byron and it initiated their courtship.

In a pub in Lewisham in July a young singer from Belfast in a red shirt, his hair the colour of sun on chestnuts, a pendant around his neck and a few fake poppies hanging by his thigh, sang:

> As he was marching the streets of Derry
> I hope he marched up right manfully
> Being much more like a commanding officer
> Than a man to die upon the gallows tree.

A kind of rallying spirit, an unwillingness to lie down, an invocation of Ireland – a madonna with blue veil and saffron belt, country women with coil on top of their heads coming in for mass on Sundays – the ability, as if from a wayside Goddess, to immure yourself and look back, picking up the sequence of the last year.

There was a strong morning light behind the bus in New Orleans and a black woman was standing beside it, engulfed in a striped blanket, as if she was in Africa.

A card had come from Dublin a few weeks before, Jan de Cock, *The Flight into Egypt*; demons doing parabolas on mountain tops; Mary in a turquoise gold-fringed cloak; the donkey's head bowed in meekness at his task; St Joseph's flowing, rich red cloak forming a rosette under the donkey's mouth.

In Alabama a black man at the back of the bus described an execution he'd seen, on yellow mama, the electric chair. He had metal attached to his body. The boy cried, screamed. They put twenty-six pellets in him. He passed out. Then he woke, coughed, threw up. It took him a long time to die.

We stopped at the Greyhound bus station in Montgomery. The woman behind the restaurant counter was addressed as Miss Mary. There were pictures of missing children behind the counter. The queue for mash and peas included a woman in a lustrous pink trouser suit and a scarf over her bouffant hairstyle, a girl on crutches, a black boy in a fuchsine baseball cap, a woman with a bathing cap on her head.

Two black women stood outside as the sun went down on a street in Montgomery. One with a straggly, Gibson-girl hair-style under a straw hat with piping around it. The other in a wavy henna wig, holographic glasses which reflected the sunset, a snakeskin handbag in her left hand.

I was travelling to Columbus, Georgia, because I loved the books of a writer born there. We arrived at ten at night. The small Greyhound bus station there was full of teenage soldiers, most of them sleeping, some looking drearily at you as you came in. They wore cocoa-coloured uniforms, a kind of East-man-colour glow to the edges of their uniforms at night, a carmine glow. Near the Greyhound station I passed a red-brick, spired church, the bricks delineated in white. There was a church house with the same style of brick beside it. The streets were etiolated.

A snowman was held up by strings in a garden; the bird cages lighted with fairy lights; a lighted Santa Claus head up a tree.

I called to a little hut of a bar where men played billiards on two tables.

'A glass of white wine.'

'We've none of the hard stuff,' the woman shrieked at me.

I stayed at the Heart of Columbus Hotel. It had a red neon heart graven on it.

Next morning a black woman with a forties scarf on her head cut my hair in Sherald's barber shop. There was an advertisement for their mortuary near the washbasin. 'Burial with compassion, dignity, integrity.' The sunshine coming through the door and the window was pure yellow.

On a bridge over the Chattahooche which divides Col-umbus, Georgia, from Phoenix City, Alabama, a man was play-ing music on a Prince Albert tobacco tin, using it as a mouth organ, as a parade passed.

Mrs Wives of America stood up, very straight and stern, on front of a Pontiac. Drill girls marched by and more disparate boys in magenta letterman jackets.

A black epileptic woman was standing on the street beside a wig shop called Woman Tree, red kerchief on her head, her features protruding blade-like, her head rolling. She was quietly talking to herself.

I'd once seen a documentary in the town I was from in which young American GIs lined up to go to war, getting into a silvery-blue Greyhound bus.

The writer's husband had distinguished himself with the Ranger Battalion in Anzio, Italy. Some years later he committed suicide. 'Il est mort stoïquement,' was his obsequy.

On the bus out of Columbus a black man had his arms around a box which contained his belongings, the words 'Milwaukee's Best' on the side of it, a string tied around the box, holding his belongings down. Someone in the front of the bus said the name 'Raymond' in conversation and a woman at the back started shouting: 'Raymond. Raymond. My son is Raymond.'

Georgia: the oak trees and poplars had turned gold, the sweet gums red, the maples electric scarlet; yellow ribbons around cypress trees and post oaks. Darkness in the bus, a last bit of the sunset reflected on a window and the headlights of cars lighting up faces. One black woman with a huge swollen eye in sudden illumination. At a filling station, just before we drove into North Carolina, the breeze fresher and even intoxicating, the radio played Willie Nelson's 'Always on My Mind'.

In the Midwest I visited an old couple who'd once hosted me in the United States when I was there for a sojourn as one of a group. A Chinese woman, a melon-orange shawl around her, wheeled an old man with wispish, almost albino hair, where he wasn't bald, over an iced lake. They'd once driven me in the fall to a Quaker graveyard, the earth organza gold, a myriad of little unnamed rocks for headstones. That trip had helped me come through much trouble with my family.

In Wyoming the bus broke down in a snow storm. We were rescued by American Red Cross women in moon boots and brought to a hall where we were wrapped in blankets and given tea.

Going down the mountains into California was a boy from Basel, in nefarious black, who was running away. His step-father had beaten him up. A bit of delicate knee was exposed.

A Cuban boy in damascened black sang 'Silent Night' in Spanish, cabaret-style.

In San Francisco, Christmas evening, I attended a party in a room dominated by Piero della Francesca's *La Sacra Conver-zione*. A coterie of professors. As they talked I browsed through a book on Tuscany.

First weeks away from Dublin I took the train from London to Florence. It was November. I returned to the monastery with the broom hanging on the dormitory wall, pictures of St Gennaro, bishop, stuck to the wall of the street leading to it.

From Florence I went on a slow, grey-green train with wooden compartments to Assisi. We stopped at barrack-like stations. There was a picture of St Francis appeasing the wolf of Gubbio in front of me. The women wore black. *'Fa lo scrittore lei?'* one of them asked me. There were fields of winter barley in the hills around Assisi. On the way back I lost my ticket and hitched through the mountains, arriving in Florence as it was snowing, warming myself in a café by the Arno where there were men dressed as women, in fur coats, resplendent wigs, one in a dress of many-hued bugle-beads. Marilyn Monroe singing 'River of No Return' was playing on the juke-box.

Perhaps it was beginning then, in a room in San Francisco, what had been overtaking me for years, a breakdown.

On the day after Christmas I walked the hills and looked into the face of an old Chinese lady.

When it came it put me with the ostracized of our town, the Mickos, the woman with the prematurely white hair and the apricot lipstick who used to shout out 'Glorio, Glorio to the bold Fenian men' on the street, and walk off with young men.

Mental hospital patients used to visit her and feel her breasts. Sometimes the price was tobacco. She lived in a house with a doll outside in a jersey of the Galway colours, maroon and white, and in the kitchen a portrait of Michael Collins. Sweet currant bloomed around it in May, and in the meadows at the back there was a refuse of broken bottles. Next door to her lived a one-legged man who was a veteran of the First World War. He sat in a cap and coat beside a pile of *Hotspurs*, *Beanos* and *Dandys*. Her business was stopped by the guards and then she sold holy pictures in the cattle mart before going to England. In a mental hospital in South London, in my mind, she was walking away on a street with a porpoise of a National teacher.

Other images of the fifties in Ireland came back in the mental hospital: boys marching to confession one side of the street, girls on the other; women queuing with Vincent de Paul coupons in a classroom on Fridays; turf mould disfiguring poor boys' nails; emerald school buses, an armament of bicycles by their sides; Children of Mary stalking the town in blue and white carrying Virgin Marys with screw-in arms which they temporarily exhibited in the homes of prostitutes or the dying; barley being loaded on to barges on a canal; campanula in front of the convent statue of Mary, the stations of the cross in Indian-ink black on the white blocks of her rosary.

And an emasculate voice whispered: 'Do you need confession?'

Years later I saw the prostitute on the tube in London. She was wearing high boots, transparent black stockings with black dabs on them, a crimson dress and a pearl necklace. She'd married a butcher and had two daughters. In a street which mixed nationalities and brands of exile the shop, which also sold Irish marshmallows, bore her husband's name and the words 'and daughters'.

Beyond the station from which the prostitute and Guy 'Micko' Delaney departed there was the bog with its cormorants, its bogbean flowers, its bog pimpernels, its St John's wort, its near-violet stacks of turf, its manic plastic covers, its pervasive rainbows. Daniel, a friend at school, who had brown eyes and a sturdily moulded face, used to cut turf there in June and turn it in July to allow it to crust. He put it out in stooks and brought it home in a horse and cart before the dew of August came.

Another friend, an old Englishman, used to come every spring and fish in the bog river. He grew up in the Midlands of England and the bog reminded him of his childhood. He'd gone to university in Birmingham and afterwards taught in Chester. In his twenties he'd go to Norway every summer but then he found Ireland.

'When I stand alone in this bog I can hear "Crimond" again.'

In my childhood you'd see Teddy boys in red jackets on the station platform against the bog. One Teddy boy was drowned. It was a man who used to steal suits in town and then parade in them on the prom in Galway, past the Grand Hotel, Commercial House, Donnellan's pub, who recovered the body.

An Irish doctor pursued me in the hospital.

'You're clinically depressed.'

He'd follow me past young male patients with shaven heads who looked like Mayakovski.

'Do you remember Olive White?' Olive White was Miss Ireland when we were very young. She used to turn the wheel of fortune on the Bunny Carr Show, and afterwards she married English nobility.

'Be careful you don't end up chasing chickens into boxes,' he said nastily one day when I wouldn't listen to him.

He liked to summon up Brendan Behan's last days, his companionship with a Dublin prostitute.

'He always said moving from the tenements to a council house ruined his sex life.'

The young doctor was sitting under a view of the Isle of Ischia.

It was the dark side of the brain; walking through it was walking through Hell. It was the genetically mad side of me, the part that clawed at me. And the landscape I was walking through looked like the landscape around the high-rises in Prague. Or it may have been the landscape around high-rises on the suburbs of Paris. When I slept at night I saw people who were half-dead. They sat on benches, drooping. They looked like Czechs, women in floral dresses and bobby socks, men with eagle or turkey badges on their lapels. Sometimes the black woman from Columbus, Georgia, with the red scarf on her head, sat among them, nodding. There were marigolds at the feet of these people. Marigolds were one of the flowers of Prague. And sometimes, instead of the near-dead, there was a young soldier in sap-green uniform, with straw hair, at a café table, a girl on the other side of the table, the soldier looking out at the amber trams.

A mental hospital with walkways between the top floors of buildings; gargoyles coming out of corners; a coat of arms with antelopes on it; disentangled tapes blowing on paths; groundsel and wild garlic in the grass.

A woman in a scarlet flamenco dress, carrying Tesco bags in both hands, walked endlessly through the grounds, as did Rastafarians with floods of hair and girls with ecclesiastical purple hair.

'Lesbian wants sperm. No commitments,' a bit of paper said on a notice board at the entrance.

There was Hyacinth Ward, Bluebell Ward, Narcissus Ward.

'Are you one of us?' a man said, doubtfully, to the sound of 'Hotel California'.

'Don't mind where I'm buried as long as I get to Heaven,' a salmon-faced Irishman said to me. He also told me about holidays with relatives in Rhyl, about the hereditary thatched cottage which had gone to ruin at home.

'PG Tips always tastes better with you,' a Polish lady informed me. She had many stories: how she'd hidden under the covers on the back of a truck and got to Berlin just after the war; how she'd stayed in a house in Berlin with some of the rooms missing; how she'd moved to a camp where the Germans, even in defeat, would only drink freshly ground coffee.

'All I wanted was fish and chips,' one silvery-haired old man in a suit smiled as he told me.

There was a boy who, in his dreams at night, always walked in Catford, a lighted sign for the Catford Gold Cup in the background. I walked through a landscape after war. It was a bog.

You feel sick inside. You feel very sick, but there is something there even if it's all over. They did everything in their power to stop you.

Just outside the mental hospital there is a drapery store with white lace roses on the suits.

I went to Brighton that spring to throw myself in the sea, like the tinker man.

First I had a coffee in a café in Soho. 'Oh, I knew Madame Valerie,' a woman was saying, almost hysterically. 'I first met her in 1924.'

'Welcome to Brighton', a sign said by the railway tracks, under purple lilac.

Last time I'd come here was the January the *Athina B* was washed up on the beach. I was with a student from the Royal College of Art I was having an affair with. When I lost interest in him he wrote letters to friends of mine, asking if they were coming to his funeral.

Schoolboys in moss-green jackets had gathered in a bus marked Hove outside the station. A girl with cat's-eyes glasses and a sixties bouffant hair-style led a shepherd dog with a Lippizaner haircut past a brandy-and-wine shippers.

There was a huge rubber reptile with green spots on him on the opposite side of the street to the beach. The sign said 'Children under 14 only'.

An Arab girl with henna hair was making a video of her family with a huge camera by the sea, a woman's and some girls' faces hidden behind Moslem veils.

I went to the spot where the *Athina B* had been and instead of throwing myself in to drown I went for a swim. The water was already warm.

The tinkers could tell you that Judas hung himself from an elder tree. They could tell you that a tinker called James McPherson was hanged in Banff on the Scottish border in 1700. They could tell you about beet-gathering in Scotland not too long ago. They'd pick up the thread of a family tale out of the beet fields of Scotland. How a man raised himself up in society with a successful plumbing business, then, on a whim, stole a Ford Orion, and ended up in a jail by the sea on the south-west coast.

A girl, his sweetheart, described visits to him. The walk from the bus stop down a road by the sea. The lemon waiting-room inside. The warden with as many keys as beads on a rosary on a chain by his side. Red-brick buildings with turrets outside and cherry trees, like dirty Guinness when in blossom. Armies of prisoners coming out all of a sudden from the buildings opposite, in pale blue shirts and dark blue trousers, a kind of exhilaration about them, as if they were going on a pilgrimage.

A woman once a beauty queen in Kerry, 'the year Canvey Island flooded', killed herself in that encampment in May and was buried with a wreath of shiny red roses in the shape of a vardo and horses. When she'd been laid out, near a rhino in a sailor suit, there was a candle at her head.

I didn't go back to the encampment after that.

Modern caravans, men hanging around as they hang around streets in Nationalist Belfast, one supreme vardo soon to be gone on the roads.

I blamed many things for this breakdown, but I could more or less directly trace it back to a night in Dublin, in the middle of an affair, a very vulnerable affair, a girl, erstwhile friend, screaming at me: 'You're incapable. Incapable of full physical relations with women.' She'd heard on the Dublin grapevine of some sexual failure. If I'd have stayed in Dublin I'd have committed suicide.

After loss, when the crying stops inside, something else starts, an alternative world. It is peopled by a tinker woman, a mad aunt, an English poet. There are squats in Battersea, squats in Maida Vale where you live. You find a body upstairs in one, and ceilings fall in on bathrooms and bedrooms. But you keep going. For a while, in a very peaceful time, there's a flat beside the heath in Hampstead. You spend a while in the United States, autumn 1981.

A Chinese lady who'd been locked for eight years in a chicken hut, where she could only write on toilet paper, was also there. Her hair was swabbed over her head and she wore jerkins and pants. She'd straddle with her fifty-five-year-old Chinese boyfriend past young Americans in shorts and T-shirts. Once she gave a reading. There was a Norwegian writer with a gipsy scarf on her head and in a décolleté dress on one side of her and a Philippine writer in an even more décolleté dress on the other side of her. The large hall was scattered by American feminists, some in crocheted hats, who ran vegetarian cafés and macrobiotic cafés which also sold turkey sandwiches. The little old Chinese lady raised her arms in the air and asked why the American army wasn't there.

There was a Polish woman with steely hair in a ponytail. When she had travelled around the United States on Greyhound buses she'd keep loading tins of food on to the buses. She had studied medicine in Leningrad during the last years of Stalin. When he died they were asked to cry and they cried. A few days later they were asked to laugh and they laughed.

Your hostess was a Chinese lady who liked wearing shawls of lacquer red and pink. She'd hidden among the skeleton firs in the mountains near Peking during the Chinese revolution and then escaped to Taiwan.

We had parties on lawns at night. There was usually a fat lady in black – black dress, black shoes, black stockings – sitting on those lawns, holding a flotilla of black balloons. She was in love with a middle-aged Egyptian doctor, with black and ash hair which fell on to his shoulders, who later married a young Polish waitress. Later, she went to New York, where she'd stand around Rubens exhibits in galleries, because she reckoned that men who liked the flushed, flaccid bodies of Rubens would like her.

You had an affair there, with a boy you met at a discotheque mainly frequented by South American girls who'd been tortured, and by gays. It was on the edge of cornfields which Amish people rode through on buggies, the women in poke bonnets.

One morning, after having made love to him in the bath the previous night, you walked past a Catholic church with him in which a wedding was taking place. It was just about the third anniversary of Eleanor's wedding.

Although it was only November, an imbecilic Santa was

swinging himself on a swing in a shop window and a Virgin Mary with outspread auburn hair, who looked like an Italian starlet of the fifties, looked aghast at the Christ child in another shop window.

You made friends there with the Norwegian writer and the Israeli writer, an Arab Catholic. Afterwards, you visited the Norwegian writer in Norway. When you arrived at Oslo Central Station youths and girls in pale blue jeans and high boots were sweeping up the garbage with brooms. Two days later, Sunday, women in fur coats had come out of Karl Johans Cathedral which had chandeliers in it. The same day you took a train to the town in the country where your friend lived. Norwegian trains are very slow. Taciturn boys with tight pouches of pubic hair on pale skin sat endlessly in saunas. You went with the writer's son to her summer house by a fjord and sailed in a boat with him out on to the lake, under the mountains. Snow came to the hilly town when you were there, falling on the houses which were set apart from one another.

You visited the Israeli writer in Jerusalem, just after the Sabra and Chatila massacres. He had a menorah in his room, five brown candles in it and two white ones with gold sequins on them.

Rabbis prayed, heads close to the temple wall.

'We sit in solitude and mourn for the temple that is destroyed. We sit in solitude and mourn.'

I travelled around Israel. There had been soldiers on foot milling on the roads near the Lebanese border, an unceasing, onward march. In olive-yellow hills black goats had bits of white like wigs on their heads. Tanks had overtaken camels in the desert behind a deserted white-brick refugee town near Jericho. An old man had played an accordion by a field of melons.

Back in Jerusalem, in the Mea Shearim district, men with *peoths*, in fur-edged *streimel* hats, had walked by in the September light.

I took a bus from the Jaffa Gate to Bethlehem. The protruding-nosed bus was old and dusty and had no colour. Geese and goats had fled from its path and some of the passengers were geese.

There was a little blue and white flag on a mast in the middle of Manger Square in Bethlehem. Sweets had been laid out on tables on the little alleys that led away from the square: pistachios, hazelnuts, almonds in the yoghurt whites, saffron reds, pistachio greens. There was a framed photograph of Tracey Ullman on a wall above a bench on which men smoked honey-soaked tobacco.

I thought of Eleanor.

I thought of my new friend, Marek, whom I'd met in a school in the West of Ireland. His mother was a German actress and his father, from whom she'd long been separated, was a Palestinian surgeon.

I walked to the Mount of Olives one night, through the West Bank, and looked down on the Garden of Gethsemane, the Kidron river.

In Acca, by the Mediterranean, I had wanted to masturbate but didn't.

After walking to the Mount of Olives I met my Arab friend in La Belle Bar. There was a picture of a grey-haired Paul Kent on the wall and the jukebox played 'We had joy. We had fun. We had seasons in the sun.' That was the song that was playing in my mind June 1974 when I walked into Easons in Dublin, picked up the *Irish Press*, a little news item at the bottom left-hand side of the front page about the death of a sister of a friend of mine. She'd been killed near Lyon, hitchhiking from Geneva to Paris. Shortly after that Eleanor went to see her brother, who was stranded in San Francisco without a valid visa.

One evening in Norway we had earthberries and cream just as Mr Haythornthwaite, the Englishman who visited our town when I was a child, would have had in Norway in the nineteen-twenties.

As I walked up the hill after arriving at the station my friend was waiting outside her door. 'Thought you'd never make it.'

An actress friend of mine died in Dublin that day.

'Once hit by it you are haunted forever,' a voice had said in a dream shortly after the girl had abused me and Eleanor had gone.

It was in Cairo, early in the summer, the muezzin's call to prayer at dawn, gurkies on front of cars on October 6 Bridge, sag pipes played by the Nile as brides in glacial white were photographed with sudden flashes by Coca-Cola stalls like munition heaps.

In London you start recovering again. You start being well again.

An old man, a neighbour, face red as a lady tulip, stands outside his door. A trough of sanguine horsechestnuts beside the door, the last green of the year lit up. Sometimes he talks about Mabel Stevenson, a girlfriend he had before the war who used to live in the oatmeal and faded mulberry-coloured houses visible just above the hill; about meetings in Lyons Corner Houses all over London, an idyll on the Cornish Riviera. She joined the Wings and was killed. A last photograph. She's standing in very high high heels, very straight, to the right of an army big band who are arraigned with their instruments in front of an aerodrome. In memory of her he observes a wartime diet in the evenings: Spam, Cheddar cheese, a slice of half-moon cake.

As a youth he worked in the Black Cat cigarette company in Camden Town. He did an evening course in photography and got a job in Whitehall during the war, working for the War

Ministry. His task just after the war was blowing up photo-graphs of quislings.

I sit on a deck chair with him on warm afternoons, beside the pineapple broom. He describes how the patch of road near us was once haunted by men taking bets. Now there's an estate agent's which is open on Sundays, painted viridian out-side with viridian fluorescent lights in the window.

That autumn, at the opening of an exhibition by a Russian painter, I saw an old friend of mine – the boy who used to take turf home with a donkey and cart before it got wet.

The landscape of East Galway behind the cottage. Beds of pearl-like rock, riff-raff of cypresses, abandoned baths for cows to drink from, verdigris on thatch, sudden illuminations on the horizon.

The Russian painter wore a crimson caftan and as if drawn by that a woman in a crimson coat approached him. 'May I introduce myself?' He totally ignored her.

'You'll probably never meet me again,' a very tanned woman with honey-coloured hair in a pigtail, in a black leather skirt, said in a kind of despair. 'I'm off to live in Wiltshire.' She was talking to a man with skimpy, shoulder-length grey hair, in drainpipe trousers, dicky bow with white mice on it, who was staring with infatuation at the painter. A woman with an entire batik trailing from her handbag very purposefully blocked his view.

I was at the party because I knew Vincent, the waiter with the canary-yellow quiff in otherwise dun hair, who was from Derry. He wore a tuxedo, a sleeper in his left ear. Then sud-denly I saw Daniel. He had not changed. Walked out of school twenty years ago and had not changed. He wore a black suit, a shirt of blue and yellow and white. He still had that moulded face, brown eyes with flecks of gold.

I'd met him once since he'd left. He'd returned to town for a visit two years after first going.

'Reason I left Ireland was because I wanted to fuck. You couldn't fuck in Ireland.'

I didn't approach him. Just looked.

This melancholic city of exiles, all races, vendors of Colombian star fruit and golden passion fruit, but always, in the wetness, the incipient sense of tribe.

Met Daniel in Salthill once and we went for a secret, naked swim. He had swabs of sores on his body and a soldier's pectorals. His body smelt of Vaseline. The day was very grey and there was an alarming number of nuns on the prom.

'I will always have Teampoilín in my mind,' Daniel said as he swam. Teampoilín was the ruined church by the river in our town where miscarried or aborted babies were buried, as well as illegitimate babies who died at birth.

Barry McGuire sang 'Eve of Destruction' from an amusement arcade which was painted in twin colours outside – tobacco brown, frog green – and Padre Pio's face was nailed to a billboard outside the church next door.

On one of Mr Haythornthwaite's final trips to our town, when he was sitting in the buffet at Westland Row Station, waiting for the train West, no other customers in the buffet, a woman in a sky-blue coat came in and sat at his table. There were many empty tables. 'There are some very nice soldiers in Collins Barracks,' she said eventually.

I visited him shortly before he died. A room in a row of council houses. It was autumn and there was a carton of Chesterfields on the cupboard – white and red with black lettering – a souvenir from the time he gave up smoking cigarettes.

In Dublin once, after you'd left Eleanor in Bewleys in West-moreland Street, you saw a young male prostitute with blond hair, in pale blue denim, being fished out of the Liffey. You felt like giving that boy some speech, some memorial, in this city of Guinness-lubricated and Guinness-agitated speech.

I got a lift to Ireland that autumn with Vincent and a friend of his, Chris. There were cumulus clouds over an Italian villa of a pub called the Ocean Queen and over raspberry haemorrhages of council houses. Chris spotted a headline in the window of a newsagents which looked like a Royal Legion hut.

'I'm not having an affair,' says vicar. 'I'm a pouf.'

Vincent had been a rent boy before he became a waiter. For a while he worked in a room full of out-of-order washing machines, where old men came to have tea and sherry and be whipped. His mother was a heroin addict who brought him over from Derry when he was very young. For a while he had a foster mother who was an East Kilbride Catholic in Appleby in Westmoreland. When he was seven or eight he confronted his foster mother in Louis XV heels with fancy bars: 'You've lost a son and gained a daughter.'

Chris had hazel hair, a scimitar of freckles across his face. He wore a watch with teddy bears instead of digits. He switched all the time from a tough Dublin working-class accent to a camp South-East London one. He came over from Dublin when he was thirteen and went to school at Sedgehill. His first sexual experience had been with a girl who'd bestow herself for Cadbury's cream eggs. Her father was a piper who played on Saturday nights in the Pipers' Club. He played his favourite tune, 'Speed the Plough', in the house as they made love in a shed.

We stopped at a church in which one of the stained-glass windows depicted a crucifix made of lilies. There was a note beside a candle. 'For my son Ben who is 21 today.' The names of the First World War dead were ingrained in the wall outside. 'Of your charity pray . . .'

We passed through a mountainous landscape of boarded-up houses, scattered rocks, dried-up rivers. Suddenly there was a Congregationalist church and beside it a Chinese restaurant, Po Lun.

Vincent had been born near the statue of Our Lady Queen of Peace in the Creggan. She had blue, upcast, lunatic eyes.

The boys in tartan kilts used come to Derry on Saturdays in buses to march.

'Are you Irish?' a soldier boy asked me at a disco the other night. 'Why?' says I. 'Do you want some Irish?'

Posters for the Wolfe Tones and the Pogues hugged electric poles in Dublin. The trees were yellow.

'Nice day in the shelter,' a woman sarcastically said.

Some men were working on the pavement outside Trinity College. 'Sure, they'll be pulling it up next week.' There was another driven bit of sarcasm from a passing woman.

Two women on a bus talked.

'And I said to him it's about time he'd be going to the altar.'

'She boils a good egg.'

'Mind you, it goes soft now and then.'

By the Grand Canal two prostitutes were fighting. 'She fuckan cut her wrists and you don't care.' One was wearing a short crimson dress and carrying a handbag. The other was wearing a fake leopardskin coat.

On Percy Place Bridge nearby was scrawled: 'Boo is a prick, but a cool one.'

There was a new motorway outside Galway city with the ruin of a castle on a circle of exhibition verdure in the middle of a roundabout.

You go back to the town you're from. An ancient sign for Kincora Plug, on the gable of a town house where the town houses ascend in size, is a mirage of colour, mainly navy.

The legend is that while a local Moslem lady, customary veil on her head, was preparing dinner recently a billygoat who'd run away from some English convoy people had intruded upon her in the kitchen.

'Elizabeth Maloney. Don't know her. But I know her aunt.'

Now that I'm here, people who ran away are called up, an inventory. A woman who ran away with a circus artiste. The woman across the road who followed her example shortly afterwards: she'd always emulated her neighbour. If her neighbour bought a lampshade, she bought one. If her neighbour bought a carpet, she bought one. The second woman ran away on a country fair day. It could have been with any of four men.

'Hope you get the weather you're expecting,' one of three men leaning against the bank corner tells me.

Once there was a virtually unbudging, save for a rota in the pub, row of First World War veterans here. 'Rue di Doo Boys' they were called, after Rue de Deux Bois.

A gargantuan one-legged man whose wife, a dress-maker, festooned him in right-fitting clothes.

One of them had deserted in the Judean Hills. They thought he'd been killed and sent home a body they believed to be him and he'd stood at this bank corner, saffron-brick then as it is now, watching his own funeral.

The smallest of them would shave his legs each year for about ten years after the First World War and box in the Connaught Under 16.

Another little fellow became an idiot, would wander about town after his mental collapse, in a cap and coat to his feet, singing rebel songs and ranting about opposing sides in the Civil War, joined the circus, was killed in a car accident.

A fellow with pitch-black hair, face always charcoaled in stubble, called Stephen O'Meara after an illustrious Limerick opera singer, would sing arias – Puccini on verdant spring days – in his malodorous black coat on the side-line at GAA matches, arms outstretched.

The gargantuan fellow, despite his one leg, had gone back to war, in October 1936, to fight on Franco's side in the Spanish Civil War. He'd never got, for some reason, very far beyond the coast of Galicia. In his last years he was the town crier. Would clang a bell on the anniversaries of Ypres and Givenchy, shouting, 'Hear ye. Hear ye.'

Teddy bears having a tea-party in the window of a guesthouse; the news that a tinker who lived by himself in a caravan by the Ash Tree has died; a blonde-haired girl leaning against a wall asks me, 'Are you Australian?'; a visit to the bog.

You feel like a trespasser, a bit of fuschia just visible in the gable window of a country house distantly, the kind of house which has a family of unmangled country boys.

He had a wife once, the tinker. She left him, 'shipped herself out of Ireland'. He died of abandonment and a harsh lifestyle in the Regional Hospital in Galway, still in unresolved youth. There is a wake, and tinkers come from all over Galway, women in expansive head scarves like East European women, and Pakistani traders. He was a rag-and-bone man, used to collect scrap on a cart and pile it up beside his caravan.

During the war, when cars were disused and wrecks of cars accumulated in the fields about town, tinkers had a glut of scrap and made rings and brooches from those cars and initialled them. When I was a child he showed me one of those rings, which a sparkle of spring sunshine had just indicated to him in a meadow, initialled by an uncle.

He lived in a white, modern caravan full of Staffordshire and Chelsea china with a prominent picture of Our Lady,

Comforter of the Afflicted. He had a mongrel dog, referred to as 'a fool of a dog', as companion.

A tinker girl in a maroon summer dress with large white spots in it sings 'Four Country Roads Leading to a Town in County Galway' and 'The Fields of Athenry' at his wake.

He was a Teddy boy in my youth, a little older than me, long locks, sculpted mouth, a pale, almost a madonna face.

'I have no mind for happiness. Just for peace of mind.'

There was a Polish woman who lived in this town once, the mother of a friend who had blonde, wavy hair and liked wearing black glasses with white frames. He had corn hair, loops of glasses, and I snatched at his corn hair outside the Boys' National School one afternoon after school and pleaded with him to be my special friend. He would concede nothing.

I was invited to their house once, for a children's party. She wore a necklace of sea-shells and a white dress with large black spots for the party. In their drawing-room was a picture of an Edwardian lady and gentleman in a chamber pot patterned with shamrocks.

The father died, and they headed to Durham in the north of England.

Years later I saw my friend on *The Late Late Show*, playing a cello.

The Polish woman came from a town near the site of a concentration camp. Recently, in Berlin, I saw a photograph of an entrance to that town, cobbled road, black lampposts, houses with dormer windows, where Jewish pedlars would gather daily before the war.

Her neighbours in the fashionable avenue in town, with its double-flowering prunus trees in the front gardens, testified that they would hear her screaming in the middle of the night.

Once a Polish film came to the town hall and she stood

outside the cinema, in a black suit, for the best part of an hour, as if advertising the film, or as if in solidarity with people she would never meet again.

It's just a memory of the dead now. But no . . . something asks me to return another time, tells me that there's room for me in as yet dark, misunderstood places.

Just before Christmas I visit an old lady in Denmark Hill whose husband was Polish. She lives on the fourth floor of a mansion of flats. Beside it is a new apartment block in the shape of a lighthouse. She met her husband early in the war and had a son by him. His brother had been one of the officers killed at Katyn. After the war he deserted her, returning to Poland.

Her son manages a gay bookshop in the Midlands and rarely visits her.

Her husband lectured at an agricultural training college when he returned to Poland and in later years also worked as a courier for Polish tourists.

She met him again, by accident, summer of 1986, in Prague. She was with a lady companion and he was leading a band of Polish tourists in Wenceslas Square. They'd gone to that café, the three of them. The band had been playing 'A Cup of Coffee, a Sandwich and You.' Afterwards, they'd walked through back streets, women standing outside doors, lights above the doors. She'd seen an old Jewish man pass by a window with festoons in it, his back bent. Or was he a ghost?

Her husband came to see her the following year in London and afterwards she sent him food packages and many gifts but then he ceased writing.

Her legs are swollen and she goes to the window with difficulty, looks out on the winter sunset over a Georgian square in Denmark Hill and says, '£35 a week. We deserve better.'

An old Russian emigré is dressed as Santa in Tesco's in Catford, enthroned on a platform. A little Malaysian man lies on the upstairs floor of the café in Soho. He holds up a crucifix with one hand, and with the other throws rose petals, which he fetches out of a small brown paper bag. Some of the rose petals hit a baby in a romper suit patterned with clowns, held by a young man whose head is barely sheathed with hair, whereupon a Greek jumps up and starts beating up the Malaysian. The Greek chases the Malaysian out on to the street.

A little serving lady comes in with a bunch of *Irish Catholics* and for some reason starts spreading them on the spot where the Malaysian had lain.

Many of the Christmases over the last years Marek, the boy from Munich, came to my flat. He's not coming this year: he's got AIDS. He's been HIV positive since 1983, the virus identified in 1984, but now he's in hospital in Berlin. Heidi, a girlfriend you had after Eleanor, also lives in Berlin. Carl's moved back to London. Eleanor's moved on to Amsterdam.

You spend Christmas with the homeless, old men with their hair curling up like smoke from a country cottage.

As you watch old men lining up for soup you think of a funeral of a ninety-year-old uncle under an East Galway sunset; second cousins, a man and a woman who lived together in the country in East Galway, whose house burned down, killing them; your step-aunt and step-uncle who died young, buried in cemeteries facing one another in County Westmeath, a road between the cemeteries.

Not her own children, my grandmother used to throw saucers at them, and my mother would cry out, 'They have a mother in Heaven too.'

My step-aunt went to the Immaculate Training College in Limerick. She taught at the Mercy Convent in Navan before she married, and later taught at a rural school where she worked right up to her death.

My mother got tuberculosis too, from germs under the bed of a woman with tuberculosis she visited regularly, but she recovered and married.

When I was thirteen she came into the theatre I'd constructed in the back-shed. I was standing in a turban with a turkey feather in it, with a tan I'd acquired from mixing some of her cosmetics, and she started beating me in a wild, frightened way, pulling down the sack curtains at the same time, pulling out lavender from jam jars.

'All this was redeemable,' Heidi said. 'It's Dublin that nearly destroyed you.'

Someone played 'O Solo Mio' on a mouth organ near Vauxhall Bridge. I remembered what the old lady had said about Christmas during her brief marriage, how the priest used to come to the house each Christmas Eve and break bread.

It was that girl. She'd wander around Dublin saying things like, 'Lizzie Rossiter is a virgin.' She was about six feet tall, had blonde hair tossed like a capuchin's, underneath an infernal, dissatisfied face. She liked wearing a flowing lavender cloak and white rubber, barred forties sandals when she walked her aunt's Irish wolfhound on Grafton Street and the surrounding streets. This dog was treated as a special guest in the Golden Spoon on Grafton Street. In her aunt's house where she lived there was a display of ancient *Ireland's Owns, Freeman's Journals, Irish Schools' Weeklies, Weldon's Ladies' Journals* on a low table in the middle of the sitting-room, and above the mantelpiece tasselled dance cards behind a frame. Elsewhere on the walls there were scenes from Ireland's past in black and white – fields being staked out during the war – and photographs with a sweetheart from the National Athletic and Cycling

Association, one taken on a laneway, the other in the Royal Marine Hotel in Dun Laoghaire. Green plants grew under pictures of St Athnacht, St Eanna and Napoleon in a maroon cloak, jabot, wreath on his head, and shoes of white with gold designs like those of Our Lady of Fatima.

The aunt wore a black mantilla or black cloche hat if she wasn't in the blue and white of the Little Company of Mary. The girl went to get her a bottle of whiskey one day and came home and found her dead, whereupon she had the house to herself.

We were very happy, Eleanor and I, when Eleanor came back from California. But after wending our way to a party this girl let fly at me: 'You're incapable. Incapable of full,' she raised her hand as it conducting an orchestra, 'full physical relations with women. It's your family. All because of your family. You hate women. With Eleanor, yeah.'

I believe that woman has a child of her own now with whom she lives in that house in Windy Arbour with its Irish, Catholic memories.

Berlin, 3 May 1991. I remember once taking the train west in Ireland on a summer's evening. Past suburbs of Dublin. Lilies on the canal running alongside the railway tracks. I thought of Russia. I had suffered a great loss. A loss I could not comprehend or cope with. But I knew something connected me with Russia, something would bring me there. Someone was there.

I have been terribly, terribly lonely but now I must call up the child. The child is me, the broken inner part of me. When you went, my love, the imprint, the ectoplasm of a little boy was left. I have almost lost touch with him at times, but now he is close.

I left Ireland shortly after the outpouring, vowing never to go back. The wisteria blue of the mountains and the talmudic shapes by the docks are always part of me.

'We teach all hearts to break,' a sign had said on a wall under a flyover near Portobello Road on my arrival in London in the summer of 1977.

'You smell of bitter almonds,' a girl told me in a café in Dublin a few days before the attack. A beautiful, blonde girl from our town who liked wearing white dresses with black spots on them. She leaned forward as she spoke and had a dangerously vulnerable openness and an almost ringing enthusiasm.

She'd had a nervous breakdown and was sojourning in St Pat's.

Now, I'm told, her mind has stopped completely, and she's sealed off in some leafy hospital in a semi-Protestant town.

At night as I sleep and dream of that girl in London there's an awkward *pietà* which forces it's way through, mother and prostrate Christ. It's at the entrance to the bad part of our town near where Daniel lived.

When we were fifteen, in 1966, a warren of lesbians was discovered in a factory by the Shannon in Athlone and Daniel went to England.

Discotheque in London. I meet a boy from our town. He has long Titian-red hair and wears a green jacket. He lists the gay venues of Dublin, where he lived until recently: the George, Minskys, O'Henrys, Fitzpatricks on a Thursday night.

In Czechoslovakia, because of 1968, the old mingle with the young, those among the old who did not conform and worked as stokers and road-sweepers. At discos in Prague you see older men sitting beside young people at long tables covered in white oil-cloth and laden with white wine as they watch videos shot in New Orleans on a small screen.

'Many were good heroes – flame-like,' a medieval chronicle said about the young men of our townland, and I see its sometimes undulating verdure caressed by pockets of rowan trees and bryony bushes aflame in autumn.

His mother had had a daughter before she married who was adopted by an American family. She turned up recently.

'When I was a child,' she said, 'when the doorbell rang I always pretended you'd come for me. My toy suitcase was always packed, ready to return.'

His family live in a cottage near an eskar, one of the strange hummocks created in the Western Midlands when the mountains were pressed down and the oak trees were razed into bog by ice. They now have an American flag flying outside their cottage.

An Italian in a shiny blue suit sold red roses on Wardour Street, the roses in a bucket at his feet. A little girl wearing a pearl necklace to her knees walked down Old Compton Street. There were violets on Ladywell Fields and two black girls in black leather skin-suits, wild hair flossed out, both of them wearing identical sapphire-blue scarves around their necks and carrying skimpy Tesco bags, crossed the Fields.

I'd just received a letter. I was going to live in the Southern States in the autumn.

Life changes: the Tarot cards on the mantelpiece are young men pulling a boat out of the sea in Portugal with ropes; a nobleman with his arm around his pageboy, a ball in the nobleman's hand, his outfit olive-yellow with patterns of girdles in it, a black hat with a silver coin on the front of it on his head; two men in thoabs and turbans conversing by a field of green barley, poppies scattered among the barley.

When you were at university your mother had you incarcerated in digs, so you celebrated your twenty-first birthday four months after the night in the flat of a friend. A woman who'd recently lost her husband and cried a lot came, a Mrs Lawlor. Two urchin boys with plum cheeks from Mountpleasant Buildings. The girl who later attacked you, in a fur coat, a blue and white striped gown like that of a concentration camp inmate, a slouch hat. You brought pictures of Bob Dylan, Carson McCullers, Katherine Mansfield, Anne Frank, the Isle of Capri and Chartres Cathedral, and pinned them on the wall.

'It's the happiest night since my husband died,' Mrs Lawlor said. 'I spend most nights crying and sobbing with tablets. Now I realize I've got to start living again.'

Shortly after that I moved out of the digs into the flat of another friend. He gave me as a gift a white, blue-embroidered Mexican shirt and not satisfied with the gift I took to wearing his clothes, especially a black leather jacket. I would sit in these clothes in Dwyers on Lower Leeson Street. I used to fulminate there – a new identity, a new shirt.

With change in Dublin you always recourse to the sea. I went every day to Sandycove, the sea at its most azure at Monkstown.

One night I went to a party held in the open air by the Forty Foot. Eleanor was singing songs and crying 'My baby. My baby', referring to a baby aborted in England, child of a ruffian songster.

> In the yellow bracken he laid her down,
> While the wind blew shrill and the river ran;
> And never again she saw Shaftesbury town,
> Whom Long Thomas had taken for his leman.

Eleanor did an inglorious wee in a corner under the Martello Tower and a girl from Irishtown swam around in the sea in a black maxi-coat, dispelling dabs of orange.

On the corner of Westmoreland Street and D'Olier Street that spring there was a poster of Chartres Cathedral.

From my friend's flat I made a foray to France in June with a girl veterinary student and we went to the Georges de la Tour exhibition at Orangerie des Tuileries.

Falling in love, coming out of the madness and cruelty of an Irish Catholic adolescence, will always be connected with those Mayan Madeleines, Madeleines gazing into sable mirrors, holding skeletons, skeletons talking back from mirrors, faces illumined by candlelight dissembled when you got up close into a myriad of cracks. A saint in geranium robes did a striptease, showing his alabaster body.

I returned to France in the autumn with Eleanor, to visit Chartres Cathedral. On our way, in London, we met a redhaired woman who stared at us and we at her. Years later I was seated alongside her at a dinner-party in London. 'Sleep with as many people as possible. James Joyce stopped having sex when he was thirty. It was no good.' Her hand was aquiline and pearl, and her slight touch called up the landscape of her youth: curling Irish streets which have flurries of leaves gathered like cornflakes in parabola-like corners in autumn, and always, pairs of girls who squint at passing cars at these nethermost edge spots.

Eleanor and I knocked around together for two years after visiting Chartres.

In the spring of 1974 I was teaching in a school in the backstreets of Dublin and one of the pupils, a boy of thirteen or fourteen, would often follow me around Dublin. One afternoon I came across him in St Stephen's Green, standing among a bed of yellow tulips, holding up a baby.

The following day bombs went off in Dublin, killing thirty people.

Two weeks later our friend's sister was killed.

Eleanor went to California and I went hitchhiking in Europe.

Passing through Arles in late July I met a girl with curly foxtail-red hair, in very faded jeans, big, broad-shouldered – like a Roman soldier.

'Will you sleep with me?' she asked. I'd only slept with one girl in my life. I only knew how to sleep with one girl.

In the autumn of 1976 I purchased a ticket for San Francisco in an emerald-fronted shop in Ballsbridge.

Following my visit Eleanor returned to Dublin for a while in the early summer of 1977. There was a poster for James Joyce's *Exiles* all over Dublin: Joyce as he was on his silver wedding, white tuxedo, white carnation. Eleanor wore dresses with epaulettes, and I wore white shirts like the white shirts from Sulka an uncle used to wear, and broad braces, in pubs where the counters were butterscotch or tallow or chamois with a fine rain of rose.

In these pubs a woman in a fawn coat and a black beret with a diamond wheatear in it gave us a pamphlet about St Cornelia Connolly, whose son was pushed into a cauldron of boiling sugar-cane by a Newfoundland dog; we met the Trinity Vincent de Paul; a youth in a dirty grey anorak tried to sell us a paper with the headlines 'British soldier, do you want to be here?'

Outside in the June sunlight of Dublin, beautiful blonde girls in white dresses walked by.

A boy is pulled out of the Liffey in Dublin. His clothes are pastel-blue like the colour of one particular pub front in Dublin. It is a grey January morning. The image creates a tremor in my relationship with Eleanor, a need to saturate myself more in her. But already there are approaching bombs and the first light falling on new trails. 'Always I sense the need of a catharsis, something not done, something not expunged.'

Shortly before Eleanor left for America we burned most of our belongings in the back garden of the house of flats in which I lived, and a postcard of a Raphael madonna I'd gotten in Florence survived in this city of young prostitutes in pastel blue, with flaxen hair as smooth as Arctic wastes.

Sometimes when I walked down a back-street in Florence, past the chestnut braziers, the purple Michaelmas daisies, a poster of Botticelli's *Young Man Holding a Medallion of Cosimo de Medici*, I was straight-backed, sometimes humped, depending on what phase of life it was, but always, even with Eleanor gone, searching for that catharsis not done, the quest sometimes becoming panoramic, as if a whole ancestry needed catharsis.

A boy from Berwick-on-Tweed who has his head shaved comes home with me one night. I've met him in the West End.

'For freedom Christ has set us free,' is illumined against the night as we take the train south-east, both of us silent.

He's wearing Union Jack boxer shorts.

We make love.

'What part of America are you from?'

'I'm from Ireland.'

'Well I'll be off then.'

Someone sends me a postcard of Sonia Delaunay's *Tango in Paris*, the women in blues, yellows, green-blues, purples, browns, siennas, the men in sombreros. The postcard turns into a tango in Prague before it reaches the mantelpiece. Chrysalises on dresses, suits, dark glasses, lime trees, a white-haired woman in white dancing with a black-haired younger woman, the younger woman looking as if she's been snowed on. The man dancing with the gipsy woman has the sun tattooed on his wrist. There's a tall white tin coffee jug on a round side-table and egg halves decorated with onion rings and anchovies.

Joe comes home with me one night. He's got an Irish accent though he's never been to Ireland – second-generation Irish. He's black-haired. Has a girlfriend. He likes to see men naked, though he's never had sex with men. 'Some day maybe I'll have sex with you.'

'In jagged coats smelling of past winters, facing a dying nation, going on because maybe in front of us there's a ray of greatness in a poem, in a film, in a bit of song.' Someone's been scrawling poetry on the walls.

But in these alleys I was in the city of incunabula, where serving ladies suddenly despoiled your spinach with a swoop of meat sauce, where dog roses blazed on metal counters, where frankfurters cooked under the lime trees, where women secretively made daisy chains in the grass for their children, where old people sat in gardens of crimson roses watching young Czechs parade by with the insignia of journeys – rucksacks, kerchiefs – where bursting sunsets drew amalgams of young people to the river, where boys skated through the light of sunsets over the middle of bridges, where war veterans wore Los Angeles Lakers caps at beer counters, where a wounded boy suddenly looked at you, his arm in a scarlet sling striped with cobalt, where there were framed collages on the walls of little buffets – a young man from the nineteen-twenties, a poem in Czech, cut-out paper wallflowers, a city which gave me a different kind of memory of my race.

My grandfather went to America on the *Queen Mary*, saved £900 in Cleveland, returned and bought a shop on the main street of an Irish town – a bar and grocery business – and managed it in a burnt-umber workcoat.

My father, with his legacy, bought a shop up the street, after doing his apprenticeship in the tailoring business in Cheapstead. A poster survived there from the previous owners, advertising an olive-yellow, short coolie-type coat. 'Two coats in one, can be worn either side out.'

He wore his hat to one side on the street, like a lid that's half open.

He'd always write over his own writing, many times, in the ledger in the shop. The pages of the ledgers created a russet effect when closed, with dapples of peacock-blue. The covers were sepia and dappled in white. His best man committed suicide in Athlone shortly after his marriage: hanged himself from a bacon hook.

He always went to see the rugby in the grounds of the asylum on a Sunday afternoon.

When I was a child he liked taking me to films in which cats spoke to mice, downstairs in the Grafton Cinema in Dublin.

He knew the people who ran Tofts the amusements, the man with the china-blue eyes who looked like an undertaker, and who would run on to the arena to collect the money as the bumpers swung round, journeying a little on the back of bumpers. He also knew many of the travelling players. Some of the players would come on the train with bits of scenery rolled up. They had exaggeratedly posh accents. They'd stay in damp rooms, eat bad food and play to small audiences in the Parochial Hall.

There were others who came in caravans and pitched a marquee in the fair green. They were more popular. A man in a tuxedo would play the violin, the strings ludicrously breaking, one by one. A woman in a man's hat with a flood of plumes coming out the front would recite Constance's speeches from *King John*. There would be a raffle at the interval and orange juice, always lukewarm, would be sold. The women of town would have their hair done for these shows.

The last time the marquee players came to town the Polish lady had a party for them. It was the early sixties, and in your imagination the Galway-Dublin train at night, whining into the distance, was a train in Eastern Europe. When you started going to Dublin by yourself the blocks of flats near Tara Street Station on winter evenings were flats in Leningrad, and always, in your imagination, there were sexual scenes behind windows.

The week before your father died you took a boat from Algeciras to Tangier. As you waited in the night for the boat men in burnouses, standing, played with *sebhas* – prayer beads – against the Mediterranean. You took a train by the coast. Men with ards ploughed the fields where Mediterranean light clashed with Atlantic light in a brilliancy which matched the south coast of Connemara in winter with its symphonies of rock which looked as if they had just been apocalyptically thrown up by the sea.

The Polish lady would drive around in a black Ford Consul with beetroot-coloured seats, always a few green Brogeen books by Patricia Lynch for her son on the back seat.

Always going back to childhood, a furniture removal lorry open at the back, goods in it, chairs with cabrioles, wide tables, green carpets, orange lino, a town house being vacated. The family were moving to a city in the south. Another friend went away when I was ten. His family had a meadow at the back, surrounded by ivy-coloured walls. We could see the train speeding to Dublin over the walls. There were birch trees over the other side of the rear wall, in the convent grounds. Once an orphan in a sky-blue shirt and navy-blue short trousers stared at me over the wall, an open fan in his hand with fat-face fairies on it.

17 June 1991. Going through Mazowsze in Poland on the Berlin-Leningrad train. The curtains by my head have patterns of pale-blue yachts on them. This morning in Warsaw as men fished in the Vistula it had been grey. But now, late afternoon, half-naked men lie by bundles of hay, women in bikinis sit by

65

rivers, some of them wearing necklaces of dandelions, women driving goats by the same rivers. The shadows in the fields are lime and cobalt and harrows lie around. Storks fly over the fields and sometimes stand in them.

There is a spot by the side of a wide river which is crowded with swimmers, mainly young boys and girls, the boys mainly in scarlet but one or two in black and white striped swimming togs, the girls in black. Black Ladas pull up, bushes with red fruit beside them.

There was a little man in the town with a cleft palate who knew everything about West Ham and the South African rugby team and Dixie Dean of the Everton soccer team. In urinals at the back of pubs he'd light matches, not only lighting up the lower regions but also the faces of beautiful local boys, making them look like the Georges de la Tour boys who used to grind colours and pose. His excuse was: 'I'm afraid my feet will get wet.' Because he worked on the railways he got pornographic magazines easily from England. The only illustration I remember is one of a nun in white leaning over a naked apache. He'd cycle through town, often with two children on the bar of the bicycle. Parents didn't mind until AIDS came. The last saga was an odyssey he made to the boys' school late one night when he'd done with lighting matches in pub urinals, hollering at the boarders and throwing pebbles at the windows. He was taken to the mental hospital and peremptorily dismissed. He died shortly afterwards, of fluid on the lung and cancer of the spinal cord, finally breathing only with terrible pain.

It was summer when he died, a time when in previous summers he'd ferret in his railway gear among the yellow irises, purple loosestrife and burdock by the river bank, in the precinct of the railway bridge, for an elegiac vision of a bathing boy in sanguine bathing trunks on a sandy spot.

About the same time he died a life-long spinster, sweet-shop

66

owner and pinafore-wearer, in whose house a woman had lived who'd run away with a man in the nineteen-thirties, ran away to Donegal, and went to live in a caravan with a vegetarian member of the Irish Army who lived on brown bread and fried bananas.

We were both English and Irish in this town, with its garrison history, its cricket grounds and its cricket pavilion, where sometimes people wound up a victrola and danced.

Something was expected of one in this town: you were implicitly expected to honour a tradition. This town, its people, were different, a people who prided themselves on a certain Anglicism. Yet when a local IRA man got out of Portlaoise jail, about twenty pints were passed down a long table in a local pub to him.

The factory was started up in 1928. There was a welfare fund, and so the houses of those who worked in the factory were much neater in the poor part of town than those of other people. Guy 'Micko' Delaney worked in the factory for a while, and he represented it by enacting the song 'In the Valley the Bells Are Ringing' one St Patrick's night concert, playing Jimmy Brown in a poppy skirt and with funnels of locks, the chorus of girls in white frou-frou dresses.

Because his mother had worked in our house he'd befriended me a little and I kept track of his life after he left Ireland. In London he had a girlfriend with a blonde beehive hair-do.

This was the time I had orgies in my head each night before going to sleep, with Vikings on board ships in the seas around Scandinavia.

From South Africa he sent me a photograph of himself

against a rondavel, and a postcard in which two elephants were approaching one another, heads meekly bowed.

Cape Town was a new shirt, a short-sleeved one, saffron with big black rectangles on it. Cape Town for a young Irishman was doll's houses of churches, Seafarers' clubs, benches for whites only, Judas trees in blossom, a young Irish sailor's grave, Islamic prayer hats, the luminous temples of black children, houses of white and azure, the ghost of a mother with hair still shining brown as it was up to her death, in a dress which suited the Cape Town climate, bolero on the shoulders, patterns of blue lilies and white carnations, a peach cloth belt with a bow on front.

He worked on the docks and was thrown out of South Africa for rowdy drunkenness.

Later on, in Camden Town and Kentish Town, it was the memory of a certain beach under mountains called the Twelve Apostles, and the memory of a young body under short-sleeved shirts that would bring him through nights of drunkenness and degradation.

There was a picture of *The Meeting of the Waters*, there was tinsel over the mirror, looped-back velvet curtains, many doilies and antimacassars in Guy 'Micko's' home, a modest but insistently furnished home like that of Bridget.

I went to see Bridget at the end of May. She is married to a policeman of Lithuanian extraction in Bromley, and has a son. On the bus to Bromley I passed the beginnings of a funeral, outside what seemed like a shell of an apartment block, so desolate was it.

Houses the colour of exotic fifties nail varnish, shops wartime colours – teal-blue, old-emerald. *The News of the World*, in smaller letters, 'All human life is there', against a smoke-blue background above a newsagent's, instead of a name.

Red skins of chestnut blossoms were stamped into the wet. A woman in a honey-coloured coat with a beehive hair-do, chiffon with the colours of streamers on top on the hair-do, passed me. The graffiti outside a hall whose purpose was indeterminate said, 'Sam is a sad lyric.' Shelley's Café was closed.

Bridget sat in a purple dress with a purple whipped-cream effect of a rose on it, under plants in bird-cages. Her husband was at work. Her son was with his grandmother. There was a photograph of him on the mantelpiece in a pale-blue romper suit with rose-madder hearts on it.

We'd lead a gang of children on a hunt for ghosts to the woods and the big ascendancy house, now a boys' school the summer Marilyn Monroe died, the summer the devil danced regularly at the local ballroom, girls suddenly looking down as the Clipper Carlton or Mick Delahunty played and seeing his feet. He wore a white shirt, braces, a black tie, had a fifties American haircut with kiss-curls.

Her father was a cobbler, had been illegitimate and raised in an orphanage. Her mother had landed with the Allies in Dunkirk, as a nurse, and had travelled as far as Berlin with them.

Her father was a story-teller, would sit cross-legged on his counter as he worked, telling stories: how a plane once landed in the fairgreen; how a tinker once stole a pair of shoes from his shop and was led back by the ear by his mother. 'Never dishonour a trader,' she was shouting at him.

On the wall of Bridget's sitting-room was a photograph of a soldier playing a guitar. I must go on and make these journeys for her, for the good people, the beautiful people.

'I know, I just know we'll have a child before the winter comes,' you said, before you took the plane to California the first time. You were wearing a cherry-coloured anorak in which you watched a mongrel who'd bitten an elderly female neighbour being shot in the Dublin mountains by your father.

When you were working at menial secretarial jobs in California, staying in hostels with Hawaiian girls and Philippino girls, singing in Bach choirs at the same time, reading Rilke, Lou Andreas Salomé and Whitman, walking in woods, collecting blue liverwort and anemones, I was playing a self-flagellating saint in a ragamuffin theatre group which eventually made a foray to the North of Ireland.

One night I stayed in a house, just off the Springfield Road, where the young and recent wife of an older man screamed in the next room in the middle of the night.

Next morning I ran along a street with side-streets that dipped with background views of cowslip-coloured hills, young soldiers in burgundy berets watching from side-streets.

I passed an orange band.

'Stamp your feet. Stamp your feet to the Sash,' someone whispered. 'Pretend.'

A few days later my host was killed, shot at close range in the lemon Ford Orion in which he'd driven me around.

First time I caught up with you you would not make love to me, had not made love to anyone for two years.

On Hallowe'en I hitchhiked up from Santa Cruz. There were pumpkins and Stars and Stripes in the fields to the left. The sunset over the Pacific was magenta. I passed a blue and white lighthouse and thought of the lady I often stayed with in Connemara, how she'd run away from Ireland and come to Chicago, not quite as a girl, in her thirties, met a man from the old IRA who wore ties with salamanders on them and drove with him to California. 'I buried myself in him in California.'

There is a photograph of you with her beside hollyhocks outside her house, your shirt out.

In a field by the Pacific there had been a crowd of children with winter mints in their mouths, mints that created phosphorescence on the lips.

We met in a café on Geary and would have slept separately at your aunt's had not a youth approached us as we were walking down Sutter Street and offered us a key for an empty flat for the night. The flat was over a laundry called De Paul Cleaners.

There had been impotence with a girl in Dublin, but our bodies found one another immediately. Dublin and the pain were cancelled out. Afterwards, you looked at me strangely. You gauged the alarm, the pain in my body, a body which had been half-exposed to the public when I played the part of the self-flagellating saint, shrouded in chains.

Some weeks later we both hitchhiked up the coast. It was America's tri-centenary. The poppies by the coast road were peach-coloured. We passed a town called Westport which the Indian summer had turned to an azure evaporation and where a couple of dogs watched us as we walked through.

Making love to Eleanor I saw a battle, a World War Two battle in the snow. It was the early forties, Russia. There was a young German soldier, slightly bumpkin face, his hair straw blond, just looking at the battle, not fighting.

The girl who attacked me at the party had had an affair with a young member of the Provisional IRA who killed a young couple who'd been informers, in a back-alley of Belfast.

'Sure it was nothing,' she said next morning. 'Nothing. I don't remember what I said. It was absolutely nothing. Absolutely nothing.' And she swigged tea as if it was Guinness, and looked as if she was listening to a song in a Dublin pub.

An ex-monk playing a tin-whistle in an indigo archway by the Liffey; Brendan Behan's song coming from somewhere else; boys in watery blue denim in Bewleys; suddenly bombs going off around Dublin; later that night a young German in a white shirt with large black stripes on it sitting on the steps of a café run by Hungarian socialists in which the ex-monk had approached him and asked him to go home with him, strumming a guitar and singing *'Sag mir wo die Blumen sind'*.

The little boy had been following me those weeks in Dublin; already there was the colour of the Pacific in you; you wanted to find a new God to the God of Ireland, a new and a more pristine spray in the air to the mouldy-coat-smelling spray of Dublin.

'You must not fall in with the manners of this world; there must be an inward change, a remaking of your minds.'

For a while when we were having an affair I lived in a small cottage in Rathmines and we would sometimes go together and collect firewood on an estate nearby. We'd light fires then, and drink mulled wine, and crawl on a gnawed carpet looking for a lost nugget of marijuana.

In California when we stayed with the Czech refugee we drank mulled wine too. The house was red-wine coloured and had a veranda with grey floorboards. Yellow meadows merged into forests of pine and mountains of blue. The ocean had secretive foam distantly. The old man spoke of the cities of Eastern Europe long ago: cobbled streets; colours – verdigris, pistachio, sap-green, buff, hazel, sienna, umber, olive-grey, rose, peach, Naples yellow; a stork on a roof-top; an accordionist with his bear; a clown with alizarin hair and polka-dotted bow; a gipsy woman in a yellow dress with blue polka dots; a peach sunset over a street of yellow, scrunched-up houses; a head on a tram illuminated at evening; lights, yellow and white, at night, throwing pools on the cobbles.

The first time I went looking for you from Dublin, I'll never forget it. The walk to the airport bus. A man raised his hat as he passed Johnson Court Church. Already some Mormons in near-fifties clothes were motioning to passers-by on Grafton Street. An old man sitting on a stool in the Star of the Sea pub looked out at me.

The plane ride from the melancholic autumn city full of damp and ill-lit basements. Up to a few days before leaving I'd been playing in a theatre company, dressed all in black, black jersey, black trousers, wheeling a doll in a black Victorian pram around a bandstand in St Stephen's Green which had pale blue pillars.

Arriving in New York, in a café at Kennedy airport, a boy in watery blue denim had looked at me in a way no one had looked at me for years.

The plane ride West into the last of a ruddy sky.

Walking on beaches, the sky blinding blue, nasturtiums running by the sides of the beaches, vines of orange and cyclamen, castellations of them by the embankments, the nasturtiums commingling in the embankments with geraniums.

'I went for a walk on such a winter's day.'

I returned to Prague midsummer 1989.

A woman wheeled a spaniel in a pram; an old lady in a yellow pinafore with blue cornflowers on it swept the street, beside an orange chariot.

I brought biscuits and salami from Paxton and Whitfield's as a gift from someone in London to a jazz musician who'd just got out of jail, after spending six years there. He lived in Hanspaulka. He brought me into a small living-room. There were posters for jazz jamborees in Warsaw in the early eighties on the wall – 'It may look like America but it isn't' over the bony houses of Warsaw, on another an umbrella metamorphosed into a saxophone – photographs of open-air jazz concerts in the rain in Warsaw, a lithograph of David standing over Goliath, on the floor beside the wall stacks of Mothers of Invention records. On a small table in the middle of the room there were cherries in a white bowl with patterns of blue circles on it.

The man and I were the same age, but he had a teenage son. The son was away in the Carpathian mountains but there was a photograph of him on a small dresser, in swimming trunks beside a swimming pool, blond, porcupine hair.

We went to a nearby *hostinec*. There were soldiers drinking beer under the lime trees outside, their flies half-open. Inside, a calendar with one of Benozzo Gozzoli's depictions of war. A mirror bordered with patterns of split pomegranates reflected more soldiers, who had surrounded a girl wearing a blouse with a hankie in the breast pocket.

Afterwards, still light, I went to the Park of Culture. In one part of the park there was a funfair. Boys with Mongolian eyes, with shaven heads, a few in flash-scarlet jackets, all with chiffon around their necks, shook hands. A middle-aged man with a monocle wandered about. The ground was covered in fuchsine tickets, like cherry blossom. Men shot at storks, daisies, buttercups. A pineapple flashed in the centre of a carousel.

There was a gallery of Minnie Mouses in pink dresses with white polka dots, purple rhinos with pink stars on them, dog-rose-coloured elephants, an illustration of infantry men in red jackets, with gold-knobbed swagger canes above them.

Around the bumpers was a panorama of women in Victorian bathing suits feeding gulls, and a caravan was illustrated with street-walkers in forties clothes.

In another part of the park travelling players had convened. They were crossing Europe, East to West, groups of players from many countries.

Washing hung between a caravan and a tree. A Lada had graffiti painted in white on it saying, 'Goodbye forever and if forever then goodbye forever' and 'God is my co-pilot'. There were posters with black and white photographs on them, one showing a clown up a bare tree, the land flooded, the other a naked and muscular clown, his face painted white, dancing in the square of an East European town.

Boys in caps, shorts, sandals, white socks played mandolins, fiddles and accordions under a tree.

A girl moved a mask on a stick from in front of her face and I saw a girl, very tall, broad-shouldered, whose hair had gone grey in her early twenties. I'd worked with her in a street theatre company once. We'd played Greek idiots on a beach in Ballyhaunis where my parents had honeymooned. Old fisher people had come to look at us. The last time I'd met her, in Dublin, she told me she could no longer sleep.

Other people who'd worked in that theatre company had gone on to make films, a boy with the black hair of the Canaries and eyes that sometimes seemed decimated by the world. 'Des.'

Suddenly I heard my name called outside a marquee. It was a black, curly-haired English boy who'd run away with an English theatre company when they visited Galway once, where he lived. I looked at the beech trees behind him and the flowering St John's wort and the knapweed in the grass. But I wasn't that Des anymore. I had broken down.

The old lady was in the café, white ballet dress on her, tutu bottom, paths of daisies running through the top, a butterfly on each of her high heels and a pearl-seed bee in each of her earrings.

'Würdest Du am Samstag Nachmittag zum Tee kommen?'

She gave me her address, inviting me for tea on Saturday afternoon.

There was thistledown blowing as I got out of the train, houses on the hills around blue blurs. A woman stood on the platform, china-doll face, paths of green wreaths and peach-coloured roses in her scarf, a boy beside her, a basket, straw-berries on one side, peas on the other, in her hand, the strawberry colour having seeped through. There was a shop beside the house, rows, one over the other, of cans of cherries in the window, a picture of the Crimean coast, a trunk of a mountain falling into the sea.

The house was immense, grey, with a hood-like roof.

I rang her bell. Markytov. There was no reply. She was not at the café that night.

I visited the Old Jewish Cemetery the following morning. A woman in a dress patterned with gentian-blue squares, scarlet flowers in the squares with yellow centres, black dots in the centres, carried a huge white poodle through the cemetery, white sandals on her with pink and white bands in front. Two American women sat on a scarlet bench. One wore a dress of peach and blue dapples, the other a white one with horizontal stripes of wrinkled green on it. They were talking of a bus journey from Milwaukee to Atlanta. They referred to a man encountered along the way, called Zachary, and one of them mumbled the name of Danny Kaye and the other the words 'country club'.

Nearby was a little museum of drawings done by Jewish children in a concentration camp:

A funeral procession, a coffin being carried, led by a banner of the Star of David, all the mourners in the pyjamas of the concentration camps.

A man in these pyjamas hanging from a bare tree, a bulldog approaching him.

A steamboat running on flurried water alongside a row of leaning synagogues.

A terrier licking a squirrel's tail.

A beetroot devil giving a little girl a bath.

A rabbi sitting by a table, a woman in a hat which looked like black mousse approaching, an umbrella over her head.

A panorama of hay-gathering, with abundant butterflies in the air.

76

Old women in the black dresses of mourning looked out of windows into the cemetery. One of them had a gold cage hanging from her window with a white bird in it.

You could smell slightly wet oil-cloth and wild mint.

A poppy in the grass, a ladybird on ground elder were good omens.

There was somewhere else now other than England and Ireland.

Before travelling to that country I was bidding farewell to Prague. But I'd come back.

Three boys in white polo necks, the Beatles, sang 'Yesterday' on Charles Bridge against the setting sun.

I remembered the sun going down behind urinals along the Tiber.

A little boy crossing the bridge carried a toy dog which had skin of red tulips on white.

On Monday morning a block of flats, mainly in shadow, was patterned with shafts of sunlight, like light on alder buds.

A gold bead of water stood at the tip of a man's penis against the light of Podolí sauna. Two naked old men played chess in the sauna.

An old man in Wenceslas Square had a walking-stick with a gold head of a swan.

And on Monday afternoon, my last afternoon, I met Honza in the square, sheafed blond hair, gleaming eyes, slightly crouched, in a white Russian shirt with a poppy-red stripe at the round collar, an azure and poppy-red stripe at the cuffs.

He'd just been to Bulgaria where the police had raided the house in which he was sleeping with his girlfriend on a mattress. They had tried to approximate, from a fleeting glimpse of them on the mattress, the distance between them when they'd been sleeping: you could sleep with your girlfriend in Bulgaria, but only at a certain distance on the mattress.

Czechoslovakia was full of crazy things too, he said. The

previous winter the president's wife had been the sole passenger in a plane looking for strawberries.

'It's a tin box that's going to explode.'

In a bank at the end of the square I signed for a money exchange for him, so he could go to a Stray Cats concert in West Berlin.

The rain in Wenceslas Square had the smell of sulphur the following morning and a bare-legged boy in a white work coat was on his knees in a shop, sweeping dust and putting it into a pale brown urn.

A girl I'd known at university who had been a nun for a while drowned herself, pregnant, in the Shannon near Kildicert, County Clare, that summer. The last I'd heard from her had been a postcard of a Gauguin boy nude about six years before: 'I am coming to be my old self again. I am sorry for not being well. I missed you a lot.'

A boy I'd known at university, with whom I shared a room when I first moved to London, turned up. He lived in New York now, working as a barman. Once, he looked as if a bucketful of coppery-blond hair had fallen on his head. Now, his hair was cut relatively short and groomed, the scent of lavender water from it.

He wore a rose-red shirt and we journeyed on top of a double-decker, heading to Kilburn where he was staying, up Charing Cross Road, past the Venetian reds, the faded oranges, the hazels, the floriations of ironwork around upper windows, the occasional signs of domesticity behind those windows, past the lime trees.

He'd had something of a breakdown after having been rejected in love by a priest in Florida – they'd taken a holiday together.

He'd gone into a Greek Orthodox Church in Florida, where

an old woman with big, black-framed glasses and a black scarf on her head was lighting candles, and decided to take a short trip home.

He came from just outside a seaside town in Kerry, a town-land of crofters. There were three scarlet pumps alongside one another on the main street of this town and in the small square a statue of Our Lady of Fatima, gold leaves on her veil, two rosaries in her hands, one signal red, one silver, doves at her feet.

His parents in their pebble-dash house had mutually become addicted to marmalade: marmalade for breakfast, for lunch, for supper. The house still smelt of ginger ale. He'd made peace with his parents.

He had some photographs with him, a long black and white ensemble photograph taken at National School, a coloured one taken in his teens in the drawing-room, he in a sleeveless jersey the green of Irish pound notes, a pioneer pin on it, a cranberry deer on the windowsill behind him. He was glad he'd gone home and also glad he was lingering only briefly in England where he'd once lived.

'So little is expected of the Irish here.'

'Near where we come from there is a beach from where a noble family once left. On currachs to a bigger boat which would take them to Europe. "Deus Meus", the monks' chant, still echoed from the hills. The noble family had imported red wine from Spain and the Spanish ships had come to this beach. Now only curlews slope there and herons. It's a barren place, my home.

'You come from a country and you try to shed it, but some-thing clings: an old sleeveless pullover, a pair of socks, a waist-coat, a habit. You dance one night in an Irish Country and Western ballroom in Kilburn and you're dancing in history. You're making your First Holy Communion again. You're making your confirmation. You're leaving Ireland in a currach that will bring you to a bigger boat, that will go to a country where there is red wine and no barren land.'

'Micko' Delaney had told his son about the ruins of Berlin, how he saw a man carrying a dead child as if it were a bit of peel, the smell of smouldering fires in the wet, black American soldiers sitting round these fires singing songs from their home country.

> If you don't believe I have been redeemed
> Just follow me down to the Jordan stream
> My soul got wet in the midnight dew,
> And the morning star was a witness too.

Guy 'Micko' Delaney had worn a short-sleeved wine shirt against the mountains known as the Twelve Apostles in the early sixties and sung an Elvis Presley song which was partly in the German language.

Before I left for America the first time I worked in the mountains with the theatre group, bringing children from the slums there. It was the very hot summer of 1976. The mountains were amber-yellow and phlox-red. The body of a young drug dealer, murdered by the IRA, was found nearby that summer. I used to see him in Captain America's dressed up as a tinker queen. I dished out fruit cocktail in rose ponds of syrup to the children. We'd stay up there until the late evenings, when the lights of Dublin were twinkling below.

On one of my first days in the Southern States Kathleen drove me to see a wooden trestle bridge. There was a golden-russet ruin of a slaughterhouse nearby, cabbage roses – pink, mauve – sweet-williams, wallflowers, dahlias, goldenrod, asters outside it. A poster on it, 'See America First'. Kathleen was half-Cuban. Her brother had been murdered in a field of yellow sage by the Ku-Klux-Klan.

She sang a song as we paused on her Pontiac:

When they ring those golden bells for you and me
They'll tell the story of how we overcame.

An ensemble of boys in wine jackets and claret ties being photographed against the verdure of a lawn; a little smoke-blue boot belonging to a young Confederate soldier killed by Wilson's Raiders; a squirrel in a tree with a hickory nut; a father kissing a son on the lips on the main street; a stack of old Elvis LPs, the beloved possession of the murdered boy. And the landscape, the clay ochre-red, a vermilion dust in the air from it. I purchased a blue bicycle and cycled the town and got to know people, the old black men beside the signs for Raisin Jacks in Woolworths window, the women with coral pink and squash-coloured hair.

'Inspired in 1857 by Dorothea Dix', a sign outside the mental hospital said. Not so long ago black patients would pull collards and mustard greens for the lunches of white patients. Nearby was the old graveyard for the mentally ill, shamrock iron crosses on the graves of white patients, stones on the graves of the black. 'The dead who died in the Lord.' A lady-slipper grew on the grave of Annie Ropp. 'Her children rise up and call her blessed.' People still came at night to leave flowers, often plastic flowers, on the graves of those who died in the 1900s and stood in the shadow of the grove of cypress trees on the hillside.

Irene had lost her two daughters when a truck went into a charity walk in Mississippi. Kathleen had lost her brother. They were my friends.

A few miles outside the town there was the ruin of a cotton mill. Right up to the fifties people, black and white, used to scavenge for wild plants here and shoot squirrels for survival. Nearby was a little shack-café with the word 'coffee' in large letters above a Coca-Cola sign.

I visited the site of the accident with Irene. There was a bed of flowers now, the yellow stars of Dahlberg daisies, purple and rose bolls of globe amaranths, the silver trumpets of nicotianas. The body of a murdered black boy had been dumped in the little lake nearby in the sixties.

Kathleen brought me to the grave of her brother. A little white timber church on a hill overlooking it, the earth liquorice-coloured, thrashers in the air and the leaves of the beauty berry turned yellow. He was buried beside a soldier, 'killed in the operation of the First United States Army in Europe June 6 1944'. They refused a service in the church because a black girl was asked to sing, so the service was held in a funeral parlour instead, and the black girl sang 'I'm Going to the Father and Will Sit'. Kathleen's Cuban mother had held a wreath of poinsettias. On the white timber cross over the grave were the words 'Forgotten you will never be.'

Once we went into a church in Italy which had amber walls and held hands in front of a huge cross on which the Christ was an unbearded and almost totally naked young man.

We went on travelling in Italy for a while, hoping for a cathartic act of sex, Eleanor, a boy, myself, but it didn't happen. Eleanor went back to Dublin and later that autumn I returned to Italy from London, hoping to accomplish this catharsis myself.

I walked through olive-coloured streets in Florence, under walled hillside gardens with cypress groves and fig trees in fruit.

I passed ceramic bas-reliefs on walls of Virgins in maroon and blue with the Child, under arches, lilies on either side of the arch.

I went to Siena on a day when Siena was flaxen yellows and Havana browns, and in the evening, when I got back to Florence, I took a bottle of white wine into a graveyard under a block of flats and got drunk.

I went south.

It was raining on the beach in Viareggio where Shelley was washed up.

The fields were hazed with sun in Etruria.

I got into Rome on a late afternoon when wallflowers, ginger, pears of old gold were laid out on Campo de' Fiori, with strings of garlic above them with slightly erect tips, the flesh of the garlic white and purple and Jesuitical black.

There were violets and daisies around the pyramid of Cestius in the Protestant cemetery where Keats is buried.

In Northern California, on our journey, we were taken in by an Indian family. The night before we met them we'd stayed with a lame boy who had brought us to a beach which was all colours, comprised of flattened glass. We slept on the floor in his wooden room, which had two pictures on the wall, both of sky-blue-eyed babies looking at dummies, but from different sides.

In the morning we stood hitchhiking by a bridge, bits of pine sticking up from rafts on the river, a little hut of a café on our side of the bridge, a big corrugated shed with an arched roof behind it.

John was the name of the Indian youth who picked us up. He wore a dusky cerise lumber jacket. The following day he brought us to Luftenholz Beach, a beach of black sand, boulders sticking up from the water, cormorants, petrels and black albatrosses flying over the breakers.

There were a couple of Vietnam veterans living in caravans

under the redwoods. Under one of those redwoods I felt a strand of this experience, of this closeness, would protect me for life.

One gesture leads to another. Before I'd left the squat in London a few years before, about to return to Ireland, a boy called Dylan, who usually wore an Afghan coat that smelt as if it had been buried in the earth, came to the door suddenly and embraced me. In the next couple of years in Ireland, before going to California, I would often suddenly remember the grey colour of his jersey at that moment, a North Seaman's jersey.

Spirit of '76 will be with me always.

It wasn't until I went to the Southern States that I found in myself the strength to understand their hatred of me.

A boy came home with me one night and asked me to fuck him. His father, who was from Yazoo City, Mississippi, had killed himself, a salesman in Chicago in the nineteen-sixties. I saw his father, hands in his pockets, in a pair of chinos and a white summer shirt with patterns of Laurel and Hardy on it.

Irene knelt on the grass beside her daughters' graves in Georgia. There was a ceramic donkey with vermilion cheeks and a creel on his back on the grave of a Victorian child nearby. 'Mama don't leave me. I won't be here in the morning.' Irene's hair was blowing over her argent anorak. I'd just been to her family home with Kathleen and another woman, a professor's wife called Marylin, and Marylin's son, Andrew.

We'd set off for Columbus, Georgia, in the early morning. It was nearing Hallowe'en and there were ghost effigies with

Spanish hats hanging from trees and cut-out witches and tombstones in windows.

Andrew wore a Hawaiian shirt with penguins on it and he carried a duck with a lilac beak, a silver lamé stole on the duck.

In a small town a lemon gingko tree flashed by.

'There was a duck who went looking for lipstick in Woolworths. He said "Put it on my bill." '

As Alabama reached into Georgia there were the reds and the golds of oaks and sycamores and beeches and dogwoods and maples and sweetgum, and of oak-brush and sage-brush.

'There were two men in the town. One man with his arm inside his shirt. I asked him "Why are you standing like that?" And he said "Because I'm Napoleon . . ." '

A man was slowly driving a protruding-nosed bus with about twelve goats trailing behind it.

In a Chevrolet parked beside a railway track two little black boys were waiting for their father who was shopping in a store which was part of a coral-pink, ginger-bread-style house. Cornflake and Muleek. They both said they wanted to be footballers.

The colours of the fall in Georgia brought back the Trieste Café on North Beach, San Francisco, sitting there with Eleanor in a white short dotted with chrysalises, listening to 'You Who Opened Your Wings to God' from *Lucia di Lammermoor*; they brought back Israel in autumn, a tree of bitter apples, a lighthouse with blue flowers around it by the Mediterranean; they brought back the Madeleines of Georges de la Tour, the patterns in his clothes, rabbits, eagles and a headdress, pink sunshaped flowers on a sleeve.

Both Irene's daughters had been mulatto: her lover had been half-caste. In the sixties they'd marched together past her plantation home in Georgia singing 'Keep Your Hands on the Plough We're Not Turning Back', 'We're Marching on to Freedom Land'.

She and her lover had marched on Washington, 28 August 1963.

All five of us walked past a parade of wig shops in Columbus. Woman Tree. Sun Wigs. Jackie La Fouche. Columbus Sister.

Over a café counter was a bas-relief of two Mickey Mouses kissing, one male, one female, tails erect, fluttering mauve and scarlet hearts above them.

And old man was talking to the waitress.

'Halfway between the houses and the runway they struck. Just beside Shercock Barracks.'

'So you don't drive a Japanese car?'

'I have a Japanese nurse. I saw that look on her face and first thing I said was "I don't have anything against the people, just the government." We traded iron and ships to Japan and they made bombs from them and bombed us.'

'Sneaky.'

'All sneak. My wife said "I want to go to Pearl Harbor" and I said "I'd never go to Pearl Harbor again." '

By the river there were cotton mills with water-towers and block glass in the windows. In Irene's childhood machine guns would sometimes be pointed out these windows.

The drive up the avenue to the plantation house brought a tangle of stories: the little black boys, presented with new tennis shoes, who were caught in a storm walking down the avenue and their shoes dyed red from the wet earth forever; Aunt Francesca who fell in love with the soldier with the trooping chicken on his shoulder during the war; the black family who cooked the foliage of the elderberry like greens.

The sky was coral white over the building which had a pedimented porch and shiplap siding.

We were served coffee from a coffee set which had patterns of acorns and green quilling on it.

Irene's father, seated at the table, wore a flash shirt, her mother, seated there too, a yellow serge dress with peach haemorrhages on it.

Irene's father had sailed with the 8th Airforce past County Antrim during the Second World War.

86

Irene's mother had worked with US military personnel in London during the war.

In a house in Georgia I saw a street in London during the war from the eyes of an ancestor, people standing around talking, a woman in a voluminous matt green scarf, a hesitant sailor seen through the crowd reminding him in blueness of wayside madonnas in Ireland, some American soldiers in the crowd. The houses on the street were serried, burlap covering an empty window, a dog with eel-like skin poking among the crowd.

We drove to the cemetery and afterwards visited the house outside Columbus where Kathleen's mother was minding the old bedridden lady.

Kathleen's mother had recently run away and hitchhiked around America, but now she was back.

There was a photograph of the old lady on a dresser in her bedroom, with a beehive hair-do which resembled in contortion the palace in *Snow White and the Seven Dwarfs*, beside a man in a string tie.

Glenn Miller and his AAF band were being emulated on television and we danced in the room to 'Jeepers Creepers', for the delight of the syrupy-faced old woman, who could only gurgle.

Northern Alabama was where Kathleen once taught; it was where, living with her grandparents, she'd had her first affair, with a young man, killed in Vietnam, who had a marble-white body; it was a countryside whose soughing trees she heard in her dreams.

On the way home through the night she drove down a side road to a ghost village – houses with vinyl chairs on their porches and advertisements outside little stores for Golden Cola, Royal Crown Cola, McCormacks Iced Tea, Nedicks Orange Juice – beside the Hanging Woods. It was there black people were hanged, right up to the fifties.

I got out and listened to the sighing of the oak trees. When I got back into the Oldsmobile Kathleen put on Gladys Knight, 'He's Leaving on that Midnight Train to Georgia'.

Kathleen, Irene and I, our faces lit up by cars coming home from a football game from which men frequently hollered, were people looking for a self-forgiveness, for appeasement for mutilated memories.

'If two lie together they have heat but how can one be warm alone?'

Early January I took the plane back to London, but something had changed for me. I didn't want to stay long in London. I'd go on to Berlin and Prague.

Shortly after we'd gone to Georgia I had a letter from Carl Witherspoon. He'd rushed to Berlin from London with the first news of the Wall coming down.

On the night of 13 November a youth stripped to blue underpants had gone up a lamp-post with elaborate curlicues, from which the SS had hanged people in the last days of the war, and waved the blue and yellow stars of the EEC from the top of it; two women kissed, the one from the West in a honey-coloured fur coat, fur hat, the one from the East with cinnamon hair, a bald patch at the back, a squirrel fur around her shoulders; a kindergarten of Vietnamese children burst into song near Glienicke Bridge; an African woman with turquoise about her mouth stared at the Trabants streaming over; girls in faux leopardskin excitedly made telephone calls in kiosks; bicycles were garlanded in chrysanthemums; people filed around with bunches of flowers held towards the ground; a Turkish girl in high heels, matador trousers, black cape fetched cigarettes from a machine as if nothing was happening; an Irish tramp sang 'Alleluia'; a man played an accordion; in a strip club near the Exile Café a Chinese boy put a reptile up his backside.

I'd also heard from Honza in Prague, where the candles were burning on the pavements. Heidi, my lover after Eleanor, was living in Berlin. Marek was dying of AIDS in the suburbs of Berlin.

It began in the summer of 1986, my journey East.

Before I got the boat to Holland a British detective with a Robertson's golliwog on his lapel had harassed me. What was I going to Berlin for? What would I be doing there? Who would I be seeing?

First morning in Berlin the coffee, strawberry jam and croissants at a pavement café seemed miraculous; there was a poster of a school of fullsome naked women on white horses on a shore outside a sex shop; lime trees touched stucco houses with balconies; there had been a blond Dutch boy on the bus, and I kept seeing him around Berlin; girls in scrawny clothes held bunches of marguerites on the East side of Friedrichstrasse; a gipsy woman with a cable of hair down her back studied the clock in Alexanderplatz; there were men and boys on Alexanderplatz in the check shirts that pullulate all over Eastern Europe.

I'd made love to Carl, duckish white of his body. Orange poppies grew outside the window of his flat, in the mulch towards the border.

I did not look up Eleanor. Marek, who was HIV positive, was throwing off the habit of heroin in Portugal. Heidi was enwrapt in her past lives, studying her time as a Russian soldier during the Napoleonic wars.

It was only a short trip, a few days. I'd wanted to go on to Prague but I didn't have the money. It would be years before I'd see the high-rises, the willow trees, the swimmers in scarlet bathing trunks in Prague.

I'd sit with Heidi in her room in the summer evenings.

'As the Wall comes down, people paint the faces of loved ones or half-remembered lovers on it.'

We'd made love in North Connemara, Heidi and I. She came to me after the wreckage of Dublin.

'So much is there inside me, longing, love, a little pain, and before I go I want you to know that I will be there when you should need me, and my love is with you, wherever you go. I shall send my love with the wind. I'll give my soul to the rain, my eyes to the night, my hands to the earth. You will find me, meet me on your ways.'

She came to one of those rooms where I lived, the walls painted combed brown, about a year after we'd met in North Connemara, and there we made love again.

'They tried to take your light from you.'

I saw candlelight at the feet of a Madeleine.

It was in North Connemara too I'd first met Marek. He was going to school there.

North Connemara, domes of bleeding azure and cobalt in turn on mountains, the lower slabs viridian, sap-green, aquamarine. Often cloud fragments are stabbed into the mountain tops. Golden saxifrage grows on these mountains, in the autumn grass of Parnassus. Also in the autumn, in the meadows below, there are red berries on the lilies of the valley. Mary's tears, they are called.

Where these mountains begin is Derryclare Lake, with its island lined with Scotch pines. Richard Martin, the last great lord of this area, died hiding from his debtors in Boulogne in 1834. His son Richard emigrated to Canada and was so haunted by North Connemara that he named his territory by the Grand River, Derryclare.

The eye is addled by lakes and rivers – Doo Lough, Lough Nagilkey, the rivers Derryhorraun, Ballinaboy – and they seem to reach not to the mountains to the south-east but to the charcoal of Erris Hill and Cashel Hill by the sea to the south-west. The red-haired lady lived in this direction. The ruins of her house are still there, with a few what local people call

'freckener' bushes outside it. She was rapacious, luring passing horsemen into her bed, murdering them, and stealing their
horses.

A lady of ninety who was half-blind commandeered the
roads around that ruin, pearl droplet earrings always on her:
'the Duchess'. She married a man with the papal title of Count
and when her son was killed in the war she vowed never to
cross the Shannon again, a promise she kept.

The last train left in 1935. Shortly after the closure of the
railway there was a funeral, and a few days after the funeral
the man whom everyone believed they'd buried arrived on the
green bus from Galway – the hospital in Galway had sent
the wrong man. He lived to a great age, finding a companion
in a man who'd escaped from the *Titanic* dressed as a woman.

'The people were always shoneens.' A town of phlox pinks,
bold lavenders, more modest turquoises. Beyond the town, on
the dip to the sea, each house has fuchsia in the garden which
on fine days autographs the almost palpable ultramarine of the
sea. This ultramarine is a miasma on the mind when you're
away from it and lures you back, again and again, as though to
a destiny.

In bed with Heidi in North Connemara, just before I left
Ireland, I had a dream in which I saw a prison cell with two
small windows and five hooks on a cross beam. I did not know
at the time that this was Plötzensee Prison in Berlin. A child
appeared in the middle of the cell.

'Because you have seen these things I will take your hand
and you will be my father and I will be your son.'

From a squat in Battersea, London, I wrote a letter to the girl
who'd attacked me at the party in Dublin.

'My children will be born in spite of you.'

13 February 1990. On my way through London to Berlin I cycle

to a squat where I lived in 1974. The girl who used to walk about barefoot had been released from jail.

Now most of the Edwardian houses have been knocked down and there are shining new flats in cubicle-effect array, with a network of undulating paths between the different blocks. A little old lady in a saffron, daisy-patterned pinafore and white bobby socks reaches up to put some rubbish in a big bin. There are towels hanging out – a train with a human face, a skiing dalmatian, a poodle gazing at his bowl, a spaniel kicking a ball, a belligerent jet – and some flesh-coloured lingerie. Someone shrieks a name . . . 'Wend.' Flowers in a Trebors sweet tin have not come out yet outside a window. A borscht-coloured Hillman is parked. A man in the blue and white of Tottenham, a boy on his shoulders, momentarily looks into your eyes. There is an advertisement for Buddhist meditation services for women on the gate of one of the few remaining Edwardian houses on the border of the domain of flats, and a biblical quote: 'And even to your old age I am he, and even to hoar hairs will I carry you.'

'Will never go back to Ireland,' a boy in this squat told me. 'It's in the blood now.'

A black man in an ancient overcoat, a black trilby, carrying a briefcase, comes towards me.

There was a woman who used to live in this squat who sang opera in Berlin in the thirties, and would pick up black men and bring them home.

Not far away in the windows of Kilburn the advertisements begin: 'Irish guy wanted for room in Irish house in Neasden. Double room near Dollis Hill. Irish guitarist wanted for Irish band.' 'Owensy from Belfast.'

22 February 1991. Going to a squat like a monastery in Battersea in 1977 was picking up the threads of a squat in West London in 1974, the inmates dressed in fiery red and fiery pink. Went to Italy from that squat. Purple Michaelmas daisies

everywhere. Didn't find that feeling of refuge until I came to Germany this year.

Going by train through snow from Berlin to visit Marek. Passing churches with onion domes, colours of burgundy and yellow. Black hares fleeing across the fields. Dark coming and the train throwing lights like a menorah on the landscape. Miles of cars held up on the roads.

Changing to a slow train that goes through the snow-covered vineyards, a boy in a green jacket and, despite the snow, short green trousers, starts talking to me. He's looking for work as a maker of wind instruments. He's been a carpenter in Cologne.

A boy I knew in Ireland in the late sixties used to visit Germany in the summers. A town of half-timbered houses, louvred houses, houses with wooden cross beams, rivulets running by the houses. After failing psychiatry at university a few years later, he took rat poison and died.

He was very tall, had hair of Indian ink, cobalt eyes, wore black polo neck jerseys.

He went to secondary school in the East of Ireland, but in the spring of 1968 I visited him in his home in the country about six miles from our town.

It was a very fine day. There were furze cutters with hooks in the fields. A boy in a maroon jersey was standing among the sheep. Outside was a tree, still bare, with a magpie's nest in it.

There was a horn rosary hanging on the sitting-room wall and a low prayer seat in the middle of the room. On the wall, in isolation, was a plate with five scenes of San Francisco, Golden Gate Bridge in the middle, around it China Town, a cable car, Fisherman's Wharf, Embarcadero terminal.

His mother, who had hair as black as he, brought a plate of pastry horns with vanilla cream. A tinker lady with a bag of goose feathers came to the hall door while I was there.

As I was taking off on my bicycle his mother shouted after me, 'If you return we'll spread the green rushes for you.'

I didn't know him very well, he was a year above me; it was a one-off day.

'I have a feeling that the people who remember the Famine are androgenous Irish boys.'

Before I leave for Berlin there is a poster all around London for Stray Cats. There is a fish pendant hanging from the neck of one of them and patterns of anchors on the shirt of another.

I have been in the end in Berlin West and I have seen Stray Cats face to face. To see such a city as Berlin West was great experience for me. It was very interesting and I found a lot of things normal which seem strange here in communist reality. Have you been in Berlin West? Truly, Honza.

A man with a crimson face and a brown hat, the fly of his trousers open and a fan of flesh revealed, plays on a green and tallow accordion near a break in the Wall.

'Underneath the lamplight, by the barracks gate . . .'

Numerals decorated like snakeskin on the Wall. A boy with amber and green hair stands on the street, a little girl doll tied to his scarf. Behind him *'Nazis is raus'* and *'Elvis ist doof'.* There's a giant surfer painted on the side of a red house.

I stay with Heidi and visit Marek, who is in hospital with tuberculosis. He's had HIV for seven years, and a bad bout of flu at Christmas a year ago, but was generally well until last spring when a doctor in Munich told him she didn't understand how he was alive.

Eleanor lives in a purple house behind a lime tree in Keizersgracht in Amsterdam.

Carl, who lived in Berlin once, is in London now, making a short film about the Salvation Army.

A woman in a burgundy coat, hat, talks to me in a Sunday café near Alexanderplatz.

She crossed Heinrich Heine Bridge the night the Wall came down. People smiled at her as though at a poor person.

She went to Sophie Charlottenburg her first morning, the buff and gold palace, and walked for hours with the boys in American shoes among the pollarded trees.

She was trained in Marxist economics. What would she do now?

'Before the Wall is falling a boy went into a shop in East Berlin and asked for a kilo of bananas. "Now it's my turn for a joke," said the shopkeeper.'

You go into a Croatian Catholic church. There is forsythia under the statues of St Rudgerus and St Josef, both with constellations of stars above their heads. A group of women pray out loud near the front of the church, under a banner which says *Servus Maria Nunquam*. They pray in German.

'*Heilige Maria, Mutter Gottes, bitte für uns Sünder jetzt und in der Stunde Unseres Todes.*'

In the porch there's a long table with a white oil-cloth on it; Croatian men with white beards, navy suits and white socks stand around it.

Marek's mother committed suicide about six months after Marek was diagnosed as probably having AIDS.

'Can I say something? Have you ever prayed? Sometimes a prayer from the repository of things can change things. Beyond medical reports there is something. That's all I can think now. And also that you'll be all right.'

As he wandered around Germany and Europe I followed him with postcards, Van Goghs, Gauguins, Leonardo da Vincis.

Turkish music comes from a shop, a golden camel with a head on either side in the window, green stars in the flat pastries.

'Tonight I think of you for some reason, or you come to my thoughts and conjectures. I sense something. I don't know what. How did the court case go? How is your life? Will this card get to you? Maybe you want to come to London for a short while? Maybe you're working. May here is lovely and I thought I'd write before it left. But as I write I can't really. Thoughts are annotated in silence and in waves that reach. But coming from you I don't know what they say. Just that I feel a little turbulence. The trees are lovely.'

There's a lotto game going on in the street, and a little old lady with sags at her neck the colour of her brown stockings looks on, and a boy in a floral shirt whose Latin-auburn hair merges into the light of the cumulus clouds behind him.

A transvestite on the Metro wears a carmine coat and high carmine boots. A terrier peeps out through a boy's luminous orange jacket. Some Polish boys in denim stand, kiss-curls on their foreheads, crucifixes hanging from their necks.

It's the blue of childhood Sunday in spring, a day you'd remember friends who'd left town.

There are rooks' nests in the maple trees beside houses with dunce's cap effects in front of them, and the cobbles of side-streets are pastel blue. A boy with hair the black of crows drags a stick on the ground with chalk in the end of it as he passes a twin-spired church.

When I was about six I used to go to the church every day about five in a blue coolie-type coat to get instalments from Heaven, voices telling me I had a mission. I often wore a wine dicky bow then, that became easily sullied.

Marek's mother, Brigita, was born in Czechoslovakia on the German-Polish border. In the Middle Ages the Swedes had burned a church on a hill there, but the ikon had refused to burn. The Virgin had turned black, however. Her mother, virtually in chador, big black scarf, would attend about four masses a day in this church. They crossed East Germany at the end of the war. Piles of rubble by the roadside, trees, bits of roofs, motor bikes, armoured cars, bicycles, trucks, Homburg hats. Women carrying their children wore necklaces of bread. Many women were violated by the Russians.

In Berlin they lived in a condominium shed that smelt of carbolic, a cherry tree in the garden. She walked around in clogs while she was living there.

Her mother worked in a factory that made Easter eggs with Indians and cowboys in them. There's a photograph of her in this factory, looking like a German woman now, seated behind her Indians and cowboys, smiling. She put bits of the Indians on to the cowboys once, and was fired.

Brigita was discovered on the street by a photographer, wearing red flannel trousers, and sent to film school.

She met her husband while he was studying in Berlin and they married in Palestine. She wears a fountain of a veil. He's a Teddy boy, white dicky bow on, a spray of ceramic white daisies on his lapel. There's a Bavarian house made of dates and red roses lined in front of a white Buick.

In the photographs that follow she carries flowers a lot, he dress is often a short, rich crimson one, a bumpkin woman always in the background. Marek in check American shirts looks at laden tables.

Then his parents are divorced.

They sit on the steps of a pale yellow building in Munich. Her hair smelt of spikenard then, he says. His hair is brilliantined. He wears a deep peach shirt and scarlet braces. For some reason there are sprocket holes around the photographs.

When he was ten and eleven, at the height of his mother's career, he lived in a pale yellow house with a blue roof, by himself, outside Rome, the woman a cypress tree-path away looking after him. There were belled goats around the house and a boy would come in the mornings with white bread.

He wore broad, cedar-green braces then, with a motif of English huntsmen on horses, hounds at the horses' feet. His favourite books had illustrations of a girl on a bed in pale blue with patterns of gold roses being woken by a prince, a woman in a snood sleeping in a rocking chair nearby, and of St Nicholas in a shako hat in a snow-covered forest, squirrels, stoats, mice on their hindlegs, looking up at him, a mouse on a red apple in his pocket, a blue kerchief about the saint's neck. He had a train that travelled through a landscape of German louvred houses, windmills, tiny sheep, stationary Buicks in this landscape.

His mother often visited from Munich, coming up the path from the railway station, bringing a sailor's bag full of gifts, always woollen stockings in the bag.

He had a German shepherd dog with long hanging ears which was killed by a train near this station.

One of his mother's lovers, an Italian policeman, gave him a pair of soccer shorts and he went to Rome in them, to see the Pope.

They'd spend part of those summers by Lago di Como. In those photographs she wears outfits like short crimson trousers with crimson braces, a gold heart on the belt. He wears panama hats, white singlets, black tights.

The trams are canary yellow and cornflower blue by Lago di Como, the houses are peach-roofed, there are cable cars over meadows of yellow sunflowers. The hotel is pale yellow with a pale blue awning over their balcony. The boats, usually with three arches on them, ferry artichokes and white asparagus across the lakes.

A man who looks like Samuel Beckett sits alone at a table in a lot of their photographs of Lago di Como.

He went to a boarding-school in Bavaria then, mountains, partly snowed over, looking like a two-coloured marble cake, nearby. The maids wore white aprons, white socks, jabots, puffed sleeves and the school was full of rustic Bavarian furniture. Coming towards Christmas there were Prussian soldiers on the Christmas tree and dragoon men in beige with long beards, carrying doves or paper trumpets. He had his first affair there, with a boy from Berlin who started early, going to Brandenburg and Potsdam to be fucked by and to suck Russian soldiers.

When Marek was fourteen he and his mother hitchhiked around Ireland together, spending a night sleeping in a red bus in the bus station in Galway. Next day they got to North Connemara. It was then Marek was sent to school there.

I met her once, in a wooden house with a loggia looking out on to the mountains. She had Venetian blonde hair – gold with darker streaks – and wore a plain beige suit.

Marek and I were lovers of sorts. The Christmas after I'd been to Palestine he turned up in my flat and we slept together.

His mother committed suicide by putting a plastic bag over her head, dark spots on her face and hands in death.

After that he went to Portugal, took heroin, sold it from Turkish-blue, *Jugendstil*, vine-trussed cafés in Alge or from his mother's house in the Algarve. I went to see him in that house in the Algarve.

There were some gipsy women in orange at the station when I arrived, white bags with peaches and bits of meadow-sweet beside them, a gipsy woman beside a motor bike, a crib with a baby in it attached to the bike, an older gipsy woman in black to the side with a baby in her arms.

It was early 1986. The last time I'd been away had been a brief trip to Italy in 1984.

I thought of gipsy girls in saffron dresses, azure belts, suddenly spectacularly appearing on a bridge in Tuscany in the autumn of 1973, under a hill of narrow three-storey houses with doors and shutters of brown and sky-blue, and crossing it in a rhythmic, a ceremonial way.

He wasn't at the station, nor was he at the pasteleria he'd designated as an alternative, full of little cakes on its shelves with mops of egg-yolk string. His mother's house was miles out and it was twilight. I started walking, but a woman in black cotton stockings told me it was the wrong way, so I crossed a little olive-yellow mountain, belled goats running about, the maize-streaks of midsummer in the sky, and I got to the road on the other side just as he was passing in a car with a drug-dealer friend.

There was a sky-blue Leeds wagon-type vardo – straight sides, curved roof – on the beach near his home, a steel hound on a lintel on either side of it.

He was withdrawing from heroin, resolved never to take it or deal in it again.

There was a lighthouse near his house and it threw light into the house at night as he lay in bed, his head in my arms, and talked about his mother.

She was always picking up bargains and bringing them home, never having gotten over the time she'd been poor. When she died her basement was full of unused bargains, dozens of pairs of woollen socks.

She also preferred staying in youth hostels to hotels. They hitchhiked together in Tuscany once in the spring, staying mainly in youth hostels, the yellow and green shoots of lentils and the thin green shoots of asparagus coming up outside, and in Sicily later that spring, staying mainly in wisteria-overgrown convents, usually a white chair beside the bed.

They spent a week together in a peasants' hut in Switzerland, pumpkins on the porch, ate pumpkin soup each evening, and heard the nightingale sing.

Once when they were going into Paris at night the man who'd picked them up thought they were lovers and gave them a tour of squares of cinnamon brown, terracotta pink, ochre yellow, copper vermilion, with hundreds of lampposts of coral-white in them.

My first time to Europe had been France, 1968. There had been a Dublin boy in a tweed sports coat sitting beside me on the plane. He'd been met in Orly by a Frenchman in a trilby. You could see mammal-like gasworks from the high-rise in the suburbs of Paris where I was staying; after the revolution the ice-cream on sale all over Paris was green *crème de menthe*; a boy and a girl virtually made love on a wall in Place de la Concorde. Then I'd gone to the Auvergne, belled goats in the valleys, the mountains conical, grape-blue.

For a couple of days Heidi's mother is also staying with Heidi. At night she makes meals – vegetable soup, red cabbage, carrots, grilled fish, baked apples filled with marzipan and raisins – and afterwards she tells stories of the war, how her brother was killed in Kiev in 1943, and how he appeared to her just before their village was bombed in 1945, wearing their mother's Holy Communion wreath which was stowed away in a drawer and never previously seen by her. In her trek through a forest to the next village she felt his presence by her side. They lived in the next village for about six months, the American soldiers giving them the fat from *pommes frites* and apples and corned beef, and in the evenings they listened to Hans Albers on the gramophone in the large room in which they were staying, as they drank tea with the GIs.

A rag-and-bone man goes by outside the hospital, the spokes of the wheels of the horse wagon very ruddied.

The hospital is a two-storey building, in two parts, one part jutting at an angle to the other. The part to the right of you as you go in has a plum-coloured Nuremberg roof. The other a medieval peak to its left side. It is encircled by pine trees. An old man in a wheelchair parked outside looks at me as I enter.

In the hall a Coptic bishop sits in a wheelchair. There are many Turkish people, women with much silver and gold jewellery on their breasts, a Turkish man with a goatee, part black, part white. Some Turkish men who look like Irish tinkers play chess under a framed jigsaw of Hohenzollern Castle in Swabia.

As I walk down the corridor I pass a dog-rose-pink Chagall synagogue, a palm tree on a tiny island with a fusillade of cirrus clouds over it, Queen Fabiola of the Belgians, a Lucas Cranach Virgin and Child, little apricots in the child's hands.

'The lion said to the mouse "Why aren't you big and strong like me?" "Because I'm sick." '

A boy who looks like a young soldier from the Korean War. Crew cut. His hair gone sand-coloured. Lurid Eastman colour spots on his face, crimson and bronze. He sits by the side of the bed in white barred sandals, clutching one white crutch, his top part naked. There is rose ageratum and yellow tansy on the windowsill. By the side there is a picture of John Lurie in a zoot suit blowing into a saxophone, a lop of dark hair over his forehead.

'Once I went to a John Lurie concert in Stuttgart. It was great. He told jokes about oil fields, masturbation, cottaging, and talked about the Isle of Antigua as he played jazz.'

Two of the postcards I sent him over the years have survived in this room: Simeon Solomon, *Carrying the Scrolls of the Law*; Antonio Mancini, *Standard Bearer of the Harvest Festival*.

'It's the winter nights; the dark winter nights bring back so many memories, anniversaries. Please be with me.'

Late in the evening we sit in the room, the candlelight reflected in the mirror as in a Georges de la Tour painting, me telling stories of times before he was born or just after he was born.

An educational tour to Dublin, March 1959. Guinness wagons, urchins, crazy people holding newspapers on their heads, white peep-toes, signal-red lamp-posts, a portrait of Maud Gonne McBride with her cheeks of Prussian-blue shadow. Getting a lift in from the train in the Beetle car of the mother of the boy who lived up the road. He'd brought a stack of comics from Dublin – *Topper, Victor, Beano, Hotspur* – and we went into the long garden at the back of his house with them, passing the pantry, the shamble of sheds, the oak tree over the pea garden, and over an ivy-covered wall at the bottom of the garden a little boy orphan, alone, looked at us from the convent fields by the river.

A production of *Oklahoma!*, Christmas 1966. You played Ali Hakim. Talks after rehearsals in a darkened room, the window stained-glass. Cigarettes dashing in the dark. The main subjects of conversation being the illegitimate children of Irish showband singers or the lesbianism of English pop singers. My costume arrived, a tartan suit. Without their clothes some of the boys had silk balls. The Bishop of Clonfert had just denounced Gay Byrne and a woman who'd discussed nighties on *The Late Late Show* and the old nun doing up my face said, 'There'll be a run on nighties this Christmas.' I played Ali Hakim with a French accent and I carried a carpetbag. The audience was a sea of nuns in black who shrieked and whinnied with laughter. Walking home, my part done, I heard those same boys singing 'The Green, Green Grass of Home' in the room in the night behind me. Later that Christmas I went to Dublin and saw a boy, half-naked, behind a window in a block of flats near Tara Street Station.

He is withdrawing from us, leaving us, no longer interested, already joining the spirit of his mother.

Sometimes a girl comes to visit Marek, a very beautiful girl, Zdena, from a town in Swabia. She has blonde, curly hair and cheeks with a dog-rose flush. She wears a black and white check scarf with a sepia rose and a sepia bunch of anemones in alternate white squares. She wears a red dress with vardos and hounds and boys in kerchiefs on it. They have a row one Saturday afternoon, something about terminating a physical relationship and beginning a new one, which ends in violence, Marek stabbing himself with a knife, although only superficially. She stops coming after that.

'I had to take tranquillizers for a week in order to be able to come to terms with things. I know this sounds like a classicl junkie case, but I was close to killing myself.'

'I saw you walk past AIDS, your mother's death, heroin. First time you broke down was when she left you.'

'After having been close to the end, I now want to live a conscious life. And therefore I suddenly realize how superficial most people are. It hurts me to see how they waste the most precious gift they have, which is time.'

'Foggio is fine.'

It was in the autumn of 1982 that Marek picked up AIDS in Verona, injecting himself, with an Italian companion. He'd run away from school in the West of Ireland about a year before.

They'd walked from a rose-madder square, filled with

umbrellas over stalls, to a bit of waste near a bridge of burnt sienna to inject.

He thought of the light on the Atlantic as he injected. 'There was a block we both came up against there, a block . . .'

The angels of death come strangely. Like the pistachio trail of the angel of death in Cecil B. de Mille's *The Ten Commandments*, which I saw from raddled black wooden benches.

Shortly before Christmas I went to the Gulf of Mexico with Irene, and we'd walk arm in arm on the beaches. A sixteen-year-old boy who was already an ex-alcoholic was also staying in the house. There was the smell of Russian olive in the air and the tutu bird hooted over the water's edge like trains going into Southern towns. At evening the horizon was tangerine, the sea pale Medici blue, with lavender sluices running along the beach. Come night-time men would put long wooden tables on the beach and clean fish by candlelight.

We sat by a table of our own on the beach one night, windows of the houses lit up like gauzed theatre. There was a candle in the middle of the table and it made the boy in his shorts look like Georges de la Tour's Sebastian.

'I don't feel whole. I wonder from the centre of my being what my relationship with you and others is. I feel like this candle.'

He blew it out.

I hold Marek's hand at night as he lies.

This city is a city of fathers with children, children on fathers' shoulders, a father hugging an infant to him, wheeling a low black pram with bubble sides. It is a city of beautiful children, a little boy, a cloth satchel slung over his shoulder with his bicycle on the Metro. Two little boys selling their toys and other items on a cloth on the pavement – a capsized baboon, filthy runners size II, a bear wearing a heart brooch, a bear with an alligator's head.

A little boy cries on the train, face against the door. Then suddenly he turns about and shouts something at two Turks who are kissing, with the mother of one of them looking on. He turns back again and cries again and bangs his head repeatedly on the door.

My first time making love I was on my way north to Donegal, hitchhiking. It was the year I met Phil Lynott in a night coffee shop in Dublin. We had cappuccinos with chocolate on the cream. Behind him were pictures of Italian houses with roofs like a bed of yellow grapes in sunlight. The lights were squashed into the rain outside. A boy with a scarf dribbling around his neck sat opposite. An actress, with apricot hair, in black, went by outside. He had a melancholy Lionel Barrymore moustache and he spoke about exile and James Joyce. His Joyce was the older one in an amber-red jacket, the one who'd lost his daughter.

It was the year I met a blond boy on the boat from Holyhead, just as we caught sight of the Wicklow mountains, whose mother had left when he was three and who'd been a detainee in Mountjoy. I made an arrangement to meet him again in Bewleys on Grafton Street.

I was picked up outside a graveyard in Strabane by a young Protestant with big, effeminate lips like the boxer Joe Louis and driven for the night to a country house which lay up an avenue. There were miniature yellow chrysanthemums in pots wrapped in orange paper on the porch. Just inside was a photograph of a woman in a hobble skirt. His mother was away. There were orange Nerine lilies in the room in which we made love, brought there from an autumn garden.

When I lived with Eleanor in Rathmines two years later, there were pictures of Hart Crane all over the wall – Crane against grained New York skies, Crane in profile, Crane with

Peggy Cowley – and pictures which suggested Crane: a victrola with a stack of records, sailors in blue under a red flag on a French beach.

We had a friend from the back-streets of Dublin that summer, a boy with a rough helmet of black curls. He came from a high-rise block of flats, with a giant Child of Prague in the window, in an area where blond boys curled up in doorways at night, and had a mother whose hair was as black as his. In early adolescence he'd been a skinhead, knocking around Kimmage and Clonskea.

Then he'd started, still as a skinhead, to read Euripides, Ovid, Homer, Aristophanes in the National Library.

He joined the Divine Light, lived in the temple in North Dublin where there was rhubarb and oranges under a picture of the guru, went to London where he lived with an old Protestant poet from the North of Ireland over a pet shop in Richmond. She had seal-black hair which she wore in a plait over her head and her dresses were of black broadcloth. There were always tears in her sleeves. The sofas in this flat looked as if they'd been attacked. She had many cats and she led them along by the Thames. He came back one day and found her dead on one of the sofas.

He'd just returned to Dublin when we met him.

A few years later he did a strange thing, returned to the flats, fungus now all over his face, and faded into his background as though he'd never come out of it. Then he changed again, ran for the Green Party, got elected, went to Europe every few weeks, wore carob-brown suits or jackets with chintz in them, became dashing and haunted again with the memory of that stubble on his face in a fashionable way, but with eyes in photographs against the Liffey that were sad, that were out of place, that were those of a shoe-shine boy in Rome.

The summer in Rathmines with Eleanor I got an invitation to visit a writer in the country. Eleanor, although she had many affairs, was jealous. I took a red bus through a countryside where the ruined cottages were overgrown with the Australian vine.

She greeted me in a black alpaca dress with snapdragons in her arms. She had grey hair, touched by ginger, and an oval, marsupial face. At night she let her hair down and spread it out and in the greyness there was char-black.

The summer after my breakdown in London I finally evaded my pursuers and started making love again, on the tops of buses at night, in parks.

When I first came to London in 1977, and there were no relatives living in London, I made love to a boy who'd picked me up, in his flat in the East End by a series of Thames-side pylons. After making love I looked out the window and saw that the entire street was filled with Salvation Army people, filing along, a march having broken up, musical instruments by their sides.

In the autumn of 1973 I knew something would irrevocably come between Eleanor and me. I got a train from Florence to Siena, through hills of cinnamon and lilac with corners of ruby. Siena was gold and papaya and rose. Boys in pale blue denim suddenly turned corners of spiral steps. Someone in a mac on the street wore a poppy scarf. Bells sounded from all directions. A funeral service was being held in St Catherine's Cathedral. Outside a little boy in a blue coolie-type coat, with short brown hair, stood holding a bunch of flowers that was bigger than him: blue, mauve and white delphiniums, auburn tickseed, purple Michaelmas daisies, poppies, goldenrod, purple speedwell.

This city of Berlin, with its greengage blocks of flats and blinking red lights on church spires, brings another subconscious. I remember the public man's wife who cut her throat and survived, and who walked about town with him in turtle clothes, face inflamed, anguished, but composed; the swan-necked woman who died young from grief; the woman, a student of singing once in Heidelberg, who threw herself out of a window.

One of my friends from University College taught English in Berlin and had a catatonic breakdown here. He came from a house in Dublin, in a street of persimmon and crumbled acorn houses, full of crenellated old yellow lampshades and large emerald ashtrays. His mother, although a very respectable Dublin woman with pictures of the Little Flower in her house, had some strange obsession with other women's umbrellas and used to pinch them from cafés in Dublin. Photographs of him with female relatives on Irish beaches, against houses the yellow of old lace and ivory, billows on them like the retreating breasts of the aged. A photograph of him with his mother on a beach in Lanzarote. He finally killed himself by throwing himself out of a train in the South of England.

In a squat in Battersea a boy from Ireland is crying. He's crying because of the way they denigrated him, tore him down for his sexuality, tried to make him less. All I can do is look on.

More than anything we seek forgiveness for having let them touch us.

Dear Eleanor,
I am in a city now where you used to live. I follow your tracks. The Romanian women crouch with small babies. Little Romanian boys sell lurid postcards of Checkpoint Charlie. A German woman in a fur coat rubs the eye of a little Romanian girl. The sky these days looks as if it has been brushed with a

pearl glow. The Turkish women stand around like huddles of nuns. All kinds of old people come out, scarves, big boots – some look as if they are characters from the Brothers Grimm. A woman with waist-length white hair. An old man hobbles in the black velvet costume of a mysterious and ancient trade, elephant trousers on. The child we would have had would have been happy and at home here. I see children everywhere, little boys with silver stoles around them locked into their fathers on the Metro, a little girl sacramentally carrying a loaf of bread in white paper past ancient houses. I hear you're pregnant. Please be happy. We'll probably never meet again, but something of you will be with me always: those old aunts of yours who used to sneak around Dublin with bunches of parsley, the mad turtle and white dappled dog your mother executed in the Wicklow mountains, the mantle of Dublin neon lights that always seemed to come and protect our love.

I see you in Ranelagh, buying veronicas for me which are mixed with twigs the flower seller has painted white.

Some things are beyond understanding – human cruelty and spite.

Our child will be our mutual journeys which have linked up sometimes for moments and said maybe there is a kind of God, a kind of protection, some sidereal banner.

I had a strange dream last night. We were back in the hotel in San Francisco. We are looking for a room for the night. A man stands beside the receptionist.

'Do you know what anarchism is?' he asks in the dead of night.

'I went to school too,' she growls.

He mumbles apologetically and disappears into the night of flagging neon while we go upstairs and make love, the taste of redwood trees and Indian air still in your silver-blonde curls, the lostness still in your eyes which was there on the front of a truck as we crossed Golden Gate Bridge . . .

'You're incapable of having full physical relations with women except with Eleanor, yeah.'

In New Orleans I am watching the funeral of a taxi driver. Some nuns in black with circular wreaths of poinsettias look on from a car. A photograph of the taxi driver and photographs of two dispatch riders were placed on a grave in Saint Louis Number 1. The taxi driver and the first dispatch rider were killed. They got to the second dispatch rider in time.

We are performing W. B. Yeats's *The Cat and the Moon* on Dollymount Strand late on a summer's afternoon for children from the Dublin slums. A piebald horse grazes nearby on a mound of grass. Some of the little girls wear daisy-chains. I am the lame man, on the blind man's back, both of us going to the saint for a cure. The big, broad-shouldered girl with grey hair is the blind man. Suddenly a little black-haired boy, in a blue cardigan with black cord bas-relief running over the front of it and patent shoes, with skin like dented crockery, breaks from the crowd and starts shouting at the saint, 'Please saint, cure me. My Daddy says I've a girl's voice and beats me up all the time. Please saint, give me a man's voice.'

Years later I visit the grey-haired girl in a mental hospital near the border.

'You're a golden oldie,' she says, as we meet in the lounge. There is a picture of a camel being dragged through a desert on the wall.

A boy with twin earrings on each ear, eagle on his belt, silver studs on his boots looks at us. At his feet is a carpet with a lozenge shape in the centre. There is coleus on the windowsill and the window is multi-grided.

We go walking, almost immediately, among the ash and alders and hazels and willows of the grounds.

'It was a fair ould boot up the arse for me,' she says.

Two nuns are walking by. 'Didn't a lord once live here?' one of them asks the other.

At the beginning of that summer of plays on beaches we'd hitchhiked together in Spain. We flew to Benidorm and hitchhiked from there – Murcia, Almeria, Malaga, Fuengirola, Seville, Granada, Madrid, Avila, Gerona, Barcelona. We even got to Ceuta in North Africa by a short boat ride. First night we stopped for a couple of coffees in a café big as an amusement arcade on a street of poplar trees in the dead of night and then went on, sleeping in the same bed in rooms with dove-brown shutters, attended by ladies with bobbed hair, in low white high heels and clothes the mulatto brown of Martin de Porres.

In the chapel of St Teresa's convent in Avila she'd said, 'Wouldn't Aunt Evelina be happy with me now?'

Someone subsequently told me of an Irish woman, in the days of cloche hats, who came on pilgrimage here and how afterwards, when she'd got to Toledo, allowed herself to be picked up by a sheep driver and had him make love to her on the side of a hill.

As we walk the girl tells a story of her Holy Communion, how her mother washed the white dress the night before and how it turned blue, and then for some reason she starts singing.

'I went for a walk on such a winter's day. California dreaming on such a winter's day.'

Right up to the end of that summer, when I left for the United States for the first time, I was still playing in the theatre company, dressed in black, looking into a Victorian pram on a bandstand in St Stephen's Green with blue-painted pillars.

In London I wasn't so much going through a bad time as feeling pressed in, pestered by family, when I went to a party at Christmas. There were soldiers there, lords, ladies, representatives from Amnesty International, all in rose-madder paper hats. I nervously fingered the John McCormack records. The only person who'd spoken to me so far was a runaway from Glasgow in a seal-skin costume. I'd drunk hot chocolate all day so I wouldn't get drunk, but champagne mixed with Beaujolais Nouveau mixed with gravy on Brussels sprouts – a gay wine bar manager had handed the sprouts to me saying, 'So you're the vegetarian' – and suddenly I felt sick and went to the little whitewashed toilet where I started throwing up. It was when I returned that some newcomers to the party, a tall, broad-shouldered boy with vagabond hair I'd known in Ireland and his wife, with snowflake-peroxide hair, in a frou-frou dress, came up to me. He put his hand on my arm and so the gesture was passed on. Dylan, an Indian boy called John, and I thought for some reason, as John McCormack sang 'The Last Rose of Summer', of an Irish woman from the country, in a black cloche hat, walking through a field of poppies after making love.

Spring comes to Berlin; women look out the windows of peach houses; lime trees come into blossom against umber roofs; a hurdy-gurdy woman in Kreuzberg, in Edwardian costume, leads her hurdy-gurdy on a wagon drawn by a donkey with carnations in his ears; a dispatch rider cycles under Marienkirche with a bouquet in his mouth; a little girl runs along a path by the border carrying a toy horse with a mane as black and fulsome as a Sephardic Jewish woman's hair; there are cowslips in the front of the detergent in shop windows in East Berlin and aftershave being sold from side-street vans; in a toilet in Friedrichstrasse Station a miniature bottle of champagne is stuck on a pin into a pot, wrapped in tinsel, of daffodils and lilies; a boy in cobalt sweeps the street, two plastic fleabanes on the back of his wagon, one pink, one magenta; a crippled Turkish boy in a black leather cap turned back to front, moles on his face, motors himself across a road, sometimes helped by a companion, and turns and throws a smile at me.

Before I leave Berlin I visit the site of the Gestapo torture rooms nears Kochstrasse, Putkammerstrasse, where prisoners were executed on a bombed-out site on 23 and 24 April 1945. There's a blown-up photograph of Dietrich Bonhoeffer in a little museum, blond, balding, in an open-necked shirt. On a side-street is a socialistic mural, girls in blue dancing and boys with red kerchiefs playing violins and accordions while wheat is gathered. In a nearby museum there is a painting of Ruth and Boaz meeting in a field of poppy-sprinkled green barley, a man in turban and thoab to the side of the field. A gull flies low over the border.

'The mighty gods forbid no one to travel the path of love.'
The train is packed. There is a young black American soldier with bow knees. A woman in a floral dress, cyclamen and red hankie on her breast, sings an aria from Franz Lehar's *Giuditta*; two women are making shirts from twenty-mark notes – 'our last'; a man with a bottle of schnapps in his fist stares into his son's eyes, his son with a big white collar and a moustache like his, except that the boy's moustache is sapling; a woman with a black mantilla on her head carries a doll with shining chestnut hair and polka-dot dress in plastic covering.

Outside men with lanterns and burning braziers illumine lambs eating grass, making the lambs look like those in Georges de la Tour's painting of the Nativity.

Candles burn in a grotto on Narodni and there are little photographs of Jan Palach and Jan Zagik stuck on telephone kiosks. 'Let us never forget boys,' a poster says outside the Hussite Church on Staroměstaké Nám.

Women on Wenceslas Square are selling lilies of the valley, threading them together for customers. The girls on the Metro wearing frou-frou dresses and bobby socks and the boys black socks with explosions of thread, lemon and pink.

'Tomorrow is coming the Holy Father.'

The old lady is not at the café. There is a table of British tourists in shell-suits near the door.

'Last of the big spenders, Harry.'

A girl with manifold, outspread hair gets up and plays *Für Elise* on the grand piano.

'Nice one, Pamela.'

I leave.

Outside, under the Air France sign, a male prostitute waits. He has one gold tooth.

Dvorak's *Te Deum* is broadcast all over Wenceslas Square.

In the Metro station near the Pope's venue, vendors tinkle little bells in your face and wave mostly French and Papal flags. A woman in a white polo neck stares at John Paul, hands clasped on her breast, as a Jack Russell barks near her.

Honza's been selling glass popes for the past few days and this evening, Saturday evening, he has a party. On the wall of a large room prepared by cranes, lions, grapes and red berries is a picture of Pat Boone in shorts, and a wooden bas-relief of a courting couple in elephant flares. His mother remarried – a communist official – and lives in the country. In the garden outside is a walnut tree she planted when he was born. They play mainly fifties American music. 'Did We Have a Party?' Billy Brown; 'Wild Wild Party', Darryl Vincent; 'Bald Headed Baby', Buddy Sharpe and the Shakers; 'Rose of San Antonie', Pat Boone.

Honza recently married and he stands in the middle of the room, arm around his pregnant wife, earrings with lemon tassels on her.

Next morning I visit the Old Jewish Cemetery.

Some children are playing with acorns on a street nearby, one of them wearing glasses with raspberry-syrup-coloured frames.

Suddenly, a wedding party comes round a corner – men with ties like bits of carpet, a bride with carmine cheeks and shocking blonde hair – and, just as quickly, they disappear round another corner.

White dead-nettle grows in the cemetery.

What brought me through? The sexuality of boys. The Southern States of America. A feeling of colour and scintillation like a beach of flattened glass. The poetry of Hart Crane. But leaving the intimacy, the sunlight of this medieval city is like a death.

'I give part of my heart to friends, to enemies.'

A woman is bidding farewell to a friend on a street of amber, buff, pistachio. In her window is a cat with lime eyes, a chimpanzee in a concentration camp suit.

She waves. I am bidding farewell to Prague.

It is a year later and I live in Berlin. Zdena comes to visit me. Marek is in a hospital in a town about sixty kilometres from her in Swabia, a town of peach roofs and marzipan buildings, houses of buff and old rose, sepia mermaids and knights and antelopes on buildings, signs of golden ships over shops, downy swans on the water, pines and firs on the surrounding hills.

We light a menorah as we have a meal. Outside, the sun is amber and grape purple on the ancient buildings of Kreuzberg.

A girl called Ursula Goetze lived in this house. She was a member of the Rote Kapelle, an anti-fascist group, and secret meetings were held here. Also members of the group were Harro and Libertas Schulze Boysen. Harro Schulze Boysen worked for the Ministry of Aviation which enabled him to get hold of vital information. Ursula Goetze was murdered in Plötzensee, August 1943. Harro and Libertas Schulze Boysen were murdered there December 1942. There's a photograph of the Schulze Boysens in the little museum nearby. She's a beautiful blonde woman playing an accordion. He wears a dapper suit. They were, paradoxically, friends of a golden-haired Irish writer who lived in Berlin during the war, teaching Modern English and Anglo-Irish literature at Berlin University. He was somehow drawn into Plan Kathleen for a German landing in Derry, helped by the IRA in Leitrim. To activate this plan a man called Herman Goertz landed by parachute in Ireland in May 1940 and made his way by foot to the writer's wife in County Wicklow. In Dublin, later that month, a party which he was attending in the house of Stephen Held, who had an Irish mother and an adoptive German father, was raided by the gardai. Herman Goertz got out the back door but the gardai got hold of a new suit. A court case was held in Dublin early in July to ascertain whether the writer's wife had purchased that suit for him in Switzers, but the woman's mother, Maud Gonne, who wore towel-like scarves on her head at that time and had a cratered facial appearance, got her off. The writer remarried a German woman and she lived in Dublin and could sing 'Lili Marlene' beautifully and sadly at parties. She was a woman of kindness and hospitality, who wore warm red dresses, and owned many white rabbits. Some-times, in Berlin late at night, on the Metro, I imagine her break-ing into song as a stranger talks, maybe a woman with a muslin frill on her shoes. 'With no border I don't know how long I've come here for. Two months. Two years. I'll go on to Frankfurt, Paris, Toronto.'

On Easter Sunday Marek got baptized. He feared it would not be possible without fierce elaboration but there was no problem.

He got baptized in a country church, with a dark gold interior, among vineyards and wine-coloured buds breaking into blossom, after a sermon about the Jews crossing the Red Sea.

In the porch was an advertisement for the pilgrimage to Santiago, beginning 23 June. On the altar were huge catkin branches, and red gerbera and broom decorated with eggs painted with flowers and butterflies, and a little flag of the Vatican colours. A little girl in a white crinoline party dress with scarlet rims was running riot around the church, cross with everybody. Eventually a boy, in a grey satin suit and black dicky bow, pursued her. The sacristan was a boy in a flash-scarlet letterman jacket. His face was full of adolescent pores. The altar boys, who were slightly crouched, wore scarlet and white. One of them had mud-marigold hair. Two little girls in sailor hats and sailor duck suits, blue and white, carried candles wrapped in silk. What looked like a gipsy boy, in a coral-pink suit, videoed the event. The lady doctor who looks after Marek carried a candle. She was the godmother. I was the godfather. Marek stood under a statue of King David playing a harp. There was a bunch of wild pansies in front of the statue. In the front row was a boy in a pearly-white letterman jacket with the words 'American League' on the back, and a crippled woman with crutches, her legs askew. Near the front there was a gipsy family, a bas-relief of black bolls on the women's black stockings. Girls in the congregation, Mediterranean girls, had lace on their heads.

When you are in love a bunch of daffodils in a glass jar outside a vegetable shop in Potsdam, beside a crate of black roots and the cats who keep passing on the umber stones, takes on a new meaning.

The days are miraculous.

I feel as if I've been dead all my life. Now I'm only awakening.

Kreuzberg, 10 April 1991. Turkish boys on bicycles lean against a *Litfass-säule*. Turkish men in suits stand around. An old woman throws crusts of bread from an upper-storey window. A man in a long skirt limps on alternate legs. A woman in chador goes by in a temper. A Dobermann has his front legs on a bench. The species barrier is broken down in murals on the wall: a duck and a teddy bear kiss in a balloon the shape of a heart; a turtle and a frog kiss; a girl cat presents a bouquet to a mouse. Outside a church the Missionaries of Charity, in white with blue-rimmed veils, give soused herrings to shaven-headed youths. Inside, a woman who looks like the Duchess of Windsor, in black velvet coat and black velvet tarboosh, prays in front of Our Lady of Czestochowska; a woman in a silver lamé turban hat chats to a friend on a bench.

11 April 1991. The meadows of Potsdam.

The tulips are red and yellow, the red sprinkled with white, the yellow with blood-red. A mental hospital patient with a big head, in elephant flares, sits beside a Harley Davidson, eating from a bag of chocolates. Two other retarded male patients walk, holding hands. A nun with a Dutch-style wimple stands in the meadows, among the cowslips and wood anemones and lambs. A little boy with defective eyesight looks into my face, his eyes all the time going from side to side.

An old lady holds Marek, like a mother, like a lover. Her black hair is rolled up. She wears a brown suit like one of the Trapp family. Beside the bed is the ladybird – *Marienkäfer* – I brought from Kreuzberg, being sold on a cloth by children, alongside a yellow duck and a red gorilla.

The lady doctor worked in Uganda for twenty years, in the latter ten years mainly with women who had AIDS. When she returned to Germany she found that no one would give her a job as a doctor so she does an administrative job, in a nearby town, getting a train through the vineyards most mornings around five o'clock. She lives near the hospital and is here as Marek's friend, having met him in a community in the mountains he'd reached from Berlin – some people mentally or physically handicapped, some with drug or alcohol problems.

'Now you see what it's like.'

Sometimes, the pain is so terrible he just cries.

He takes *temgesech* for the pain, with a thimble of water.

He gets infusions from three bottles attached to a contraption by his bed – glucose, minerals, antibiotics. Pink rosettes are appliquéd to him.

When he walks, with the contraption strung to his body, his face has the charcoal of death. When he's in bed again it's a young boy's face.

Zdena came yesterday. She brought a pool of tobacco which lies by the ladybird. She'll return in a few days.

'It's a strange life, hospitals.'

Old people sit in wheelchairs in the lounge. There are pebbles and artificial plants around the side and a Nigerian mural of the Flight into Egypt on the wall. Through a wide glass window you can see the town below. Snow has come again and it falls on the peach blossom, the cherry blossom, the redcurrant, the hedge flowers, the buttercup hills, the peach roofs, the swans. Blossom is messages of white through a mist of alders. The town, with its towers and parapets, becomes a lavender-blue blur with late afternoon.

> Now I lay me down to sleep,
> I pray the Lord my soul to keep.
> If I shall die before I wake,
> I pray the Lord my soul to take.

I hold his hand.

He cries from pain and I cry from loneliness. His hair has turned colour again. It is the black of Palestine. In Palestine, shortly after her wedding, his mother had seen the moon and the stars being blessed by rabbis, in slouch hats, with snowy beards. In the light of Galilee in the fall Marek was conceived.

Against the glamorously lit-up medieval town I see a boy from Ireland, dressed in black, black polo neck, who used to come to Germany. 'How lovely are thy tents, O Jacob.'

A child of the West of Ireland who died in the early seventies.

Last thing Marek talks about, before falling asleep, is Ireland, the winter roses in January by the sea, the sunsets, the sudden view of an entire meadow of snowdrops across a stone wall, a cake with royal icing of blue and white made by an old lady and he quotes her, 'God be with the lovely days and nights.'

19 April 1991. I was in that room when the white-winged reapers were there. There were a few of them. I was not afraid of death. I'd been near death many times but they were asking of me, asking of me. I sat calmly with death and I put the blessing of love and peace on Marek, my deepest blessing, and I went on.

The lady doctor unweaves her hair. She stands very straight.

In the little room in which I'm going to sleep on a couch there's an ikon of Our Lady of Vladimir, a squirrel-like child held by the black hands of a mother against a gold and copper patchwork like fallen autumn leaves, pendants of stars on the rose-bud-lipped mother's wrists. On a dresser there's a photograph of children in coats around a kitchen-stove – kitchen witch – in Berlin in the thirties, a photograph of a Third Reich ballerina on stage, a colour photograph of a little boy in a top hat, yellow shirt, short blue trousers with straps.

A candle lights. It throws grape-red light on the boy's ankles.

There's a white towel for me on the radiator.

She asks about his burial. What potter's field among the cherry blossoms, the peach blossoms, should he be buried in? Her family live in a village high in the Swabian mountains, with a view of the Alps, and I suggest that he, a child who knew Europe, would be happy there.

Last time I was in Alge a woman, in a white coif and a scarf of fuschia and violet with a border of black berries, was selling gold rings with the Portuguese Queen Victoria on them in a square splintered with orange peel. A man was striking a canary in a cage over a spread of ceramic bullterriers and cats. Above the square a banner announced for a few years hence 'Europa 1992'. Young heroin dealers with flap-fronted shoes went by.

20 April 1991. Early morning I break down on a bridge. Shane McCowan's and Bob Geldof's photographs are nearby, advertising a concert, alongside a poster for an Indian experience multi-vision show. There's a male nude in a kiosk with the words 'Budapest mit Paprika'. Girls with hair polished on their heads, a boy in boots and camouflage trousers, a woman with a poodle whose coat is trimmed around the neck like a

lavish fur stole, a man with piping hot cheeks who looks like Curly Wee, all stare. None of them approaches. There are swans on the water in the rain. My friend is dying. In Leningrad I have met someone and, despite the fact that my closest friend is maybe near death or perhaps because of it, I am going there.

The moment's serenity asks:
　　Was it worth it?
　　And it's up to you to answer:
　　Yes, it was the right path.

　　　　　Death at your throat.
　　　　　You have loved life.
　　　　　Yet your soul is weary
　　　　　Of what finally pushes you now.

　　　　　Even though we will die
　　　　　We know the seed will blossom,
　　　　　That people will see,
　　　　　The spirit will force the State.

　　　　　The last arguments are neither rope
　　　　　Or guillotine knife,
　　　　　And our judges today
　　　　　Will not be our final judges.

This poem by Harro Schulze Boysen was found under the floor of his cell after his hanging in December 1942. Plötzensee haunts my sleep at night – its maroon and oak colour, the river around it, the turbines on islands in the river; so does the figure of a boy in a black capote, purple diamanté on him, a cross, his hair blue, his lips blackberry-coloured, who begs in Kreuzberg; so does a witch on a cloth on the pavement, a skull in her hand; so does a hurdy-gurdy woman in Kreuzberg, in a maroon capote, wide-brimmed black hat with bedraggled black feather on it, black paper roses on her breast, black teddy bear hanging from the hurdy-gurdy; so do the punk boys going to work early in the morning – '*Hast du etwas Kleingeld für mich*? – some of them letting out a strange cry as they walk, as if they are selling wares at a marketplace.

27 May 1991. A grey day in Berlin, Germany. A lorry from Warsaw, Poland, goes by.

Marek suddenly improved and the doctor started taking him out in a wheelchair. Then one of his friends came from the community in the mountains, put him on the back of a motorbicycle and took him for a ride in the mountains, on the roads lined by rowan trees. After the trip the strength went from his body.

In the courtyard of the house where Ursula Goetze lived there are red geraniums, lace curtains in the windows. The chips on the walls make a ruddy and silver tracery. During the day there are always children playing, and frequently the sound of jazz comes from the lime-shrouded street outside.

We leave our friends and keep going. Once you've found a country you love you want to go back there no matter what.

Before I leave Berlin I get frantic letters from my mother, injections of melancholy, and then, on an evening when the cobbles are blazing with vermilion, Turkish couples out walking, a crazed telephone call. I understand now why for some members of Irish families there's no choice but to go to the Antipodes or die.

When I was a child I purchased my mother a necklace for

Christmas, big gaudy beads. I saw beauty in it. When I presented it to her she started hitting me.

In a photograph she's a raffish, voluptuous little girl in booties, white socks, knickerbockers showing under a white dress, holding a chair against a South Sea Islands scene. Once she came on her way from the South, where she was having an affair, in a black Morris Oxford and presented a gift – a handsel – of a bunch of golden tickseed to my mother. The gift was rejected.

'Bog Irish,' someone once turned and said towards me in a café in Soho. But the bog-myrtle grows in the bogs, and in the spring it is very beautiful with orange and red catkins.

At a wedding party in Ireland on a cement carpet at a crossroads this woman of the Midland bogs, in a suit of the near-biscuit brown which covered armchairs all over Ireland at the time, in block high heels, got up to dance with a young man who'd been an orphan in an orphanage where most of the orphans had been mulattos. A year or so later she was dead – had died of a broken heart.

On one of my first nights in Dublin when I came to go to university I went to the Bailey where a row of people sneered: 'Up from the bogs in a nipple-pink shirt.' In a far corner was a poet, fat as a rooster.

Marek went to visit a teacher he liked, who lived in a yellow wooden bungalow with a brown door, mauve rails on the porch, and a loggia at the back, to read a passage of Herman Hesse:

... he nailed his senses to a cross, bowed his head to the stern rule of obedience, resolute to serve only in spirit, offering his body as its sacrifice; had become, through and through, *minister verbi divini*. There like a corpse he had lain, half-dead from weariness, with white face and pale thin hands ...

The teacher had just stared at him.

Shortly afterwards Marek had run away from school, gone first to Scotland, then back to Munich, from where he started visiting Verona and where he became HIV positive through injecting heroin.

Because they had rejected the gift I offered I went on, past that town, to the West, to a landscape I could identify with, the savage little shores with beaches of beaded splinter, where long ago raddled black tinkers' kettles would be left.

So it begins, a country you love, a country to live and die for ...

On my way to the Leningrad train a woman in a trouser suit and high heels plays with a hula-hoop; a woman in silver lamé high heels, white hair outspread, stands in the middle of the road; Kurds in saffron costume do a dance in flank-formation on the pavement, arms on one another's shoulders; an American boy stands talking to a German girl, the sun hitting off him; a begging Romanian woman rubs her nose with that of her child; 'Sadeness Part 1' by Enigma is blasted on to the pavement.

There is something to be listened to there, as one listens to the sound of the sea in a sea-shell.

Fields of white rye; a blond-haired Virgin Mary leaning forward, lilies on her white veil and dress, a gold orb in her hand, cochineal-coloured streamers from her head to the ground; women in fiery angora jerseys staring at the train; girls in drummer-boy hats with green lollipop indicators at stations; bushes of red dawn by the railway tracks.

My mother brought me up to Dublin to see a pantomime at the Olympia and Jack Cruise at the Royal. Ireland was an aviary of priests and nuns and snogging couples at the time. On the streets huddles of women would suddenly burst into 'We Will Be True to Thee til Death'.

Her hair was mussed raven, her lipstick geranium, she wore a black serge dress and in the lounge of Wynne's Hotel she chatted to frumpish spinsters from Kimmage and Templeogue and Phibsborough. We stayed in the Castle Hotel, a bony building like the house of Warsaw. She took off her clothes and I saw her naked. She put on a pink nightdress and slept in the bed, with her arms about me.

There are rotted lilies of the valley in the attendant's cubicle; two little red flags crossed under Mikhail Gorbachev; a birch-twig broom outside it. She had a plate of little pink cakes with dabs of cream on top for tea with the attendant of the next carriage.

A country just coming out of civil war; a group of young hockey players, brave faces against an ancient building.

Someone gave me a little photograph of a woman who ran

away from the town in the nineteen-twenties, leaving two children. She sits in a deck chair, in a cloche hat, her friend, in a narrow suit, immaculate shirt with narrow collar, paper flower on his lapel, to the side behind her, she leaning towards him, a man in shorts and kerchief is on his side, further back.

A young Irishman and his English girlfriend in the mid-forties on Brighton Beach against a merry-go-round. They liked to see Max Miller at the Lewisham Hippodrome and come to the open-air music-hall on Brighton Beach on summer evenings, girls singing 'Daddy Wouldn't Buy Me a Bow-wow', men shifting around tailors' models in red polka-dot dresses, and coloured lights strung up.

Asleep, I see girls in summer dresses of the nineteen-forties – dresses with patterns of twin bars on them, slabs of different coloured polka-dot patterns – girls with the tubercular beauty of Gerard Majella, against a white country house, crying like a Greek chorus. There's a sudden strophe-like wail.

A sister of the man of this house whom my mother's sister had married lived in France during the war and walked around it for a year with the family for whom she was governess, eating turnips. The house has a river near it bordered by oaks, sycamores, copper beeches, and there are frequently swans on the river.

Young men with beautifully coloured ties – Moroccan red, laquer red, cyclamen, garnet – a misty maroon tie with white polka dots.

A wedding scene – priests, bridal couple, sisters so close they look like a locomotive.

With a husband who went to the asylum grounds on winter days to watch rugby, chatted in a room thronged by naked men afterwards, she thought to get a divorce, go back across the Shannon, go to her people, but she stayed in the West of Ireland town.

Queen Elizabeth, the Queen Mother, in the little British Legion hut, oak trees outside, tables and chairs arranged as if in a restaurant.

'Of your charity pray for . . .'

In Lerici once on a blue day I saw the child I'd been in a crinkled swimsuit with straps in the water at Salthill, against the promenade buildings which looked like an airport in wartime.

In the country, a group of young men in suits back from England on holiday in a sitting-room, a storyteller, gangly as a spare-bodied cow, who'd been coming for centuries.

A country lane at Christmas, a lone magpie's nest, mummers coming along the lane.

> The wren, the wren the king of all birds.
> St Stephen's Day was caught in the furze.
> Up with the kettle and down with the pan.
> Give us a copper to bury the wren.

The Artane Boys' Band coming out to play in Croke Park before a football match involving Galway – all orphans.

A boy in trousers like rainfall, sandals on him with cross bar, bar down the middle. They tried to make me a Boy Scout but the day before I was to be inaugurated I became too frightened by the nationalism they were purveying, and opted out.

There were the women who died or tried suicide. If one of them protested about the erosion of their dreams their husbands would say, 'Ah sure, I adore the ground you walk on.'

A woman who used to make sweets of green and pink coloured marzipan in a flat at the top of a large house had a picture of Romy Schneider in *Sissi, Mother and Empress* on her wall and died during a heart operation.

A woman who had studied singing in Heidelberg, and would sing 'The Last Rose of Summer' at parties, threw herself out of the top window of the house she was living in, a red brick house in an alcove.

A raven-haired woman lived in a courtyard beside the mortuary and a little shoemaker's shop that smelt of black polish. She wore black bejewelled suits even for sweeping up. One day when she was sweeping up and I was passing she took a fit, and started wielding her brush at me as if I had the look of someone who'd do something unforgiveable some day.

My aunt, who lived in a vestal orange house out of town, had a big picture of a geisha girl, entertained priests a lot, gave words and admonitions in fruity Gaelic. One day she showed me an illustration in a book of cranes flying over vermilion turreted palaces, and that was the first stage of my journey to Russia.

A woman in a broad-brimmed hat, emerald coins on white, ribbon around it with a bow, her eye-shadow Nile-green, looks into the train.

The fashionable avenue of a town in Ireland where the Polish woman lived and the children you always wanted to be. The attempt to coerce love from a wheaten-haired Polish boy who looked like a white poodle. He shook you off. You weren't satisfied with being a good Catholic Irish boy like you should have been. A woman who made firescreens with embroidered flowers on them also lived on this avenue and died young.

A girl who'd just lost her virginity crying, bent over, hands on her face, in Butlins, Mosney, County Meath. The Dutch College Swing Band had been playing in Butlins that night. A few girls in red jackets looked on.

A school which had once been the manor house, a pyramid in the garden like the pyramid of Caius Cestius in the Protestant Cemetery in Rome, an avenue of poplar trees cutting through the garden. We were asked in this school one day what two people in the world we most wanted to meet. I said Carol Baker and Jackie Kennedy. Daniel said Harold Robbins and Tennessee Williams. Next day he vanished to England.

Your mother tried to destroy all your friendships. She didn't like the look of the boy up the road. She wouldn't let Daniel into the house. She beat you up and locked you in a room for seeing Bridget – 'a tinker'.

You were the leper boy with the leper's rattle then.

You meet a friend who'd gone away in Cork in 1968, went to Blarney with him. The daffodils and the narcissi had withered. At Cork Airport, where you also went with him, a young couple held hands.

Your passport photograph before you went to France, freckles like bullets, a prisoner's haircut.

The first view of the pale blue twin spires of Chartres Cathedral across the wheat fields. That summer, you met your art teacher and her husband, by arrangement, in a Paris hotel with a faded carpet. Later, you took a train through France, from the Auvergne to Paris.

(In Berlin, years later, you saw this Europe again. An old lady, maybe ninety, in a brown coat and scarf, fluffy like a beard, skin already dead, tripping along outside Gedächtniskirche, glove falling off her fingers, joyously looking up at the plane trees about to break into blossom.)

'You must forgive. It was history,' an obsidian-haired woman from Washington, with a great bun at the back, said to me in the Russell Hotel, which had a cerulean door.

'You've got to go through Poland to realize what we did,' a German boy told me. 'How business-like it was.'

Your first time in England; a pound for accommodation in the house of a black woman in Notting Hill; an Irish girl going up to you next morning on the street and saying, 'It's different for you coming over like this. For us it was awful'; an address your mother gave you of one of her loves, a man who lived in West London, hair askew, face inflamed, holy water from the Jordan on the cupboard, a picture of the miraculous draught of fishes on the wall.

In Dublin, a city where as much as possible was painted green at the zoo, where girls in moss-green convent uniforms would sit endlessly in Bewleys, you came up against something.

Plötzensee, two windows, a cross beam, five hooks. An American woman hanged there translated Goethe before she died.

> Noble be man
> Helpful and good
> For that alone
> Distinguishes
> Him from all beings
> On earth known.

Waiting at Dublin airport for the coffin of a girl, a truant of Ireland, killed while hitchhiking from Geneva to Paris.

The intellectuals who lived in houses with sitting-rooms with lachrymose forties lampshades, who tuned into a hatred of England brewed over the centuries. These masters of war with their many books.

A boy on a platform in Ireland, petunias on the platform, a plane going by in the sky.

To take the life of teenage British soldiers, of a young couple who'd informed, is evil, is a contumely.

There were British soldiers garrisoned in the manor house

in the town after the 1916 rebellion, many of them from a countryside with wild service trees still in it, and girls fell in love with their firm pectorals as they bathed in the swamps surrounded by loosestrife, burdock, yellow irises.

The last lord of the manor had married a London music-hall artiste and, to celebrate the wedding, there had been fireworks over the town of immense sheaves of wheat falling downwards.

As a teenager, I'd meet a little old lady in a black coat, black beret, on a red bench on a hill overlooking the town. Although she never married, she remembered what were, for her, the dulcet days of 1916 and 1917.

Before the train goes into Russia the wheels have to be changed and people get out and sit on the grass. A female attendant walks along a corridor with a great plunger. A male attendant holds up a bunch of wild strawberries he's picked from the railway tracks. He introduces himself and shakes my hand, strawberries in the other hand. His name is Darya. Lemon pepper also grows on the tracks. Women in felt boots grease the tracks. A woman in gold lamé high heels with a stippled effect, plain gold strap, plays a lemon-gold accordion and young people dance. They dance in circles around individuals and couples parade in succession under sporadic bridges made by the dancers, the bridge all the time lapsing as couples break from it to advance under it. A man with a white beard to his chest and a gold and cobalt moustache, broad braces of gentian blue, flamingo and white with bunches of flowers embroidered on the white, looks at the dancers from a bank. A woman in a red cloth hat, red dress with white polka dots, stands and looks towards Russia. The sky, with its high clouds in the heat, is chromium blue.

A meadow of black cherry trees in fruit; a flock of cranes by a river; a woman in strawberry scarf fetching water from a pump; a woman in a big white scarf and tattersall pattern coat of black and white looking at the train, a girl beside her in a summer dress with patterns of little ducks, mauve with blobs of brown on them; an old lady with patterns of nosegays on each side of her shawl also looking at the train; a graveyard with three pairs of arms on the crosses; houses secretive, diminutive, often with families of geese pleading outside them.

A railway station, a booth on it, with cobalt weighing scales, which sells sugar-freckled buns in boxes with patterns of spider chrysanthemums and dandelion heads, lemonade, jars of pickled kohlrabi and beetroot. A Red Army man carries Vecchia Romagna in a box. There's a gipsy woman in a red flounced dress, with gold bracelets on her wrists, a girl in coat, trousers and wellingtons as if dressed for winter. A boy in an anorak who looks like Marek.

That evening, Marek passed into a coma. He looked very beautiful, strong before this, a young soldier, sitting up in a wine jersey. But the thalamus of his brain had irreparably degenerated, and although he was in great pain that evening he spoke in English about forgiveness and gratitude; he said it didn't matter how long, that it was like passing from one room to another; he spoke of *Liebes-schmerz*, the grief of love, *die dunkeln Machte*, the forces of darkness; he spoke of Italy, an open-air dance on a wooden platform outside Rome, tangos, polkas; the pastelerias of Lisbon; cormorants crying on a rock in Connemara for a labourer buried in the Midlands of England; a memorial stone in the middle of an Irish square for the Connaught Rangers.

Irland war ein schönes Land aber ich bin dort gegen etwas ge-stossen. Manchmal habe ich so eine Friede gefühlt. Jetzt fühle ich diese Friede noch einmal. Es ist genau so wie eine Insel zu

135

finden, wo das Wasser hinuberschwemmte. Diese Insel ist deine Kindheit.

He said goodbye to life, to his short life, and thanked everyone who had held his hand in life.

Late evening, azure of lupins at the edge of the forest, yellow of rape, juniper bushes and the smell of caraway and hemlock in the air. In a dark compartment, a boy with his shirt off plays a red bayan over a glass urn of apricot juice, rye bread, toffee sweets, and a vaudeville lady in a bewhiskered mini-coat with muff wrists and a carpet-like mini-dress stands at the door and does a little dance, lifting her legs. The bayan is still on the table next morning when we begin to see the high-rise buildings of Leningrad.

A ladybird on a stalk of ground elder in waste land in Prague; high-rise buildings; a plywood room, gauze curtains blowing; memories that had nearly been killed coming back. An aunt long ago who wore sandy suits whose worship had not been mass or prayer but sex. Sex was her path to God, sex with young men who listened to Mick Delahunty, with young men who were box players, members of brass bands, with young male nurses in mental hospitals. She liked men with small penises best because they were usually the most beautiful. She liked boys in 'their birthday suits'.

Down Burgh Quay and George's Quay to City Quay and Sir John Rogerson's Quay, over the River Dodder to Pigeon House. Boys in anoraks waiting against the Irish Sea. I always wanted to take one of these boys to safety, not England where they'd be maligned, but Europe – maybe Amsterdam, put them on Rembrandtsplein or by the Schinkel Canal. But the hair of an almost albino-looking boy, boy blue in denim, blows this morning in Leningrad against the lavender blue over the

Irish Sea, a ghost. Then suddenly, on Nevsky Prospekt, at the corner of Sadovaya Boulevard, there's a boy in powder blue with cobalt eyes selling American T-shirts, and the sound of an accordion.

A woman with a yellow wig falling down her forehead, little American flag on her lapel, playing a black and white accordion with black on white by the sides; a soldier on his knees dancing with a little girl; a man turning towards me and showing off all his war medals; an old lady in Hare Krishna costume selling Hare Krishna books on a little table, the books surrounded by dill, wallflowers, sweet william and parsley; the rays of the rising sun on a shop sign; women staring at a pineapple in a kiosk; a woman selling canaries in cages; a man in a wheelchair with blackberry-coloured streamers attached to the wheelchair; two dwarfs walking along together; a little girl dressed like a Valasquez Infanta; a woman, mussed raven hair, glimpse of an earring, cherry lipstick; a little boy in a short-sleeved blue shirt; a little boy in a white cambric shirt with a blue dicky bow, patterns of birds on it.

Dublin, as a child with my mother; a man playing an accordion and singing 'Kevin Barry – Just a Lad of Eighteen Summers'; a queue to see *Esther and the King*; meeting, at the Royal Marine Hotel in Dun Laoghaire, an orphan from home who'd married a Dublin doctor and become respectable, in a blue beret with a white jewel in it.

Long escalators, globular lights in the hands of tribute bearers; a coronet of illuminated eggs on a little stand with a bulb in it at a market-place; the eternal flames by the Neva.

I never thought I'd know happiness. I never thought I'd look at happiness in the face again.

Graffiti on the wall – 'I knew it would be bad but I didn't know it would be so soon'; a poster for a film, a knight in a landscape of skeletons; a ragged old lady suddenly talking to herself.

Everyone is a mystery; that's why those women didn't fare well in the fifties, because Ireland makes everything part of community. But that's a lie. Community leads to fascism, the swastikas in the churches, the lilies of the valley under Hitler.

'St Sava, the founder of the Russian Orthodox Church, was promiscuous,' a Puerto Rican woman who is studying translation at Leningrad University says to me at the Saigon Café, 'That's why the Russian people have a different attitude to their bodies.'

Boys wait outside the Kirov Ballet towards evening; a woman in black crouched on the pavement sells pornography on Nevsky Prospekt – 'Your boobs against mine'; a street is incandesced in light, with the grass coming through the pavement.

The Jazz Club of Leningrad; outside, with its steps, it looks like a cinema in Cork; in the porch there are celestial flushes in the ceiling. A group of boys not so much welcome you as determine who you are, all in mod shirts that were popular in the mid-sixties.

Photographs of Bert Hardy and Dinah Washington on the wall. Men in carob-brown suits and women in gleaming satin décolleté sitting around tables on which there are burgundy lamps with burgundy tassels. The smoke ascending against lamps on the wall seems to be a secondary code, a secondary meaning to the conversations below.

In the lounge a boy from Bettyfield, Alabama, wearing a shirt with the words 'Hector Pierce Academy 1954 Jackson Florida' at the back says to me 'Well, son, how does it feel to be in the Soviet Union?'

In the upstairs bar, against the midsummer light, a sailor in white, with a V of blue and white stripes at his neck, is drinking lemonade.

The singer, who wears a black chiffon dog-collar, sings 'Ochi-Chyorniye', 'Sinner Man Where Are You Running To?' and Elvis Presley's 'Love Me Tender'.

> Love me tender
> Love me sweet
> Never let me go.
> O darling I love you and I always will.

A young man gets up to waltz with an older woman and they are the only dancers on the floor.

He wears a summer shirt with mauve peonies and red sorrel on it, and she wears a summer dress, gold roses which have black centres on it, long green beetles with black feet.

My mother's and my father's favourites come back: Woody Herman, Guy Lombardo, Glenn Miller, Maurice Mulcahy, Billy Cotton, Oscar Rabin, Victor Sylvester. 'La Paloma', 'Melancholy Baby', 'La Mer', 'Wish Me Luck As You Wave Me Goodbye' played at the County Hall in Mullingar.

'Desmond.'

A boy with a GI haircut, meadow-amber hair, in a summer shirt with cerulean daisies, poppies, sheaves of wheat on it, a gold ring of four-leaved clover on his hands. He greets me on the upper balcony as I watch the dancers. Gavriil.

He is a student of architecture in Leningrad, from Syktytyvkar. His grandfather was a one-armed communist from Kleistpark in Berlin who escaped from Anhalter in 1936, ended up in Moscow where he joined the Red Army, got to the Polish concentration camps. His father works on the black market, brings goods between Leningrad and Skytytyvkar, and is something of a playboy, dressing in blue serge suits, red serge shirts, black suits, black silk shirts, and brings young women to Simferopol on the Black Sea.

We leave the Jazz Club and walk in the midsummer night.

First we call on Laveus on Vereyskaya Street. He is a small, chubby sailor and his wife has just left him, taking their son, so, sitting in a sleeveless vest, he laughs that this is a *novoseley* – a housewarming – for his being alone.

There are big crimson cushions, a screen with men with shako hats on them, washing hanging up, and the small room, its shelves, is packed with toys. A squirrel with a mushroom. An orange Donald Duck with real bird feathers sellotaped on to him. A dog with an aeriel coming out of his head. A rabbit with a carrot. A bulldog in black panties with a necklace on. A bulldog with a bib of green and white. An Alsatian in an apron. A mouse on the telephone. A mouse in a little bed. A teddy bear with Mickey Mouse pattern skin. Five teddy bears in mulberry dicky bows, with red sashes on them, on rectangular blue tasselled cushions. A blackberry-coloured rhino. A donkey in a cardigan. A row of little Cossack puppets. A belly dancer puppet with a girdle of coins, black horsehair on her head. There's an inchoate animal with hair like Dolly Parton. A pair of clogs with windmills on them. A quarter moon hanging above with a doll on it.

In this small room there are two clocks, one with a man's face, henna rolls on either side, little legs with pepper and salt trousers. The other in a bell-jar, held up by slim pillars with pink roses on them. On the dresser is a photograph, in an oval frame, of his son.

In the wedding photograph on the wall, everyone looks

sixties, bouffant hair-styles on the girls, shingles under their ears, the suits striped, trousers flared, moustaches walrus, red sashes on everyone.

Also on the wall is a picture of the King and Queen of Sweden, a picture of the Château de Chillon, a painting of a mansion, wheat fields in front of it, an ikon fretted in silver – a saint giving his blessing with three fingers, a picture of Elvis Presley and Cliff Richard.

Laveus presents tea in a white teapot with red polka dots and a red line on the rim, pickled mushrooms with chopped chives on them, a bowl of brandied cherries and a plate of profiteroles. The tablecloth is white with blue stripes through it.

To go walking with us in the midsummer Laveus goes to change and comes back in a white shirt and a brown jacket peppered with orange. It's raining outside now and with the rain the colour of the air is blue. A boy with a cleft palate noiselessly passes.

We call on Valeri on Izmaylovsky Street by the Fontanka Canal.

She's a Jewish girl, a pianist, and she's just about to emigrate to Israel. She has long mousy hair and wears a shamrock-green dress with long, white peaked collars. We sit in her kitchen. 'If it's a stranger knocking at the door always make him more welcome,' she quotes a Jewish proverb.

There's a poster '100 Fires' on the wall – one hundred dalmatians looking at a fire, foreign toothpaste boxes pinned up – Nautica, Panda, Pepsident, Colgate, a photograph of a palm tree with white flowers among them.

An den Wassern zu Babel sassen wir und weinten.

The lids of biscuit tins are displayed on a shelf. Queen Victoria sipping tea. Two polar bears on an iceberg. A boat entering the Panama Canal. A bear on a drum, being tamed by a Cossack. Prancing majorettes with plumes.

She serves tea in a teapot with yellow stars and green lines on it and semolina on a tray with has tansy and eighteenth-century figures on it. She puts the tray on an oil-cloth with patterns of blackberry blossom and blackberries and yellow flowers like rancid buttercups.

To go walking in the midsummer night she goes and changes and returns in a dress of lapis lazuli with uneven black lines running across it, and in peg-top shoes. The rain is falling, the light is cornflower blue. Women pass us noiselessly with huge poodles, imbecilic-looking Alsatians, muzzled Airedales. '*Salve*' is written at the entrance to a tall eighteenth-century house with ironwork railings outside it, and Gounod's 'Ave Maria' comes from an upper window of one of the houses further on. Lights of windows are reflected in the canal, like the streamers of candle-flame in Georges de la Tour's paintings. A coral red truck goes by, one of the few vehicles that have passed. We go, all four of us, into a courtyard with a floor of black and white tiles, pillars, the top half blue, the bottom half orange. 'We had grown sick and sinful, had to recover ritual, closeness to God at any price.'

Tonight is a night in Ireland, in Dublin, in Cork; it is the night I went to a convent reunion dance with the girl with whom I used to play a Greek idiot in a chiton and we danced to 'Meet Me on the Road to Nenagh' and afterwards walked home with a girl who threw a smile after us as we said good-bye and who was drowned a few days later. It is a night of beautiful ghosts.

The woman who cut her throat, the swan-necked woman who died young, the woman who studied in Heidelberg and threw herself out of a window, the woman who made marzipan sweets and died during a heart operation, the aunt who came with flowers once and was rejected, Irene's daughters, Marek's mother, are all out in their most beautiful clothes, georgette, satin, party dresses. The doll-faced Madeleine puts her arm through a candle-flame.

By a bridge a boy is playing a guitar and singing 'Universal Soldier', surrounded by a small hushed group.

We wait in a small bakery in a peach-brown courtyard for

the first bread rolls of the day, an old woman with a cloth bag patterned with shell-pink roses heading the queue, Gavriil and I then say goodbye to Valeri and Laveus and get a taxi to his place near Park Pobedy, his head on my shoulder. We go into his flat, a painting of a liner with war-planes above it on the wall, his landlady's high heel on the carpet – blue with white hatch effect and a pair of gold beads – and he takes off his clothes, lots of cotton underclothes, and he stands naked for a moment, genitals red like the red blemishes on Irish pears in the autumn, and then we sleep in separate, narrow beds across the room from one another in a light that hasn't failed, dreaming dreams that seem to come from a mutual remembrance.

A ship, still lit up, reflections in the water, goes up a river into an Irish town at dawn. It passes a row of tall creamy white or light green houses as if the citizens had demurred against any strong colours. All the houses have transoms on the doorways. There's a convent near the water's edge with a statue of a nun in black over the entrance as if she'd flown up there. It is the ship of death.

26 June 1991. Marek died. In Kreuzberg a group of nuns in white, who looked Jewish, passed me. A blond-haired boy, with plum cheeks, fell off his red bicycle and I picked him up. A boy in bafflingly large trousers, with brilliantined hair, looked on. The cobbles were violet and pale blue, overlaid by rain which had begun to fall about twelve o'clock when he died. There were many lime trees in blossom up those side-streets, Trabants parked. They could have been side-streets in many East European cities. There was kohlrabi outside the shops and old women in pinafores of rosebuds and hydrangeas looking out the windows, and the rain smelt of sulphur as in Prague. In a corner café, with a conical tower above it, by the window, two women chatted, cloth hats pulled

down over their heads. They had strings of beads about their necks. Further in was a soldier with blond hair. An old lady, in a white blouse, with heavy breasts, a pheasant feather in her hat, carried a suitcase. 'You are the red thread in my life.'

10 August 1987. In Ruzyně in Prague a man and a boy walk along a row of low, red-roofed houses, with dormer windows which with evening have shaded into blue. They both wear donkey jackets. The man's hair is long and unkempt. The boy is tow-headed. The man wears pink sneakers, the boy green. The man carries a corrugated aluminium suitcase. Suddenly the boy looks around as if saying goodbye to something both father and son are leaving.

Norway, November 1986. Oslo covered in snow and soldiers in red outside the Royal Palace, a little café near the palace which has marzipan cakes in banana shapes in the window; apartment blocks often with a pub at the entrance to the courtyard, a red plush curtain at the doorway as if for a performance, a stove and old prints inside, the solicitation then.

'Once hit by it you are haunted forever.' A dream after I'd left Ireland in 1977; St Bonefatius Church in Kreuzberg now, its twin spires. A walk across Eastern Europe.

'You know the story of the Archpriest Avvakum and Dame Avvakum and their walk across Russia and she says "How long, Archpriest, are these sufferings to last?" And he says "Till our death." '

A black dress on a Turkish woman with fierce white polka dots on it, a geranium coat on another Turkish woman and white scarf; both seem to be looking at me in the evening as I walk in Kreuzberg, having heard; the marigolds – *Studentenblume* – aflame in the middle of the road near St Bonefatius.

Yellow agrimony and purple speedwell by the tracks; a change of trains and you are in Swabia, the country of the soul. A river dividing in a valley, heather by brooks, buff cows, half-timbered houses and timber houses.

First Zdena and I went with the doctor to the house of the doctor's sister. A daguerreotype on the wall of a man beside a drayhorse and wagon, and one of a man holding a twig against the Swabian Alps. Then, with the sister who had the key, we walked up the street, mountains all around the village, to the little hut where Marek lay alongside an old lady. Both their faces had jaundiced somewhat in death and a stubble had come above Marek's lips which appears when the facial tissue has peeled away. I left a card in his hands, posted in Leningrad during the siege, the Egyptian Sphinx at the Quay of the Academy of Arts.

There were striations in the rolling meadows around the cemetery, the rowan tree and pine and beech grew about it. Yellow lion's teeth, yellow key flowers, white goose flowers, white bell flowers by my feet. The church at the top of the hillside cemetery looked like a biretta and, as was the custom in this part of Germany, black chiffon scarves were attached to the headstones – dots on them, hems of black cloth – and they waved in the breeze.

The distant meadows were mussed with summer flowers and the sky was clouded with pearly and blue clouds. Zdena's hair, alongside me, scuffled against the sky. The doctor stood with her sister at the bottom of the cemetery.

Titus van Rijn, Rembrandt's son, died at twenty-seven.

Georg Trakl died, at twenty-seven, from cocaine poisoning in a garrison hospital in Cracow which smelt of carbolic acid and where victims of war were ending their misery by blowing their brains out. Marek died at twenty-six.

Wild geese flew over, against the Alps, as I stood there, as I had once seen them fly over Vltava in Prague, or the Moldau as it is called in German, and they seemed to be saying good-bye to Marek but also perhaps welcoming me to Europe. The Wild Geese were the Noble Irish who went to Savoy, France, Piedmont, Austria, Lombardy, Flanders, Alsace, Bohemia, Russia in the eighteenth-century – Count Browne was the com-mander-in-chief of the armies of Maria Theresa, Peter Lacy, governor of Livonia, Count O'Rourke commanded the Rus-sian Army. They were also, by reason of their great journey, the tinkers who were deported to Barbados and Virginia.

A street in Ireland in my childhood, bathed in gold, beech and elder on the fringes of the village, the May devotions going on and young men in black patent shoes outside the court-house. I felt that peace again in the paths of the Wild Geese; a town in Galicia at evening, children carrying bread along by canals; Kreuzberg on Sunday afternoons with the Turkish men standing around in suits.

They'd tried to maim, they'd tried to destroy, but people, strangers, brush against one another as true families, attracted to one another perhaps by the chimera of a piece of clothing or a glance, and create, away from totalitarianisms, true posteri-ties, based on love and kindness.

A friend of Marek's from the school in Bavaria, Erhard, who'd since lost a finger, came by plane from Berlin for the funeral in a new shirt. The villagers gathered as if burying nobility and in the showers sang Byzantine hymns. There was the smell of wild thyme in the air. The doctor wore a crenellated, ebony fur coat which made her look like someone from the Berlin of her childhood. A boy played an accordion which when it opened looked like a festive lantern, with patterns on it.

The priest prayed: '*Das Korn wird in die Erde gepflanzt, damit der Weizen emporspriessen kann.*'

Afterwards, there was a gathering in a house full of faience – polka dot cups, square petals and petals set on squares in the cups – and in the evening there was a service in the hospital chapel attended mostly by nuns from Africa with a few Missionaries of Charity sitting on the carpet in front, in dark blue cardigans.

Zdena read from the Koran in English:

Men ought to have a part of what their parents and kindred leave, and women a part of what their kindred leave: whether it be little or much, let them have a stated portion: and when they who are of kin are present at the division, and the orphans and the poor, bestow somewhat upon them therefrom; and speak to them with kindly speech. And let those be afraid to wrong orphans.

I saw the orphans on the other side of the convent wall and heard the whine of the Dublin train.

The Swabian mountains at the top are like Pacific waves rolling in – the blue of blue lines in exercise books when you were a child – greater, more grandiose waves beyond. My first time in Europe I saw the French Alps from the Auvergne, with white peaks which were rose with evening light. I also saw those Alps from Savoy in 1974 when I feasted out of doors with a young French family, a plate of almond cakes in the middle of the long table and the snow at the top of the Alps, which I could see more clearly with evening.

Prague, 11 August 1987. A little boy in a go-cart holds a yellow dog with a tail so long it drags on the ground and he laughs up at me, sharing the joke. On the riverside tram no. 17 there's a little lady in a cream beret, with cream bobbed hair which has fuschine shadows in it. A family picnics on the path of sand by the river. The tablecloth on a little table is black with gold squares. Two policemen check the identity papers of some travellers on Maje Bridge; early evening jazz, 'Hong Kong Blues', comes from a corner café; wild geese fly over the Vltava; hundreds of swans sail by the fan of a lock.

When I get back there's a note under the door: 'We already had to leave because of the train. Have a nice time and see you. Your Canadian friends.'

Prague, 8 August 1987. A couple waltz at the top of Wenceslas Square, under the lime trees, she in a daisied navy dress and white bobby socks. A man in a white work coat rushes to put a lighted cigarette in the male dancer's mouth. The accordionist plays 'La Paloma' and a small group gathers and begins, against the lights of Traktoro Export, Balkancar Bulharsko, Machino Export Bulharska, Telecom Sofia Bulgaria, Lucerna Bar, Licensintory Moscow USSR, Licence Know How Engineering, Fiat Olivetti, to sing Carmen Miranda's 'La Paloma' as if it is the national anthem. Some of the women in little boots, in berets, hats with feathers in them. Some of the men in baseball caps, some with tattoos at their necks. They come like the cast from the raddled black cheap benches at the cinema, on which we children were seated to watch 'Mise Eire' – the heroes of Ireland, Michael Collins, De Valera, strutting around in quick motion on silent newsreel – all in magic lantern now, the man who sang Puccini at GAA matches, the Rue di Doo Boys.

At Easter 1979 I went to Portugal with the old lady I used to stay with in North Connemara. She drank aniseed liqueur and told filthy jokes on the plane over. We took an old train up

148

the mountains to Fatima and stayed in white-washed rooms divided by plywood. One morning I looked in on her and there was a young American in the double bed with her. He'd come in the middle of the night, and the only space in the house was in that double bed.

My first summer in Prague I noticed images of Mary all over the place, the annunciation above a doorway, the Virgin appearing over a cornfield, and the colour of corn was my first impression of Czechoslovakia, the fields by the airport, the yellow of corn also woven into the green colour of the Czech summer, the urgency, the innocence of a beautiful girl's blonde hair in this hue.

'Wash yourselves clean, spare me the sight of your busy wickedness, of your wrongdoing take farewell.'

At university there was a Siamese-looking girl from Cornelscourt who had dates every lunchtime with a blind man called Mr Clarke and she used to steer him round to a little café run by the Irish Country Women's Association. 'I'm tryin' to convert him,' she'd always say in an exasperated Dublin accent to the sedate customers.

And in the little family house in Churchtown where my mother insisted I spend my three years at university, Francesco, Jacintha, Lucia were depicted in the hallway, having their vision of Our Lady of Fatima. Women divided little pictures of Our Lady of Fatima in the rain of Grafton Street as the colours ran amok – olive yellows, roses, verdegrises – and the indigents stood haplessly over their money boxes. So even on the worst of days in this wet city, with its often cornflower-blue mountains, with its harbinger boats forever bringing its runaways home, with its Murillo back-street children, with

149

its mallards, with its lament of a Phil Lynott song forever in readiness on the juke-box, a miracle was proposed.

So afterwards all cities became places where miracles were expected. I entered every city, sized up the first feeling of it, hoping, like the little boy on Dollymount Strand, hoping for the real boy's voice, and every embrace with every stranger became an act of expiation, and every act of kindness became an act of atonement, and the city's orphans became the only possible friends, the only possible mirror, a candle always reflected in that mirror if the liaison, if the friction, if the exchange of depth of hurt was a true one, like the candles in the mirrors in Georges de la Tour paintings.

But it was in Eastern Europe that the mirror was most exact, that the Madeleine I brought from Ireland saw herself most clearly and most remorselessly, for here prostitutes were the town's holy women.

When I was seven I was cycling along at dusk with no lights on my bicycle and was arrested by a young, virginal guard, and brought to court where I stood with the town's criminals, young men with holes in the backsides of their trousers. Whereas they were sent to prison, I got a fine. But in my dreams I was circumscribed by the town and the country from that day on.

In my dreams, back in London, I am walking across a flat landscape. At first the houses I go into have cuckoo clocks, one or two pictures on the walls – a grandfather, a grandmother – altars with Mary and Jesus on them in a corner, tables spread with salads, pickled vegetables, vodka, decorated with sprigs of plastic flowers. But the further East I go the walls of houses become more crowded, all kinds of pictures on them, big and small, collages, and the collages become something to make sense of, the puzzles people create in order to try to divine the mystery of their lives, in order to try to hear the tempo of their feet.

My friend Miranda writes from Berlin. She is a Croatian stained-glass maker. There is a stained-glass window of hers showing whales in a church in Berlin. 'Berlin makes us foreigners somehow more present in ourselves than our own countries. This is a paradox of being an unhappy, dispossessed being.' Berlin, she says, is now like the Raft of Medusa, the raft with the alabaster bodies on it. In her own sad and ruined country she says buses arrive in villages at night to find they have suddenly become empty. Men play football with children's heads. In Zagreb people are thrown from high-rises in the middle of the night by terrorists. There are bombs in bins. Apartment blocks are riddled with bullets. Her parents have lost their life savings, which were in a Serbian bank. Women in black march in Zagreb with the blue and white of peace, the green moon of Croatia, the blue, white, red with the red crest in the white. It is a time of pain and suffering and yet strength. She nearly died last year, having an open heart operation. ('Why do doctors conduct operations in Latin in Zagreb?' 'Because soon they'll be speaking a dead language.') Having survived she can't go back to Croatia, not because of the war, but because, having been touched by Berlin at this time, Croatia is too small. Like Hart Crane's mother after his death she feels 'like a wanderer on the earth'. Further East in Russia the yellow moroshka berry (the berry Pushkin ate before he died) is to be found now under small bushes in damp places. Cranes are gathering in Eastern Europe. The swans are gathering by lakes in Ireland.

Miss Hanratty who studied singing in Heidelberg had a picture of the Little Flower in the alcove of her room in the London brick-orange house. Her memento of her stay in

Europe was the romantic postcards from the time of the Anschluss in her album, an SS man, hands behind his back, on many of the romantic, lime-tree-crowded streets.

Once I went into a church, surrounded by a white fence, in Norway in November. It was filled by old ladies in black like the bits of black chiffon blowing on the headstones in the cemetery in which Marek is buried. They all turned around and looked at me.

30 December 1991. Jazz Club of St Petersburg. A girl, Kzenia, at my table, with sanguine curls, in tall boots, mini-skirt, a huge, festive chrome-yellow ribbon at her breasts, takes my hand and asks me to dance to 'Moonlight Serenade'. Around us are photographs of musicians who look like the young Tennessee Williams. 'You are very gentlemanly. You dance – *pravda.*'

Afterwards we watch a couple who dance solo to 'Boogie Woogie Bugle Boy', the girl in a tawny woollen trouser suit, the tall boy in black jacket, white shirt, cedar-green trousers. He tosses his quiff, his kiss-curls back, then continues to shake his arms, clench his fists. He has those fragile St Petersburg cheekbones, the mime-artist-pale skin, the small, almost obfuscated mouth, those telegrammatic liquid-black eyes like the eyes of a madonna in an ikon. He smiles at me, sharing a joke, like the little boy in Prague with the yellow dog which had a long tail.

Gavriil comes in then with some friends, a girl in a red dress and black stockings, and two boys, one of them with a silver chain with a medal of Mary around his neck.

The afterglow of a summer's day in Leningrad is still in Gavriil's smile, a day in last June, as if a summer's day had merged into a winter night and all between it – Marek's death, return to London, hundreds of Irish tramps, some of them in cowboy hats, by fires alongside the Thames – not so much cancelled out as postponed.

On a day in June I'd taken a train with Gavriil to Komorova. The ticket office at Komorova had walls of shining grey and Havana-brown, cracking as a medieval painting, a tiny hole for tickets, a little old lady in a scarf behind it. 'Fuck off' in English was scrawled on the wall opposite the old lady. We stopped at the ticket office to make an enquiry about return trains and on the other side of the railway tracks, beside a powder-blue store, Gavriil waited outside a skeletal telephone box to make a telephone call to his gym. There was another little old lady in a scarf in it and she stuck her head out and said, '*Poshel na hui.*' 'Fuck off.'

An old man who heard us speaking English stopped and told us he'd sailed to England once with the navy.

We walked through a forest of conifers, past the pale Madonna-blue cottage of Anna Akhmatova, to the Lake of Pikes where we swam in the coppery water.

Although he himself was child-faced, child-limbed, Gavriil, like many Russian boys, already had a child, a girl, Bashkirs, who lived with the mother in the Urals. On the way back two little boys with shaven heads, buckets in their hands with windmills on them, asked us '*Horoshay voda, ili plohay?*' 'How's the water, hot or cold?'

In the evening I had dinner with a young couple. Looking through their many books I found an inscription by Anna Akhmatova in one of them. We were having tea from a samovar shaped like a Matreshka doll, patterned with white daisies, black-eyed Susans, green tambourines. I remarked on the inscription and they immediately began denigrating. 'Anna Akhmatova was vain. A lesbian.' Finished with her they started on Pasternak. 'He wouldn't look at Olga Ivinskaya when she got out of the camp.' It's just like Dublin, I thought.

Georges de la Tour was forgotten for centuries, his paintings ascribed to other people. The first book about him was written in Paris during the Occupation. When the biographer looked through the records of Luneville he found that the citizens hadn't a good word to say about this creator of beautiful Mayan-looking Madeleines; he'd refused to pay taxes for the poor, he'd set his spaniels and greyhounds among other people's crops.

Done with Anna Akhmatova and Pasternak, my hosts not only flailed Andrei Tarkovsky but his father. 'He wasn't a good film-maker. He wasn't a good poet.'

I thought of Andrei Tarkovsky, modern ikon maker, not tempera on wood, but still the art of the catacombs, film-maker, who'd given meaning to our arid age, to the vistas of thousands and thousands of high-rise apartment blocks surrounded by cypress trees.

Beyond this room, beyond this city, was Komorova and its lake with little bands of swimmers alongside it on summer days; beyond Dublin on summer days were the mottled beaches.

I left and walked through the midsummer streets, many old women on their *passeggiata*, to the Jazz Club which was not far away.

The female singer was singing 'Shenandoah'.

> O Shenandoah I long to see you
> O away you rolling river
> O Shenandoah I long to see you
> Away I'm bound to go across the wide Missouri.

In the upstairs bar, against the midsummer light, was not a sailor, but Andrei Tarkovsky, dark hair on his forehead like a wing, Mongolian eyes, Tartar moustache, mod shirt, and another Russian who lived in a high-rise, Nadia Mandelstam, her large gipsy's mouth, her gipsy's eyes, and I thanked them and the medieval ikon-makers, the men from Novgorod and Constantinople, the makers of madonnas with beautiful eyes in amber oranges and sulphur yellows, who despite the denigration and the spite of the crowds, of their own countries, went on to create a beauty that linked up through the ages, like a pattern of fleur-de-lys on Russian wallpaper, and redeemed, put a charcoal brazier in a world where Irish tramps died of cold through the winter in the streets of London.

On the afternoon before I got the night train to Berlin in the summer, a couple of days before Marek's death, I'd sat in a café with Gavriil, near the Moyka Canal, the wall papered with dolphins. Nearby was a park in which little girls sat on ponies or carried shoals of balloons, most of the balloons round, the top ones sausage-shaped. We talked about London, why I had to leave it. Couldn't live in Ireland, couldn't live in London; flee the small-mindedness of Ireland, find yourself surrounded by an abyss of racism in London.

'I blew out the candle on London. London extinguished for me.'

On my way to the station, walking by the Fontanka, I saw a woman in a sarafan against a bridge. It could have been a de la Tour Madeleine, with long, black hair, a straight fringe, and sad, lighter eyes. It was Anna Akhmatova.

'Goodbye. A strong, strong kiss. Gavriil.'

Dear Volody,
Since leaving you and Iveta and Pyoir and Gavriil my heart has been sad. I felt on Monday night never in my life was I in the company of such lovely people, filled by God.

Since I met you, I have thought about you, and I feel, I hope, I trust my thoughts and prayers will go with you. Gavriil is a very good friend for you. Before the Feast of the Epiphany love to you.

The road outside the tinker encampment is a one-way system

now and the trucks shake the aluminium caravans. People peg stones from the railday station above and even a ladder is thrown down one night. The fumes have become unbearable and children can't sleep at night and are prescribed sleeping pills. Sometimes when you pass there is a bunch of flowers high on the lamppost, with his photo, that of a little boy with a fitful head of hair; near where the little boy was killed, in spring a bunch of daffodils, in summer a bunch of marigolds or stock or wallflowers, in autumn Michaelmas daisies, in winter carnations or chrysanthemums.

More difficult for the travellers to move in summer, parking places were always privately owned but now people are more possessive about green places.

A blue umbrella lights up on the railway tracks as I pass the tinker encampment; there's a teddy bear on the tracks with a blue dress pulled up over her head; below, many-ribboned traveller girls play school, most of them sitting on a bench, the teacher confronting them.

A traveller woman comes out of one of those caravans in the afternoons now as the children are playing and puts up a picture outside her caravan, a concave picture behind glass of an angel guardian standing behind a little boy and girl going for a stroll.

People's lives touch less often than we think, like lighted ships passing one another at night on the Irish Sea. I feel like someone, socks going around without legs, shoes without ankles, arms, head separate, bits all over the place. At night, often the lights of Catford Greyhound Course still blinking, there's a child in the sea. Is it Marek in somewhere like Porto Nuovo or me in Salthill? The rhizomes of grief go deep into the earth but there is also a contradictory joy. Missing someone, someone's face, is like missing a country, the sky of another country. You think in January that the only real way to fight evil is not prayer but to hold someone's hand. Touching can so often be rape, molestation. Real touching comes from love and love happens so rarely. You have to fight for love, the way Ursula Goetze, Libertas and Harro Schulze Boysen, Dietrich Bonhoeffer, Etty Hillesum fought fascism. In London I see Rembrandts everywhere; he brings tenderness to old people, mostly black, queuing to take part in an old people's talent competition; to a maroon and blue bomb-disposal van stopping and a man getting out to look at a parcel; to people entering a hotel for a pawnbrokers' conference; to a funeral gathering outside shelled-looking flats; to a group of black women singing 'Abide with me . . . Fast falls the eventide' in a shopping arcade; to two young Irish lovers, holding hands, looking at pictures of Padre Pio in a window; to an old Irish tramp praying before a picture of Bernadette Soubiroux as a nun; to a Killarney brick-layer in a hospital, about to have a hernia operation, the lights of South-East London high-rises outside – 'I feel like an old woman's blouse.' You pick up a second-hand blue jersey, from a pointillistic chair, like the one you wore in the first squat you lived in in London. There's the continuity, the faithfulness of paupers about this city. The city itself is a second-hand jersey. Always, at the worst of times, an echo, a pastiche of the Second World War. A woman puts a scarf, turban-style, on her head, puts epaulettes on. A boy says of his father who has cancer: 'It's the most exciting thing that happened to him since the Second World War.' The city itself seems to have cancer now, ragpickers in the West End, wartime colours in West London – Santa Claus red, teal blue. Loved it once, too close to kin now, must take off. In you there is a longing for life, a longing for Europe, the invocation of the Flight into Egypt – the knowledge that there's never any going back to Ireland. The violation has been too horrible, too spiteful, the connivance too wicked.

There was your own wickedness too, the inability to fit in, to obey the rules, say the right things, the tendency always to flit, not to concentrate, to aggravate people.

When a friend dies they leave you their life's images like the bits and pieces of Kreuzberg. To put them together is not just to relive their life but also to enter a stronger, braver life. There's a bequeathed shirt to fit into, a flamboyant purchase in Amsterdam. I feel in January that there were people who tried to murder me, to murder the children I'd have. But my children are you Marek now, you and your mother, and the bits and pieces, the mosaic like an East European high-rise apartment block, the precious array in any of them – a Red Army man with a clock on his breast, a disgruntled doll in Victorian cap, dress, knickerbockers, a puppet of a girl cobbler.

It was as if in Ireland I'd seen the face of evil and travelling in Eastern Europe in those years, in the cities of mustard yellow, amber yellow, persimmon trams, of welcoming verdure, the vision was corrected; I saw the face of God.

'He was from Ireland. Used to box there. Then came over here. Lived in Clapham, Battersea, Peckham, places like that. Then he disappeared.'

> *Denk ich an Deutschland in der Nacht*
> *Dann bin den Schlaf gebracht,*
> *Ich kann nicht mehr die Augen subliessen*
> *Und meine heissen Tränen fliessen.*

People hold hands in London, put their arms around shoulders. Miranda writes to me about starvation in Zagreb, about the concentration camps in Serbia. The letter is posted from Warsaw, which she's visiting for a few days, and the stamp shows a crane flying low over a cornfield speckled with corncockle.

In my dreams swans take off from lakesides in Ireland and helicopters come from the skies, landing in cities of corrugated red roofs and cypress trees, to take the dead and wounded aboard.

'The second question cannot unfortunately avoid a time of force, suffering, asking . . . why? Which flies in our heart since ever. So many deaths . . . '

Once hit by it you are haunted forever, I write back. Your life will be full of dashes around, subterfuges, other people piling spite on you to try to quell your disturbance, your chaos, even; people, cities becoming part of your flight. Occasionally you look back, to see the others there in their safe lives, smoking their pipes. But you keep going, cities, streets, avenues. Occasionally when there's a candle lit for you in some church someone touches your hand, your face. You might even make love for the night. But there's a knowledge that won't go away no matter how much they pretend it's you. You see beautiful places. You're assuaged by beauty, but always in you there's a crying. What comes if you keep going is faith. A faith that's wholly different from theirs. That finally divorces you from them. But which links you to people who have suffered like you, remember like you, seen what you've seen. There are far cities for you and maybe even peace sometime, peace that comes from the fact that you accepted and didn't pretend. And if your faith is great enough there's love. Love comes and puts its arms around you and love, against these wars, against the hatred, is the only answer. But the price we pay for love is high. We pay it with every fibre of our being. At the cost of alienating almost everyone. Must keep going. Must keep going. I reach for you and you don't answer. I try to tell you about my loss but you don't understand. I seek to communicate it and you repudiate me, try to eliminate my statement. Yes, we're part now, Miranda, we're part of the hordes, the refugees, the ones who have seen and lost and yet gained everything.

First time I saw Chartres, the molten aftermath of childhood scapulars still on my breast, coming back in the car, it began to rain as we entered the suburbs of Paris at August dusk, lights over motorway bridges, funnels spangled with lights. It was over, the excitement of a vision, but something of that day, of Chartres, its portal statues, its roundels, would last forever, a gift from my parents.

'Where Do You Go to My Lovely' ricocheted from the café on the main street early that autumn. I hung around outside it, hoping to see the woman who gave French lessons. I willed myself to be as beautiful as some of the boys of Paris and I was beautiful, masculine, smartly dressed for a while but there was no one around to see.

First sight of Big Sur on a journey from Dublin; then back for attack, denunciation. That was the way, progression, regression. Big Sur like Chartres would stay with me. Another link in the loveliness of things, another link with the river of my childhood, with the photographs of vulnerable women in cloche hats, something they ultimately couldn't destroy.

The child I saw in Lerici, near a dog-rose village, it's hall-door steps which came to the sea, me in Salthill, alternated with another child, a boy in very short shorts, blue and white striped T-shirt. It could have been you, Marek. You would have been about eight then. Boats swayed on the very blue sea, women sold postcards right by the sea edge, and a lateen took off to sea.

An aunt of mine visited Berlin in the nineteen-thirties, just after Hitler took power, the aunt who died two weeks after I was born. When she'd been training at the Immaculate Training College in Limerick, Maud Gonne had come and lectured about her time in Holloway Prison and how she managed to speak nothing but Irish there. Not the Maud Gonne I saw in the portrait on an educational tour to Dublin in 1959, a muss of hair over her elegiac features, but a Maud Gonne with blanched face, still in the coal-scuttle hat of the twenties. My aunt stayed with an Irish woman who was a governess, in a nougat-coloured street. There had been witchhazel under portraits of Hitler, and she'd seen Ashkenazhi Jews leading their children along, something frightened about them. They'd have afternoon tea in Kranzlers, they walked by the traffic of coal barges with their heavily smoking chimneys on canals, listened to a group of boys in tam-o'-shanters, most of them with blond hair and pinched faces, sing '*Deutschland über Alles*' at the tables outside the Maison de France on Kurfürsten-damm, the orchestra resuming when they'd finished with 'I'll Send You Some Violets'. She'd met her husband while she was teaching at the Mercy Convent in Navan and gone to live in the white house in the country. A sister-in-law walked through France during the war. Her hair had turned white when she returned to Ireland, and she was very silent, sitting around a lot by herself, always in a blue dress, taking the red bus to Dublin occasionally to meet old friends at Mitchels Tea Rooms or go to the pictures at the Rotunda Cinema. Then she'd returned to France and my aunt never saw her again. 'I never go out now. Miss Holly does the shopping for me. I feel just middling. Have just heard from Saorse George in Berlin. Their biggest fear is the Soviet Union's atom bomb now. Had a letter from Father Louis on the Divine Word Mission. They hear nothing but martial music in Seoul now.'

When I lived in the squat in Battersea in 1977 there was a boy from Belfast there. He'd been summoned to the house of a prominent Irish citizen in South Dublin in the early seventies, given a gun and some money. He discarded the gun and went to England where he got a job in a vegetarian café run by gay Divine Light people from Ireland and had a few children with a West of Ireland girl. Last time I saw him he was with the winos in the bar at Galway station. 'Thank God for the nuns this side of the Shannon,' he said. 'If it wasn't for them I'd be dead.'

A nun, a distant cousin, passed away in Brooklyn last year and in the way of these things, the stories staggered now, I've just heard. She'd been suffering from a brain tumour for years. As a child she'd cycle into town and addictively purchase bags of liquorice allsorts. Her mother had opened a sweet shop in the house after she'd become a nun, sold bottles of mineral water and lemonade, sweets in jars and, on the counter, in open boxes, tins of fruit. Last visits back to Ballyhistle, to the house with the clock which did a gavotte, people had come to regard her as a saint. Boys would come on their bicycles to see her, and a country and western band had welcomed her on one occasion with 'One Day at a Time'. A local man had sent a bunch of yellow bog-asphodels to Brooklyn for her funeral. For years she'd cared for the terminally ill in Brooklyn, and of late worked with AIDS patients. Hart Crane befriended a young mystic tubercular case called John Squazialupi, who had visions of the twentieth century's wars in a sanatorium in Brooklyn in the nineteen-twenties. After his death Hart Crane's mother worked as baby-sitter, cook, scrub-woman, invalid's companion, in a world whose light was caught by

Edward Hopper, using her earnings to collate his poems and his writings, the way Nadia Mandelstam gallivanted around Russia, on the run, using her earnings from her work as a teacher of grammar to hold intact her husband's life's work. Grace Crane died in the Holy Name Hospital in Teaneck, New Jersey. My distant cousin lies in a hillside cemetery in Brooklyn now, not far from the house where Hart Crane had pictures of sailors on the wall, a house with a view of Brooklyn Bridge, a house which echoed a house with a tower room in Cleveland where the first sentience had come as he listened to victrola music. In the spring I light a candle not for, but in celebration of my distant cousin, at Bonefatius in Kreuzberg, the way the lady doctor on a ramble through Germany last summer lit a candle for Marek in the Church of Our Lady, Nuremberg.

In the Chapel of St Teresa in Avila I'd lit a candle for all of them, the women in cloche hats, the soldiers, the tuberculosis cases, the pub-owners, the grocery-store-cum-pub-owners in their ginger-sandy coats the herdsmen, the vendors of silk ties, the nuns, the priests, the missionaries, the navvies, the runaways, the lost forever.

'Patrick went to America, died young.'

13 February 1992. Back in Berlin. Afraid to look. The lights all around, yellow, green, red, white, poppy orange, electric blue, Aegean blue, sky blue, grey-blue, aquamarine, magenta, lavender, mulberry, blood.

It is quiet like an East European city.

As I walk to another temporary address the lime trees are so bare and wet you want to put a coat on them. There are birch trees against tall apartment buildings.

'Sarah (Bobby) went to America. Never heard of again. Esther went to America. Disappeared.

'Austin went to America. Came home on holidays twice.

'Alfred and Elizabeth burned alive at the home place in Carrarea.'

In a family bible in Swabia, next to a name, are the words *'Ausgewandert nach Amerika. Verschwunden.'*

Krzysztof, a young doctor friend, who is handing over the keys of the apartment, has made a meal, and we eat it by the light of a menorah.

'What are you running from?'

On a dresser is a photograph of the owner of the flat, who has gone away to Africa for two months, in a kippa hat, in the Jewish Cemetery of Senefelder in East Berlin.

On the wall is an oval photograph, edged in platinum, which is going to be my companion here; picked up in one of the junk stores of Berlin, it shows a little tow-headed boy, in the wide trousers of the nineteen-thirties.

The lemon trains go by on elevated tracks against the red lights on the edges of high-rises, bare willow trees brushed against the wet sky, in the city my aunt visited sixty years ago. 'Old friend, what are you looking for? What do you keep looking for?' A black hare runs through Marx-Engels Platz. On a Saturday afternoon an old lady on Oranienburgerstrasse brings home a life-size ceramic Dobermann, with his tongue hanging out.

25 February 1992. It is Marek's birthday. 'New World Symphony' plays from a street of tall houses, with a scattering of lights. An old lady suddenly stops on the street, remembers something, then walks on.

God protect me, I think. Before I left London a shadow of a man came to my door, to the French windows on which the panes are circular, some of the wooden circular frames crossing one-another. I was sitting in the dark so he must have thought there was no one there. He went away again.

In a junk store on Fasanenstrasse, where a synagogue was burned down on Kristallnacht, 9 November 1938, there is a black baby box from an Irish school. The head of the baby, kneeling in a gown on the box, is blue and black like the scrotum of an old man.

Maud Gonne said of the Nazis: 'I am not sure had I been a German after the Treaty of Versailles that I would not have become a Nazi; except for the Nazi exclusion of women from a share in the direction of affairs.' Krzysztof, my doctor friend, says that for his patients, memories of the war are returning. The syphilis of a woman who was raped by the Russians resurrecting itself. A man with cancer of the liver talking about Matthausen. A man with a tube in his throat recalling the two young French Resistance workers whose throats were cut on a truck in Alsace, minutes after he'd conversed with them in French about a favourite church in Paris, Notre Dame des Victoires. Snow and frost have briefly returned and at Grünewald a boy skates on the ice, making a long resounding sound underneath it, the sun going down in old gold scraggles like in a Flemish painting, and Krzysztof suddenly puts his arms about me and hugs me.

Yes, the memories of the camps are returning.

When Marek's mother had reached out to him after he'd been diagnosed as having an infection – B-plus contagious – he'd just kicked her away and gone off to the house in Portugal for a few months. When he returned, she was in a hospital and he didn't go to see her; he got work on a building site in Munich, then made money as a male prostitute. She killed herself, he said, 'in her madness, and in her fear of having to grow old'.

She killed herself with the knowledge that her son had AIDS, that he'd rejected her, and with the memories of a walk across Germany at the end of the war.

The memories of a family I didn't belong to were returning, maybe even of a country I never belonged to, the violence that was brought out in me when too much closeness was forced upon me, the madness that came out in me – the cruelty most of all to myself.

'Keep on running,' a Welsh boy said to me in London, and here I'd run into the camps. I could see what they were like. I saw the fires burning. I saw the piled-up corpses. I saw the bits of beloved garments among the corpses – blue and white check, red anemones. I saw the dead children. I saw people hanging from trees.

What do you do about all this? And then I remembered Marek's love of cafés, talking to people in cafés, how he'd once spoken to Andrei Tarkovsky in a café in Berlin and I thought, yes, that's it. Keep fighting for love. Even when they've all but destroyed language in you, pick up the pieces and make collages, continue making collages – some meaning will come out of it. Even when they're pushing you into the grave scream, scream a statement.

In the little bar Krzysztof and I went to after walking in Grünewald there was a jingly song on the jukebox: 'Für Mich Wirst Du Ein Neuer Anfang Sein', 'You'll Be a New Start for Me'. We sat by a little table with a red tablecloth, a yellow lampshade on it, paper flowers, ferns in a yellow band, and a waitress with scalloped curls brought us guava juice.

A friend of Krzysztof's, an architectural student, had hung

himself in Münster that week. He'd just wanted to paint. Do nothing else. But it wasn't possible.

And I remembered Marek telling me about the number of heroin addict friends of his, HIV positive, who'd killed themselves in Germany. He'd shown me photographs: beautiful-looking young people in beautiful shirts.

Must go on. Must go on. Running creates its own momentum. If you keep doing it a bravery comes which is a meaning, a cohesiveness in itself, a mirror for others to look into, however briefly, a magnet for someone to reach to against figures in the snow.

At night, they're in my dreams, a film with sprocket holes on the edges, a film with no sound. Marek and his mother at a table by the turquoise sea in Sicily, he in a black summer shirt patterned with white skulls, the two of them laughing over a pitcher of wine which has little squiggles on it.

Also in my dreams, I'm driving through Swabia, the countryside where Marek is buried, a man looking back at his life, stopping at the little cafés in the villages with louvred houses and towers. It's as if this landscape will not only bring the bits and pieces together, but also give you a new, secret life.

Whereas once I told Marek about adventures in my life – an educational tour to Dublin 1959, Oklahoma 1966 – he now tells me about adventures in his: a wedding in Rome 1978, Marek in a sea-blue zoot suit doing a mazurka with his mother to the music of a Hebrew band, a Venus de Milo in the hall with a black broad-brimmed hat on her and circles and circles of pearls about her neck, vases of purple Michaelmas daisies mixed with purple, pink, lemon feathers, a girl outside, scarf around her neck, selling purple Michaelmas daisies; travelling with a Finnish girlfriend in a bus through the DDR in 1980, passing pairs of strange old lovers – in berets, woollen hats, hair askew, with side whiskers; stopping and having a drink in a pub where all the waiters wore black and white and where the men were drinking green crème de menthe, fluorescent in the walnut-brown darkness; standing with his mother, arm around her, by a lighthouse in Sicily at sunset in 1978, looking to the sea.

Miranda and I sit on a bench by Grünewald Lake.

She is currently making a stained-glass window for the dead of Croatia, dozens of tombstones in the shape of sand-dunes with crosses above them, against a sea of kingfisher blue colour.

Near us are some Polish women in wheelchairs, one of them with an umbrella patterned with elephants above her head, though there's only the odd drop of rain in the air.

We don't speak of her war – it's too terrible – but a remark of hers – 'You're a nineteen-fifties person. Everything about you is nineteen-fifties' – prompts me to tell her about the young American with Venetian blond hair, who looked like Tab Hunter, who came to our town in the nineteen-fifties. He'd fought in the Korean War. In his brown suits or letterman jackets or button-down sailor's jerseys he'd smelt like Gold Flake cigarettes. On a frayed armchair at the guesthouse down the road he told us about the dark green trams of Seoul and about the many lepers.

'I've been to war and I never want to see violence again.'

The fishermen at the pub loved him, mixing their smells of river crowfoot with his tobacco ones, and they exchanged stories but those stories I never got, just echoes of songs from the pub at night, which hinted at what they might be talking about.

> My wild Irish rose.
> The sweetest flower that grows.

He caused my first wet dreams, dreams nearly as intense as those caused by a half-naked boy in flats near Tara Street, Dublin 1966.

I wrote to him, in a letter that would never reach him.

'I miss you very much. I wonder often about you.'

When *A Hill in Korea* came with George Baker we all thought about him, but then he was gone far away.

Things would suddenly remind me of him over the years: a photograph of Mamie Eisenhower; the rifle drill by Irish soldiers at the funeral of President Kennedy; a song, 'The Yellow Rose of Texas'; Coretta King playing the piano; a boy at Kennedy Airport, New York, October 1976 – 'No one looked at me like that for years'; a blond-haired boy in a café by Bay Bridge 1976; a Quaker graveyard in the Midwest, 1981; a soda fountain in a café in Columbus, Georgia, December 1987; the red earth of Tennessee 1987; a group of bare-chested young soldiers jogging on a coppery fall morning in Alabama, singing 'Look at 101 rolling down the strip. Heave up. Heave up. Big Daddy's going to take a little trip'; yellow grapes on a table in the fall in Alabama; a boy riding a motor cycle on to a truck in Yazoo City, Mississippi.

He is my war story for you today, Miranda, my stained-glass window.

Afterwards, Miranda and I walk to the Russian Church in Wilmersdorf where, a service going on with a small congregation, a little old lady insists we join our hands and then goes to fuster with candles, pulling them out of where they are for no apparent reason, putting them elsewhere, ferrying them between candle stalls, plucking out bits of wax in an increasingly agitated manner.

A monk in a silver stole, facing the congregation, recites a prayer with a candle in his hand, and the choir sings, magnifying glasses to the texts.

Miranda kneels on the tiles to pray for her country, and I remember the boy from Korea, here in Berlin in a Russian church with a Croatian woman, just as I used to periodically recall him as a child.

He was my first and most enduring lesson in courage, courage to face memory, hypocrisy.

He was the mirror to all that was good in life.

He is conjured up in a Russian church in Berlin, but only by mutual volition, by the friction, the reaching to one another of two minds, Miranda's and mine, clear as the memory of the poster for Walt Disney's *Bambi*, the stubble over his mouth not unlike that of Marek in death, a power against evil, a renewed talisman, and he turns and looks at me and I am again the child I was then, the child is recaptured with all his dreams and all his openness and all his fearlessness and a path that was concealed is open and a strength is passed on, like an irrevocable candle.

In Berlin, on the Metro, Turkish men incessantly tell their beads – their *sebhas* – and a mantra is created, a mantra of consciousness, and things are brought to mind here which would not be possible anywhere else, and things are remembered, a young ex-soldier, pinks pinned to his lapel, holding a boy's hand in a small town in the West of Ireland in the nineteen-fifties in the season of cranesbill, in the season of croaky versions of 'The Maid of Mooncoin' for gatherings of tinkers in the local pub.

After he left I went to the films as often as I could, to the two cinemas in town and, on Sunday afternoons, to the hall in the orphanage where we sat on wooden benches. Once, shortly after he left, a teenage orphan, in grey rather than the blue younger orphans wore, got very excited at a film which ended in marriage.

'Oh I love the films,' she said, clapping her hands.

'But he's a divorcee,' the girl sitting with her posed an objection.

'It doesn't matter. They're not Catholics.'

Outside the church in Wrangelstrasse, beside a big basket, slanted on both sides at the top like a roof, a little Asian missionary of charity is wiping the face of a shaven-headed, heavily tattooed young man, which is covered in blood. He's been wounded with a broken bottle by a gang of skinheads from the Marzahn or Hillesdorf districts of East Berlin.

I go into the church and there's a crucifix with a young Christ on it, a pot of poinsettias underneath him, and I remember the crucifix I saw with Eleanor in Italy and know that this was to be our lives.

Outside, there's a liquescence about the scene with the nun and the young man, as if it had taken place in early Christian times.

She rubs his face almost rhythmically, then lithely stands back from him to see the effect. Everything is calm for her, everything is as it should be.

His shirt is open now and you can see his marble-white pectorals.

To the edge of this city are the high-rise apartment blocks of Marzahn and Hillesdorf and beyond them high-rise blocks all over Europe, slits of sunset above them come evening.

This was to be our lives, to become part of one of them, a number, a window, a room with its own brand of exile, with its own individual *bricolage*.

The car keeps driving through Swabia in my dreams, stopping at the little towns, the driver still trying to collect, to make sense of what has happened. Sometimes the landscape, the beauty of it, is an end, a cohesion in itself. Other times nothing coheres, there is no coming together and he still tries, knowing that this life has been beautiful, like the landscape, and must make sense.

My first summer in England I kept hearing a song:

> I haven't got the love of the sweetest boy in town.
> But I've got the silver of the stars
> Gold of the morning sun.

And I remembered a girl who'd been in love with that young American soldier who had since died.

Something that was smashed, something that was destroyed is coming together again, a town, a connection.

A group of labourers run naked into the river. There is a black Victorian coach in a shed in a blacksmith's yard. Mrs Delaney sits under her picture of *The Meeting of the Waters* in a pale blue dress strewn with coral-white daisies.

A connection is being made again, is being resolved with country of birth, but not with their country but a country beyond it, a countryside of Country and Western parlour masses; of trees on which beautiful crofters' sons hung themselves, for unfathomable reasons, with extra-long laces, standing on their bicycles, and were given funerals with arches of hurleys over their coffins; where little girls, destined to be nuns, open lucky bags with thick tablets of sweets in them and a message; a countryside of churches with saints with broken lilies in their chipped hands; of people who continue to go into exile for reasons unknown and spend lives drifting through rooms with other people's settees in them, the spoor of other people's exile on them, on the diamond-patterned cushions; of people, all of whom have a relative who went away on the *Queen Mary* and was never heard of again.

Two people dancing under lime trees in Prague with lights coming through the trees, two people on a cement carpet at a crossroads in Ireland.

'I have looked into your eyes and seen the horror in them and understood.'

Years ago in Ireland, often at the end of a journey – a boat journey, a train journey – somebody would be waiting on the other side. For years, going between England and Ireland, there was never anybody. When I travelled in Germany suddenly people started waiting on the other side again – having mathematically deduced the arrival time of a train.

After we'd gone to see Marek's body in the mountain cemetery, in the evening, Zdena and I went to visit a blind girl in a little apartment block a few miles outside the town of louvred houses. In the surrounding meadows was the pink of weigela and the white of the beauty bush. She was sitting over a tomato salad she'd prepared, all in black, her hair newly curled, radiant, waiting for her lover.

We drove then through Swabia, Zdena and I, as the sun was going down, through the little exact villages, past one which had a red English telephone box in it, and she said, 'Nobody will be as glittering as him.' She was soon to be off to the United States with a boyfriend; they'd hitchhike around. She showed me a photograph of the boy, already prepared, in a pale yellow summer shirt with palms and poinsettias on it. I told her to be sure to go to New Orleans and the states of Louisiana, Alabama, Mississippi, Georgia. And she said, although she'd never been there, 'Yes, return to Georgia.'

She'd stopped the car and gone and collected a bunch of wild flowers in the meadows and when she returned, scraggles of her hair over her blue denim jacket against the green fields, she took my hand and pressed it.

It was like when the Liverpool boat would come into the Mersey Canal, the sudden jolt when you'd be sleeping on the floor; touching something, making a contact now with another being, with other beings that wouldn't go away.

From those women, the swan-necked woman who died young, the woman who cut her throat, the woman who threw herself out the window, the insistence of them in Berlin, came a lady, an answer, Our Lady of Berlin.

She appeared above a side-street of tall houses one evening in the spring, some of the houses dark, some light, matchstick corridor effects of lighted windows, the sky murky.

Something that came from the purity of those women's lives remembered in Berlin, from all the journeys, from the bits and pieces of this city – a gold Immaculate Conception in a frame with some red plastic flowers in a Turkish hairdresser's shop, two old lovers by an oil-cloth-covered table, a Kurdish lament, Elvis Presley singing 'Wooden Heart' on the nickelodeon.

A figment of the imagination, yes, but no less real for that, a notion, a counterpoint, a return to a childhood when we were geared for the continual possibility of such apparitions, a drawing together of my times here and a knowledge that my sojourn here was a right one, that there was a token of safety, of protection over my presence here, and that Marek's death was leading me from one path of search to another. The paths were cross-reaching, but where the new path was going I didn't know yet. All I knew was that I'd have to take the courage of a tinker woman, who refused to die at ninety, with me.

When I was travelling through the Southern States in a Greyhound bus December 1987, a woman was loaded on the bus by her husband and son at a small depot in Tennessee. She was a very big woman, huge bun at the back, on two crutches, dressed in what could have been mail-order clothes. They were sending her, alone, to a hospital in Iowa City, where she was from. She kept telling me she was thirty-six, though she must have been much older. At another stop in Tennessee we got out – I was helping her. It was sunset. There was an advertisement showing a cowboy riding a pig outside the timber café. She said, 'You speak American real good,' and then for some reason, by instinct, she raised her right hand in what seemed to be a blessing against the *rose doré* sunset, and I knew that, because of this, I would come back, again and again, to the Southern States. I would return to Georgia.

At the bus station in Chicago, where we were stuck for thirty-six hours because of a snowstorm, she collapsed and was taken away by ambulance. I panicked. My things were in her locker. She had the key. But she managed to throw it to me as she was being taken away. Sitting there, alone, I watched a little black boy play with a miniature Greyhound bus. One morning in Alabama a girl who dealt in what-nots – voodoo bits and pieces – came and left a miniature Greyhound bus on my doorstep.

> Slowly and slowly I'm changing my life.
> Sweet Jesus, slowly I'm changing my life.

On Oranienburgerstrasse an old lady in an apron-coat

speckled with little flowers, bent over, coming out of a tiny store, says to me, *'Nehmen Sie mich bei der Hand,'* and I take her hand. It is a spring twilight. Golden trams are swimming, are wraithing out of one another. Little boys surf along on skates, one of them with a Davy Crockett hat on. We pass a synagogue with a gold and almond-green dome. Someone at the end of the street is playing a barrel organ. There are corner parks with benches as in any Eastern European city and already, though cold, some people sit on them, conversing. Above those parks you can see the lighted rooms of people's homes, the kinds of lampshades, the shadows of creatures at the windowsills – a furry bird, a raving crocodile.

And in this city you meet them now, the people like Grace Crane, from middle-class houses in other countries, far countries, once with good jobs, living in tiny rooms now, cleaning toilets, scrubbing stairs, washing glasses. In Havana there's no food, someone who's just come from there tells me. There's a boy from China. Can't go home. Will wander the world. Miranda will go on to the United States. It rains heavily and the lights mix on the pavement by Gedächtniskirche. In the window of a shop is a poster showing a café in Havana, with a lemon awning outside it, a woman with a microscopic dog on a long leash.

Lou Andreas Salomé said something like the cloaca and the genitals must be reconciled before we find a path to God.

In the spring Krzysztof and I went to Worpswede where Rilke lived after his trips to Russia with Lou Andreas Salomé. At the old border to the DDR the police were holding up a Russian family, grandmother in huge scarf, husband in sneakers, young mother with red velvet bow at the back of her hair, children with the pale blue of hunger about their eyes. The women wore watches embroidered with flowers.

Gavriil's father, though only fifty-two, had died of a heart attack, just after the New Year, in Russia, and his relatives – fifteen people – had come, according to custom, and stayed for forty days in the three-roomed family flat.

Gavriil had sent me a photograph of himself at these unwanted festivities – a tie with ice-skating seals on him.

His friend, Iveta, whom I'd met just after Christmas, had written from St Petersburg: 'I waz very glad to meat with you. I want to visit you. It will be very nice.'

She had come and stayed for a few days, on her way to Munich and, in high heels with gold knobs in front of them, the girl who frequently worked as a prostitute in Leningrad, her father having been exiled to the other side of the city when she was a child because he'd made love to her, joined the queue for confession in the Russian Church in Wilmersdorf, the choir singing as the people queued.

'What Are We Living For?' played on the car radio. Starlings swooped over the fields.

'After its success in Vienna, Bonn, Munich, Antwerp the circus comes.'

Once, when Chipperfields' circus came, a woman who knew she was going to die, who'd been in love with that American soldier, stood in the middle of the green in a long, old-rose coat, the elephants and crocodiles around her, her head bowed.

Berlin had taught me that the way to destroy evil is to forgive, but one must never go back.

In my childhood there was a gang who lived down a cellar in a yard, a steel plate on top of it, and frequently came up, by way of a wooden ladder, to attack; my friend and I arranged a funeral procession for a cat, my friend dressed like someone from the Ku-Klux-Klan for the occasion, a girl, who'd gone bald, heading it, sprinkling flowers on the grass; my friend performed a play outside the British Legion hut, playing the fairy queen, 'Dismiss. Dismiss'; when he'd gone I wrote down what I remembered of the play in a fat, green-covered copy book with pale blue lines, imagining the fairy queen to look like Romy Schneider in *Sissi*; the oak trees which flanked the British Legion hut were cut down before I'd finished putting the play down, so it was as if their green went into the words and green would always be part of the words, the green of a row of oak trees cut down in May.

Kites sat on heaps of earth near the motorway as we got to the North and the meadows were trickled with black earth – signs of the burrowing of moles.

In small towns crowds of boys, many of them with baseball caps turned back to front, returned from school.

Ugly duckling boys, crouched, returning from school in the West of Ireland, destined to become beautiful for spells.

A little boy with green-framed spectacles looked at our car passing.

Marek had a photograph of himself, a little boy in sunglasses, jiving with his mother on a balcony with urns on the wall, against the sea, in Taormina.

A boy, porcelain-skinned, curly, beige-haired, in a thick argent T-shirt, against a house, purple crocuses in front of it, a message over the door: 'O God above protect this graciously given house from fire, gale, burning, and shelter us, and one day guide us into Your Heavenly Home.'

'We are always looking for someone stronger, braver, more compassionate than us,' I thought, as I looked at Krzysztof in Worpswede.

After the visit we stayed the night with his mother, who lived near Bremen with an American – a deserter from the Vietnam War – she married after divorcing Krzysztof's father.

It was dark as we took the ferry across the Weser and Krzysztof's face was lit up by the red lights of the harbour on the other side.

Berlin was the city of Georges de la Tour's most beautiful painting, *St Sebastian*, the irrevocable arrow in him, four figures above him – three, one above the other, one to the side – the red of the robes of the woman nearest him passed on to the dead body, an act of love, the flame in her hand doing an orchestration, the figure to the side like the figure of death, a deeply bowed head, a sickle of a moon in a black hood, and the colour of night in the clothes, all around them, just as the colour of night had enveloped the desolate grandeur of this bog countryside, crossed by narrow roads flanked with giant birch trees.

Krzysztof's mother, Bettina, crouched on the ground in a flash-crimson blouse decorated with Chinese mountains, and skirmishing clouds and tall pagodas with spiralling rods on top of them. His step-father, Shannon, was in the same position; he wore scenes of Honolulu on his white shirt: Kawaiahao Church, Ioliani Tower, the Royal Mausoleum.

The room, which was papered with a pattern of a goose chasing a dog, had little shelves on the wall which were built at all kinds of angles to one another and all kinds of little objects on the shelves – box gipsy wagons, a little louvred wooden school, a little louvred wooden bakery, a louvred stable with tiny horses in it, a dwarf – palette in his hand – painting, a little dresser with patterns of flowers on it, a honey-coloured witch on a broom, a family of elephants, a glass ball with a richly brown view of Prague sunk in it – Prague Castle above a myriad of gabled houses.

There was a sofa reserved for teddy bears – teddy bears with glasses, a teddy bear in black leather shorts, a teddy bear with earphones, a teddy bear in a jogging outfit with a red kerchief around his forehead, two elderly teddy bears – the woman in polka-dot scarf, the man in trilby and dicky bow – ancient, orange-ginger teddy bears, a grinning sailor thrown among the teddy bears, a bald doll with a suggestion of saffron hair, a mulatto doll, a pink devil with silver lamé horns and a brown loop on his head kissing one of the teddy bears.

On the wall was Elvis against a vermilion background, a Hieronymus Bosch picture of a writer getting inspiration from the Virgin Mary in Heaven and a man with the legs of an ant, coat of armour on his middle, spectacles on his nose, jealously looking on, a photograph of Wilhelm Busch of the German

Confessing Church, a lithograph of Jesus with Mary and Martha, a placid dog looking on and large earrings on one of the women's ears.

Bettina and Shannon were born-again Christians and there was a stack of *Der Wach Turm* on the floor.

On the demi-partition separating the room from the kitchen were mainly American photographs: a youth on a beach against boulders in the sea, three boys with surfing boards, a boy with strawberry-blond hair in a panama hat, a herd of deer on a cliff.

Shannon's younger brother, featured in those photographs and who'd worked as an architect in San Francisco, had recently had a devastating breakdown, his mind, the flow of it, having stopped. From doing intellectual work he now had to do something physical, at the same time moving from an apartment on Anza with sliding doors to a small room on Vallejo. Working as a labourer, he usually dressed in a geranium-coloured jersey or in white singlets. Sometimes, during his work he lay spread-eagled on the ground, face to the earth. Such it was with the human mind, one day intact, the next day a wreckage. Such it was with life, one day peaceful, the next day in chaos.

'To everything there is a season, and a time to every purpose under the heaven.'

The postcard he'd chosen to convey the most recent news about him was a Rembrandt, a woman with a gold ring on a leather string about her neck, a band of pearls on her wrist.

When first I went to California, when first I went to this country, on a lonely beach near Big Sur, the breakers coming in, cormorants and petrels above them, I suddenly fell on my knees in wonder.

Shannon had come to Germany in the late sixties and lived in Quakenbrück where he'd met Krzysztof's mother, getting a train to Bramsche in the mornings where he worked as a mechanic.

'We had no time for friendship in Vietnam,' Shannon said.

Then, drinking tea, we silently listened to records. 'I'll Leave This World Loving You.' Ricky Van Shelton. 'Remember Me When the Candlelights Are Glowing.' 'Always on My Mind.' Willie Nelson.

That night I dreamt of a part of the Old Jewish Cemetery in Prague where the tombstones were particularly golden. There was a woman with large earrings weeping among the tombstones and then a boy stood over her, naked above the waist. It was Marek.

'You were wounded in flight.'

Next day as we drove through Hamburg there were women in black coats, black hats, men in antique-looking coats, who could have been people of the nineteen-thirties. Cat Stevens sang 'How Can I Tell You That I Love You? on the car radio when we reached the motorway and buses and trucks from Amsterdam and Rotterdam went by.

Spring came again to Berlin, its light hitting the big grey buildings, the left-over Stalinist apartment blocks, coming through the lime trees, franking snogging lovers by Metros. In the evenings the sky was lavender mussed into peach at the end of the Kurfürstendamm.

In November 1974, around the time of the Guildford and Birmingham bombings, I headed off to Venice. There I picked up a letter from Eleanor in *poste restante* and read it in St Mark's Square, which was partly flooded, a youth with a monkey on a leash walking through it.

Dear Des,

Must we always be up and on the move? Am staying temporarily here but will shortly go to Sacramento for a few
weeks. A Russian girl lives in this apartment. The walls of
the sitting room are gold leaf. She made tea tonight in a
golden samovar. She told me the Russian word for crane:
'guraul'. On Hallowe'en I went to a performance of Giovanni
Gabrieli's *'Jubilate Deo Omnis Terra'* in St Francis' Cathedral
and I felt an ineffable sadness. I thought of a chapel on an
island in Mayo and of the Earl William crossing the Irish Sea.
As I walked home the paint of a mime artist conducting an
orchestra against the sea was running in the rain. I bought a
bunch of roses for you tonight, pink and red, and put them
against the ocean. You are stronger than you know.

After reading the letter I went to the flat of the Italian boy I was
staying with, in one of the tiny streets just behind the
cathedral, a lithograph of a male nude with heavy buttocks on
the wall.

I'd had a call from her, by arrangement, about ten days
before in a ramshackle telephone booth beside a box of a pub
on the street of my dungeon of a squat. She'd told me that she
wasn't coming home and that she'd joined the religious group.
I was wearing an electric-blue jersey which had become loose
and which had slashes in it.

For Eleanor, joining the religious group in the fall, golden
sunlight in a city where young men strode the hilly streets in
shorts, was like going from one city to another, a Western one
transient as the gourd of medieval paintings to an Eastern
one, one of labyrinthine streets, hammams, cafés filled with
the smoke of incense, old people with many rings on their
wrinkled fingers.

In one of the cafés of this city she met an old man who'd

been in Buchenwald. He showed her the tattoo. Each day in San Francisco was a thanksgiving for survival. She put up the barrier of deafness to my letters, to my pleas.

Years later, in Amsterdam, beside a house with a sickle of a moon with a human face over the door, she would cross another border, go back to the girl she'd been before she entered that Eastern city.

By then, on a train going through Poland, her image had faded for me.

We'd once slept together in an apartment in Amsterdam and she'd woken in the night crying, the same way I was to hear a new young wife of a man shortly to be murdered in Belfast crying in the middle of the night. It was the apartment of a young couple, a boy and an older woman, who'd picked us up when we were hitchhiking in Connemara. 'The trouble with Irishmen,' the Dutch boy had said in a pub, 'is that they put their penises in their pints.' Children, dressed up like German children for *Fasching*, had passed us on the street as we reached the apartment in Amsterdam. An old man, smoking a pipe, sat on a bench under an autumn tree.

When Dylan put his arms about me at the end of my sojourn in the squat my body had felt as if a pit had been dug in it for a grave, but something of the warmth of his body, of his condolence, would take me through the next few years in Ireland: chips wrapped in the *Republican News* in Belfast, British Army tanks rolling along the Springfield Road, the scream of a girl whose husband was about to be murdered. And it would take me through more.

'Must we always be up and on the move?' Eleanor became Heidi, and Heidi, Marek, and then touching became ever more chancy and dangerous.

And always the resort to journeys to solve the crater left by Eleanor.

A journey through Europe the summer Eleanor went, culminating in the Camargue, storks rising from the marshes, horses galloping against the varicose blue of the sea, bathing huts on the beach at Saint Maries de la Mer, blue bushes on the sand dunes and a boat with mouse-grey sails taking off to sea.

A journey to Italy the year I returned to London, to a squat in Battersea – the words of a girl at a party still screaming in my mind – climbing to a chapel on a hill above Assisi, wending past the fields of winter barley and, having reached the top, beside the chapel, raising flowers to the sun – violets, poppies, white carnations, purple Michaelmas daisies – and then descending to a village where flotillas of children walked by with white bread and where, at a funfair, boys stood around the bumpers in beautifully coloured jackets – peach, burgundy, strawberry – and ties of jade-green and cedar-green.

When you were under attack by family, under threat of molestation, the journey to Palestine – Jerusalem to Haifa to Tyre to Capernaum on the Sea of Galilee to Tiberias to Nazareth, to Nablus, to Jericho – tanks passing camels in the pitted whiteness of the desert near Jericho – and then back to Jerusalem, men in streimel hats going by in the blue voltage of the fall sunlight in the Mea Shearim quarter. And then when you'd nearly gone dead inside from loneliness and the insistence of kin, something brought you to Prague, to a bare plywood room on an eighth floor where you began looking back, the smell of balm-mint in the room from somebody's balcony herb pots, and the remembrance, by lulling association, of a song, 'There is a balm in Gilead', sung by a black girl in Chartres Cathedral on an evening when, long unkempt locks on you, your back crouched, you walked back to your room, past the boys, in narrow sloe-blue jeans, on mopeds speeding by kiosks squashed into fire-gold, to your room and, a plant on the windowsill, turned and saw the twin spires of Chartres against the summer night sky.

> If you're going to the North Country Fair
> Remember me to one who lives there
> For he once was a true love of mine.

In the spring of 1992 she would frequently wheel her child, Aoibhinn, down Javastraat, over Flevoweg bridge, into Flevopark, and stand with her, under a background of high-rise apartment blocks, by the old Jewish graves.

When she first came to this city in the fall of 1988 and lived on Muidergracht she met an old lady, with hair dyed blonde and looking like an elderly Kim Novack, in the café near her home. She had been in Belsen.

A boy in an amber leather outfit had bent over the jukebox as they'd spoken. There was a pattern of Mickey Mouse heads on the oil tablecloths in that café.

'You come back, you go to the old cafés, you hear new songs: "Symphony of Love", "Bessa Me Mucho", "Don't Fence Me In". But the only one that matters is "Saturday Night Is the Loneliest Night of the Week". New music, a new world, a new kind of human being. Those who came back from the camps.'

First time in this city she'd come with him. They'd approached the flat on Gerard Doustraat of friends they'd met in Ireland and children had passed, dressed up, and looked at them. Maybe an omen that she'd have a child in this city one day. A little boy had worn pink lamé horns, a pink lamé jabot. Another had on a black half-mask with a greatly beaked nose.

Her child always carried a tin ladybird with a key coming out of his behind, given to her by one of the former neighbours in Muidergracht.

Eleanor would stand there, by the tombstones – the *matseiwa* – near a canal and, now that she was returning to the United States, remember him, the gristle of his face.

When I first went to Prague and used to sit in the Old Jewish Cemetery, I'd think of how the old Jewish town reflected my life, sometimes the double-tailed Bohemian lion flying proudly here, sometimes the inhabitants having to wear the yellow star.

And in the spring in Amsterdam, sea-light in the cemetery, the first swallows flying around, she would be back in the Dublin of her childhood, Rathmines, near the old Jewish quarter of Dublin and, beside her child, the sequence of her life would commence for her and its unfolding would try to tell her things and her life try to make sense of itself.

It would be like the windowsill of a neighbour when she first came to Amsterdam – Goofy in an A-line skirt and ankle socks, Mickey Mouse in cornflower-blue trousers, holding out a bunch of red carnations, monkeys in Honolulu skirts and Chinese hats, a China man on a donkey, a strawberry-nosed hedgehog with prickles of mohair, a white goose with green polka dots on a white ribbon, a clog decorated with a line of blue windmills by a sherry-gold sea.

A large room in Prague with a bunch of golden knapweed on the table in a green vase, a band around the vase with a pattern of red and yellow roses on a check tablecloth, a print on the wall of Hendrikje Stoffels, Rembrandt's lover, looking out a window into Jodenbreestraat. A walnut tree in the garden outside. Near the window a picture of Mary, Queen of the Angels. The room is like the ashram in North Dublin of our friend who joined the Divine Light. There is the invocation of feminine peace here, of autumn, and the listless smell from the garden that there is from many gardens in this city where nude old ladies with many rings on their crinkled fingers sit under pillars of glazed majolica in saunas, an autumn smell that snuggles itself out from the back gardens of old houses in Dublin.

She'd often pass the Seder on St Kevin's Parade as the children were engaged in their Seder sing-song, a lemonade pitcher on the teacher's desk; on Lennox Street was the Jewish bakery where her aunts would purchase gingerbread men, honey and curd cakes, sugar pretzels.

Her mother's people were traditionally from Rathmines; her father's people were poor, and they came from the North of Ireland.

In their home in Rathmines as much as possible was green; there was a painting of a maroon-garbed Arab with his arms around his dying steed, a photograph portrait of her mother in a black dress with a choker at her neck and, in her hand, a

186

cigarette in a shining cigarette holder, a photograph of her parents in mackintoshes beside St Germain's Abbey on the Isle of Man during their honeymoon, a photograph of herself in a swimsuit being led by her father on Curracloe Beach, he in an old-fashioned black swimming costume.

Her mother's aunts smelt of Ashes of Roses, Chanel No 5, Evening in Paris, and for a simple visit they would have sandwiches covered by a cloth and biscuits with pink icing on them. After her father's funeral in November 1990 one of his aunts, who was aged eighty and had swollen legs, had spoken to her.

'We came from a very poor background. The land was poor. You couldn't raise crops but you could sheep. Black-faced mountain sheep. All the girls went to America one by one. They borrowed the fare and sent it back, bit by bit. They were only working as servant girls so it would take eight years or so.'

At family gatherings it was the Dublin relatives who had the stories; how her mother saw an IRA man escape from Mountjoy Jail, dressed as Rita Hayworth, in 1942; a love-affair which commenced in Irish House on the South Quays where people were retreating from a vitriolic sermon given at Francis Xaviour's on Gardiner Street. A little girl in a dress with a honeycombed front, she'd be led by her father so far down the South Bull Wall and then she'd have to stand there when he went for a swim in the nude in the Half Moon Swimming Club. Maybe that was why at a certain stage of her life, in London, sexuality was a pogrom for her. She was picking people up almost daily. But they had to be English boys, Pre-Raphaelite English boys, from Birmingham or Swiss Cottage, with names like Darren or Encombe, who wore cord trousers and made love to her over launderettes.

Going West to a convent on an island in Mayo was emancipation for her; it was also connivance with another Ireland. It was leaving her father behind, the lecturer in the College of

Art, who'd stand outside Marsh's Library, in an old suit like a young man, a Franz Liszt haircut on him.

A convent with a monkey-puzzle tree outside it and elms by the side of it; nuns singing 'Roll Out the Barrel' on a drugget at a Christmas concert; cakes every weekend – Bakewell tart, French sponge, cheesecakes with strings of coconut on top, Battenburg cakes – and during the week the trip to a little store for tipsy cake which came in plastic wrapping, and had soaked mottled sponge – dark and pale brown – almond paste on top and pink icing over that.

Sister Camisias spoke of marvels and it was from her that she heard the story of the Children of Lir.

Fianoula, Oodh of the Golden hair, the twins Fiachra and the blue-eyed Conn were bathing naked in Lough Derravarragh when they were turned into swans by their jealous step-mother. They retained the ability to converse in Gaelic how-ever and at another convent when she heard the story of Oscar Wilde she thought it was similar – after being humiliated he lost the power to write but he retained the power to make dazzling conversation.

The children of Lir spent three hundred years on Lough Derravarragh, three hundred years on the Mull of Kintyre and three hundred years in Mayo on the Erris Peninsula and on Inis Glóra.

Then they were blessed by the Christian missionary Kemoc, turned back into human beings, but human beings aged over nine hundred years, and died almost immediately, Oodh buried in front of Fianoula, Conn at the right, Fiachra on the left, their names in ogham.

In North Mayo also lived a bird frequently referred to by Sister Camisias, the Crane of Iniskea, which had been on that island since the beginning of the world.

Perhaps her parents felt she was getting over-enthused with her location as they brought her back to a convent in Dublin.

The intervening summer, however, she spent in Paris and lost her virginity there to the father of the children she was minding. If anything, nuns in the West of Ireland, with their insistence on the Gaelic body in their stories, the hurling-playing, Atlantic-healthy body, had inspired her to sex.

But it was not her first experience of sex she remembered most from Paris but the city at the beginning of the autumn, old people sitting in fold-up slatted chairs in the Luxembourg Gardens, the *café au lait* in the sidewalk cafés, the first sense of the aura of exile.

He said that they'd met on a train going west that spring, but he was in Paris at the same time, he too was walking in the Luxembourg Gardens at the end of that summer, he too was entranced by the first lights in the Seine come evening.

Back in Dublin there was a multitude of boyfriends, and even though they only lived up the road from her she'd get Rembrandt postcards in Mulvanys on Wellington Quay to write to them – seated rabbis, prodigal sons, Slav princes, por-traits of elderly ladies, girls at half-doors, tortured Christs, shy scholars, young women at mirrors, Sibyls of Cumae, Joseph telling his dreams, Jacob blessing his grandchildren, Christ with the woman of Samaria, Titus with lipstick lips, King David with his harp, lavishly embracing David and Absoloms.

She turned up in University College, Dublin, in a cherry-coloured anorak and jeans, and it was during her first year there she had an affair with a folk singer who lived in London. She met him in Galway city. They'd known one another from a dance hall in Dublin. He was the son of a Dublin builder and he'd moved between so many schools – Marion College, Sandymount, Sandymount High, Presentation Glasthule, Willy Martin's school in Mount Street – that he contributed to his father bringing the entire family to live in London.

He was with a girl from the North who had bonfire-orange hair, a reputed bomber, in a pub in Galway. He sang '*Athá mé in mo codhladh agus ná dúisigh me*' and 'The Waters of Tyne', abandoned his revolutionary girlfriend and went off and made love to her.

In the fall was the abortion in Brighton, and her first night ever in Amsterdam, on Gerard Doustraat, she woke up screaming, remembering it.

So the secession truly commences from bourgeois Ireland into which she was born, from the congealed consciousness.

Driving to Mississippi once from California with her second husband, Jesse, in a café under the mountains of New Mexico which had glitters of snow in them, illumined like a studded ikon, Willie Nelson singing 'Always on My Mind' on the juke-box, she thought of him.

After they'd left Amsterdam that first time they'd hitch-hiked to the South and were picked up by a Moroccan truck-driver with a moustache who brought them to his flat in Monte Carlo, in a cluster of Moroccan-looking houses. He gave her a white T-shirt with a Moroccan soccer player kicking a ball on it which she was wearing in Dublin, he in Italy alone, when she betrayed him and started making love to another boy from the West of Ireland, banshee-pale in nakedness.

So the break-up of an affair begins which lasts a lifetime, through two marriages.

'You are to me the little sister, the friend, the child, the future and the fulfilment of the past,' she tells her daughter in the old Jewish Cemetery in Amsterdam. And perhaps this child started being born one autumn in San Francisco when she left her old life, her old way, her old self, to join a religious group.

Coming to live in Amsterdam recalled those autumn weeks, the way there were pictures over houses like in the Tarot – a coppiced tree, a berried rowan tree, an old-clothes man with tiers of top hats, the blessing of the new moon, the gibbous moon over the sea, a swan on lapis lazuli waters, a leopard, a green bird with red beak among shoots of grass, a pelican feeding her young with its own blood.

She was told in San Francisco that Jesus had studied the cabbala with the Essenes and for a girl who'd had an abortion, for a girl who'd walked into a bombing in Dublin in which thirty people were killed, such random information, thrown out in the San Francisco air, opened an opportunity to expiate, forget, become new. The hold they had on you was terrible, but you had to fight your way out of it, become yourself, but in doing this you had to know that there was no way back, that you'd be an exile going between the cities of the world, half the time unwanted, but you had to try to hold on, keep your own mind, and a new religion, a religion which quoted the time there was a gymnasium in Jerusalem where boys performed naked, seemed to be a way of enabling this to happen, to let her have a new identity, a new soul which was safe from them.

She met a man in a café who picked up a first knowledge of the cabbala in Buchenwald – crown, understanding, severity, imagination, harmony, wisdom, clemency, justice, prudence.

And still, in spite of all this, there was a longing for a city where a catharsis could happen, but it couldn't be an American city.

She stayed on Lombard Street when she first joined the group and worked with delinquents in St Gabriel's Youth Club on Lupus Street. She had a letter from him, from Calle dei Specchiere in Venice, above the mirror makers, in which he described Venice in flood and a young man crossing St Mark's Square with a monkey on a leash, and then she moved north to Sacramento for a few weeks, and then back down to San Francisco before the new year, staying on South Linn Street, going to North California in early summer, staying in a caravan beside a lake. The Essenes had lived on the west side of the Dead Sea, away from the shores. He'd written to her about the fulguration of candlelight in Santa Maria della Salute in Venice, about bombings in England, how terrible it was for Irish people, about runaway English girls in black Juliet hats and black maxi-coats hurrying along streets of peeling Edwardian houses to meet boyfriends who were wearing school straws and spectator pumps, about women leading poodles in tartan outfits on other streets in this area, of the sudden eruption of song from an Irish drunk with cream sherry in his hand, how an entire street of squats was converted to Islam, how, at the door of the squat he was vacating, an English boy with pansy fine hair, in a mouldy Afghan coat, had put his arms around him before he'd returned to Ireland – the Irish stamp on the letter, Christmas 1974, had shown a Gaelic Madonna and Child, the madonna in infant's blue – of British army trucks speeding down the Falls Road and murder off the Springfield Road.

'I was fond of the times with you.' She put up a distance with him and yet his travels, the travels of the previous summer immediately after she'd left Ireland, insisted on coming in on her; Stockholm, Geneva, the statues of Mary, Mother of James the Less, Mary Salomé, Mother of James and John, and Sarah, their gipsy servant in a church on the beach in Saint Maries de la Mer.

Her first husband, whom she'd married a year and some months after her first return visit to Ireland and who was also in the religious group, had visited the basilica of St Anne de Beaupré in Canada when there had been a pilgrimage of North American Irish tinkers to it. He saw an Irish tinker playing the mouth-organ on the steps of St Anne de Beaupré, emphatically stamping his left foot as a woman sang 'Spancil Hill' beside the Canadian goldenrods in the autumn.

> Last night as I lay dreamin' of pleasant things gone by
> Me mind bent on ramblin' to Ireland I did fly.

After her divorce, she went to Europe with her second husband, living in Berlin where she spent most of the nineteen-eighties.

It was in the fall of 1988 they moved to Amsterdam. They drove there in a Pontiac with the American flag on front. Approaching it they passed a row of illuminated windmills by a canal, which, in the rain, made colours on the road like American football pompoms. She'd been in this city before and it was from here she prepared to go back to the United States, to Northern California, with her husband and child.

Yes, her first night ever in Amsterdam she'd screamed, just as in Belfast the young wife of an IRA man about to be murdered had screamed. She screamed for her lost child, for her fading bourgeois identity, for her presentiment of journeys, journeys always to be made and her own country always to be circumvented, for her search for solid identity beyond them, for her lifetime of exile.

'*Glór mo chroí,*' he said to her in Amsterdam and her fingers which touched his face were already touching other lovers, men she'd meet her first summer in San Francisco, men in shorts striding the hilly streets, whom she felt obliged to sleep with until she went to a lecture on *The Book of Splendour* given by a young man who held up a copy published in Lublin in 1872.

The Book of Splendour says that God is on earth and my first summer in Prague I contemplated this summons to carnality in the mildew of Podolí sauna, among the nude bodies seated in lemon light.

'*Tréigí amanánacht, agus maírigí: agus imigí ar slí na tuigsiona.*'

It was among the dead and mutilated bodies on Talbot Street, May 1974, that she knew she had to leave Ireland, find another city, find an identity more solid than the one that came from the presumptions and intimacies, however seductive and literary they were on one side, which bred unyielding versions of nationalism.

'Ireland, maker of wounds, tormentor of youth, ultimately breaker of all that was sensitive and enriched by sun, rain, wind.'

June 1977 in Dublin, among those houses of persimmon and crumbled acorn, which had garden houses of liquid gold glass where flowers were tended with Huguenot zeal for possible exhibition at the Royal Dublin Society, a girl attacked his sexuality. He never really recovered from her; she returned to the United States and married and he left Ireland and maybe their paths would cross again for a moment and come morning that girl talks poetically, as you're urged to in this city, but behind that poetry is a savagery which attacks anything not vetted by the tribe.

She returned to the house where the attack had taken place in November 1990 for her father's funeral – he'd had a heart attack while inspecting their turf patch on Djuce Mountain. Mary Robinson had just been elected president of Ireland. A tinker woman came to the door while she was staying in the house, in a polka-dotted white blouse, copper cocktail jacket, skirt of rhododendrons, black booties with pompoms at the back, a silver bullion on the front.

The black-haired boy who'd committed suicide told me the day I visited him, in the spring of 1968, that when a tinker woman comes to the house she brings luck, when she comes down the road there's change in the air.

Perhaps she'd had a premonition of her father's death at Zandvoort aan Zee, men running into the winter sea at dusk.

A tinker encampment near my home, by high-rise buildings.

A tinker girl under a photograph of the boxer Dave Proud in poppy shorts.

Tinker boys in a fish and chip shop at dusk, beside the bowl of Japanese koi fish.

A petrol can burns after a tinker wedding. A boy with a porcupine haircut, in a bristled cream jacket and scarlet dicky bow, and a youth with long locks and cigarette trousers look on, lit up.

At a funeral party in Dublin, cloth over the sandwiches and plates of biscuits with pink icing on the table, Eleanor thought, there'll always be a quotation of him in my body, that everyone is a mystery and that that mystery has to be accounted for, and she walked out of the house to the nearby tinker encampment where they were loudly playing Jim Reeves's 'I Love You Because You Understand', where there were chalk greyhounds and empty swan-shape flower bowls outside caravans with Valentine festoons in the windows, and where a terrier was darting among little girls in crab-coloured blouses.

One road takes shape out of another, but sometimes, because it is a side-road, we don't see the direction.

While I was staying in the high-rise apartment block in the Midwest a boy called Vance, half-German, half-Choctaw, invited me to go for a ride with him into the countryside. He had guinea-gold hair and scars on his face like smallpox scars. Earlier in the autumn we'd all partied on the loggia of our host's house, which was on a hill alongside the apartment block, Chinese people singing Chinese opera into the gold and scarlet maple trees, Eastern European people reciting poems, copies of which would mysteriously appear in the police station in Cracow within ten days, Uraguayan men who'd been tortured smilingly drinking but never getting drunk. Recently, the parties had been indoors.

A few nights previously I'd slept in the room of a Venezuelan boy who'd been visited by demons at night. The demons left that night.

The countryside was under snow. There were gold ribbons around tree trunks for Thanksgiving. An Amish man with a lambchop beard passed us in a buggy, his wife in a poke bonnet beside him. Although it was winter little stores prominently advertised Midwest ice-cream.

We stopped in a little pub where the graffiti in the lavatory said: 'The anus is not a proper receptacle for the penis,' 'The pope said no to faggots,' 'Fags die,' 'Troops out of Northern Iowa,' and we played two songs as two men with backwoods beards looked on in the darkness: Connie Francis, 'Where the Boys Are', and Bobby Darin, 'You're the Reason I'm Living'.

'You know the poems of Louis l'Amour,?' he asked me as we drove on. 'Poems that tell stories. Well, that's what you remind me of. Everything connects up, becomes part of a story.'

We got out and walked. Vance was wearing a short wool coat of green and amber. There were lemon lights in isolated Norwegian houses. Lone figures were collecting firewood and someone had lit a fire in the snow. Cars were going by, to a

195

local football match and to a Rolling Stones concert in Cedar Rapids, faces in the cars lit up, cherry-coloured football caps.

In the winter of 1830 14,000 Choctaw Indians died trekking over 1,200 miles of swamps from Mississippi to Oklahoma after being cheated out of their lands by President Andrew Jackson at the Treaty of Dancing Rabbit.

On 13 March 1847 Pushmakaha, chief of the Choctaws in Oklahoma, sent $710 to help the victims of famine in Ireland.

Six years later, a lonelier person, under snow again, I would return to Iowa on a Greyhound bus, crossing the Iowa river from Illinois as Dolly Parton sang 'My Tennessee Mountain Home'. And as I'd continue that journey the bus would be stranded at the Greyhound station in Cheyenne.

Some weeks later, back in London, by chance I'd meet an Indian couple who lived near Cheyenne. The girl quiet like Vance, with thrusting china eyes, wax hair, near-celluloid features.

But now I thought, to recover your dreams you've got to go through the snowy wastes. Nearly always alone. But sometimes there's someone who volunteers to walk alongside you for a while. This time an Indian boy. He touches my shoulder and uses the Amish 'thee'. His dark eyes are sad because soon people will be leaving, most of them back to their countries.

But I won't be going back to my country. I eschew the tribalism of my country in shame.

'Ruby Tuesday' was her favourite song.

It was of Galway city she spoke in the weeks before she died, before she killed herself. The city she arrived in with her son.

They'd both peeped through a window into a hotel where a room was arranged for a wedding reception, sherries in little glasses lining the table, a cake with a coach and cantering horses on top of it on a little table of its own.

A tinker lady, scarf and coat on her, one of her front teeth missing, was sidled up against a wall with a sign in her hand: 'Have your fortune read by Mada Brigid.' There were pictures of Padre Pio all over Galway, inviting you on pilgrimage.

An American band, in grey-green uniforms, with peach drums, had marched through the narrow streets, playing 'Oh Suzanna'.

In a church was a statue of Our Lady of Galway, with her symbols by her feet – a ship and a star.

Further out the hills of Clare were blurred beyond Mutton Island, a football match in progress in a field by the bay.

It was in this field, a football match in progress, that Eleanor and I had first kissed. After spending the night with her son in a red bus they hitchhiked to Connemara and stayed in a guesthouse in North Connemara which had a picture of Vincent de Paul in a kippa in three-dimensional lamination on the hallway wall. A window in the hallway looking to mountains of the palest blue she'd ever seen which brushed with scraggly marshland which was allowed a brief lemon colour before it was usurped by water the pale blue, the human blue, of Renaissance madonnas.

She fell in love with this countryside and chose that her son go to school there. In the school he was taught that Tir-na-n-Óg, the Land of Youth, lay near Greenland. But the loveliness of the place could not save her nor him. He ran away to Scotland, then returned to Munich from where he started making forays to Verona where he injected himself with heroin and became HIV positive.

In her last weeks there was her and him a lot, the couple, sometimes just herself as she looked in Berlin at the beginning of the fifties, flossed hair, skeletal thin legs. Interspersed with the images of Galway were tiny DDR postcards of Buchenwald in Weimar – the watchtower, the crematorium – which had circulated at the beginning of the fifties. In between had been the glamorous years – clothes, films, travel – but HIV and Buchenwald seemed connected somehow, the same bleak toll of existence when the glamour was done with, when the

197

colour photographs had been dispersed, the same account if some great effort were not made to redeem it.

A mental hospital in Munich, a suicide in the first month of 1984, a song, 'Ruby Tuesday' – the keen along a corridor.

Miranda returned to Zagreb for two weeks in the spring of 1992 before flying on to the United States. She took a plane from Berlin to Vienna. There was time to look around and she visited St Stephen's Cathedral where she'd never been. A black woman with a hat on her head in the shape of an ibis was praying in front of her under a painting of Christ, in something which looked like a gold strapless evening dress. Then there was a plane from Vienna to Ljubljana. From Ljubljana she travelled by a red and white bus to Zagreb.

Chess games, candle-holders, crucifixes, garlic, apples, oranges, bananas were sold by candlelight in the bus station. Most of the women wore purple-blue angora hats as if these were a product of the war. Soldiers had cotton underwrapping coming out from under their boots.

Outside the station was a cluster of gipsy women, in spring-green smocks despite the war, in matador trousers, white socks with Slavic writing on them.

Just a little on the way they passed a long mule-drawn gipsy cart with gipsy women walking alongside it. The almond blossom was coming out and you relaxed. You took deep breaths. Then suddenly there was the meander of war through the landscape. Eaves of roofs exposed and mashed like birds' nests, with scavenged pines alongside.

Immediately afterwards, going through a mountainside of pines, deer and boar peeped from the trees as if the times were serene.

In an arcaded town a soldier with a rifle on his back sauntered along and entered a café.

In the next town they stopped. A barge of refugees arrived by a pier and she was reminded of the way barges were so popular during the Third Reich, and how you see photographs in junk shops all over Berlin of SS men on barges with women in fox furs or cheetah coats or in pork-pie hats.

It was raining a little on the damson roofs. They had Pepsis and Fantas and coffees in a café where there was a black and white poster of a young Croatian punk, killed in the war, his face a web of blood – he used to mutilate himself during his performances. They entered Zagreb along an avenue double-lined with lime trees. A scarlet Coca-Cola sign was lit up on a high-rise.

She wasn't going to linger long in Zagreb, not because of the war, but because this independent Croatia was too small for her. She wanted to hold on to distance and she'd go on to the United States, teach, become a professor, use all the right, utterly debased and debasing jargon. After Berlin she'd never be satisfied again with soirées over an oil-cloth of rose-hips and blue roses.

But no jargon could tell of the raping and murder of children, the torture of youths, the bombing of old people. Maybe a stained-glass window, made among the cornfields and the Quaker graveyards and the dirgeful autumn land-scapes of the Midwest could get it across to someone, some-where, that these things were part of her now, waking and sleeping, and always would be.

The women pushing prams in the suburbs of Zagreb looked greatly more stooped now, and a small group of refugees, old people, the women in black, slowly moved along, their ikonostases in their bags now.

Krzysztof went to Amsterdam, spring 1992, with Jo, a mulatto girlfriend who worked as a nurse in a hospital in Düsseldorf now. A boy had spat at her on the street the day after her arrival in the city of Berlin. 'You're not of the pure German race,' a honey-haired receptionist at the hospital had told her a few days after she'd started working there.

On the bus to Amsterdam there was a group of German men in Tyrolean hats. On a bridge across the Rhine in Düsseldorf three women stood in fedora hats, short fur coats, pressed slacks, just like women in the nineteen-thirties, while the bus radio played Leonard Cohen, 'Hey, That's No Way to Say Goodbye'.

In Amsterdam the lime trees were coming into blossom. The gable fronts of houses by the canals were like screens when the light was translucent. At other times there were different strands of colour webbed in the air over the canals. The first swallows had come. He imagined that this was how St Petersburg felt in the spring.

Women held their vaginas in windows by the canals.

The spring sun skipped along the bridges.

Coming in on the train from Zandvoort aan Zee they passed a field of swans.

They frequently called in on a café run by two black American twins in kilts who had lines of brightly patterned knitwear hanging up in the café.

In the Russian Orthodox Church on Utrechtsedwarstraat they stood beside a Russian Orthodox nun for devotions. A little boy in a gold lamé dalmatic held a candle in front of an ikon which showed two figures kneeling before a tree which enclosed the Madonna and Child.

There was a great peace in this city as if it was the most peaceful place in the world.

They stayed in a house with a hedgehog over the door, the medieval sign of the gipsies – *Wij Zigeuners* – and there was a jar of dandelions on the doorstep.

Etty Hillesum had once looked out of the window of one of these houses and seen a squad of green-uniformed young Nazi soldiers, and never been so frightened of anything in her life.

'Your body feels very familiar to me,' he whispers in his sleep to her at night in the House of the Hedgehog, and it is as if her mulatto body is the body of many people whose lives he has briefly crossed or almost crossed.

One night all the neighbours came into the kitchen with banjos and guitars and there was singing and recitation. On the table were plates of Passover bread – bread with marzipan and currants – and bowls of beet salad. Jurgen had come, a friend of Krzysztof's who'd been HIV positive for eight years and who'd just cycled from Berlin to Amsterdam in two days. 'The marigolds of the New Testament,' Jo said. The phrase had come out of nowhere and she did not know what she meant by it.

Carl Witherspoon visited his mother in Berlin, spring 1992. She lived in a street of stucco houses and chestnut trees in Friedenau. She sat, this grey-haired woman, in her customary solitude, in a black dress, in shadow, under Qian Long plates on the mantelpiece showing a crowned, black-faced boy, with a halo, surrounded by angels, the figures enclosed in silver fretwork. The ikon had been a gift from her Jewish father who escaped the Germans in the South of France by crossing the Pyrenees on foot. She was shortly going to leave Berlin and go to live in Zurich.

He could see why.

In Babelsberg in Potsdam, where he'd gone to meet a film-maker, two Hell's Angels were striding along, chanting 'Sieg Heil. Sieg Heil.'

The Wall was gone now, the years of safety. She would live beside some bougainvillaea in Switzerland. He looked at two cows on a cabinet with bells on their necks and scarlet ribbons, their cheeks plum-coloured, and at a Victorian scene of caramel cows, by a pine-lined brook, not far from raised wooden houses, under gusty Alpine-looking mountains.

'They have never been resolved, those camps,' she said. 'In the East the memory of them was suppressed by the drab routine of socialism. In the West they threw a little glitter and American slang on them. But very few German people resolved them in their minds. And they passed this lack of resolution on to their children. These children who go around the streets with headphones and have no culture. You must have culture. I don't want to know these children, to look in their faces any more.'

Her husband, from whom she was divorced and who taught in Columbia, South Carolina, now, once called her accent, when she spoke English, Weimar, picked up from listening to Joseph Schmidt arias in English.

They discuss his current girlfriend then.

'She's a Catholic and she's got bad teeth.'

And they have schnapps and, as the light fades through a stained glass showing the crucified Christ, very like the one they had in the chapel of Eton College where Carl went to school, they play Lale Anderson singing 'Fernweh'.

The time Eleanor and her husband had set for return to the United States was May 1992. In March they visited Berlin together, where they used to live, and from there went on to St Petersburg for a week.

They left their child in Amsterdam with a rabbit who had a lachrymose stitch for a nose and a yellow key in its backside, a black walrus with a long rubber tooth, a head-scratching rhinoceros, an elderly teddy bear with long Arctic hair and spectacles, in blue dungarees, who looked like a Big Sur hippie.

They stayed in Reinickendorf where they used to live.

What would it be like to be back by a lake in Northern California with their daughter? The mystery and inner glow of religion had diminished in her – her husband's fervour was undiminished. But she had a daughter and a comfortable life. Her husband was rich.

Her mother, whose hair was champagne-coloured now, had written how the spring days in Dublin were fine and how she travelled to Dunlaoghaire each day to catch the sun, where she encountered her aunts, who wore spring dresses of hydrangeas, red daisies, blue braids and peach roses, who were militantly doing the same thing. She had to be careful not to become just another one of them.

Would you and Jesse and Aoibhinn not come to live in Dublin? We have Mary Robinson now. I feel sorry I never travelled like you. The Isle of Man was our honeymoon. Lawlors in Naas was a great night out. Jimmy O'Dea and Harry O'Donovan kept us happy and many is the seditious pre-kiss we saw in the Regal Rooms. People rode bicycles as if they were on liners and Eszteryom, Cardinal Mindszenty's archbishopric, was a place we could all see, alike, in ghouls and in palaces on steep hills, to Dracula's Transylvania.

But I have a longing for travel now and I've no one to go with – just the shadow I often look around and see now that your father is passed away, a young man in a beret by St Stephen's Green.

I need the child I gave birth to in you.

Why does that city haunt me day and night, Eleanor thought in Grünwald forest which was full of Russians and Poles, a Polish lady being pushed in a wheelchair. Wherever I go. Wherever I'll go. The bombs of May 1974. The little back-street boys with Mediterranean faces and eyes that adhere to you. A young Carmelite in a cassock with the desire of a Caravaggio boulevard boy. A tin whistler's medieval army march by the Liffey. The way the aquamarine skies attack you at the arched ends of alleys. The pejorative smell of a seaside urinal in the reverential rain. Something unresolved there. Something undone. It will always be the only city, wherever I go. The city I'm trying to come to peace with. The city I'm trying to forgive, but no forgiveness will come, will ever come.

Remember the blond male prostitute Des and I saw being dragged out of the Liffey? He'll always be Dublin for me.

But there was the shape of a boy almost born there. A cherub like Nathaniel Hone's *Piping Boy*.

As fate had it, it was a little girl I was to have, in another land far from Ireland and I'll soon be taking her even further away.

But I give this to Ireland, the land of Mary Robinson, a kiss for my unborn son, the idea of him.

When she'd first gone to the United States and passed over Yosemite National Park she'd thought: all the possibilities there are in life now, all I can do. Now she'd passed those possibilities on to a child.

The cabbala said:

He who dies without leaving children will not enter within the curtain of heaven and will have no share in the other world and his soul will not be admitted to the place where all souls are gathered, and his image will be cut off from there.

She'd assured her place in Heaven. A child born out of travels, a report back to the day she saw dead and mutilated bodies in Dublin.

A letter from Venice long ago; boys in amber jackets and rolled-up blue trousers in paddle boats on the floods of St Mark's Square.

Then a person forgotten forever.

A little boy with black crimped hair, in a shell-suit, looked at her on Nevsky Prospekt. There were booths along the pavement.

'Before, it was easy to survive,' the hotel receptionist told her. 'Now everything must go through corruption. And before, it was easy, corruption. Now the corruption is dangerous, violent and still there is the KGB, the army, the navy. They have the money.'

Nevsky Prospekt was still covered with slush and some Irish tourists demonstrated the currency of their country to street vendors.

In his last few days Marek had a persistent trance of a trail of mules crossing a hill of pollarded trees in medieval Swabia.

'It takes all my strength to live, all my strength to die. If this is death my life was beautiful. I give to my friends *das Zimmer, das ich immer gesucht habe, das ich niemals gefunden habe, wo sie ihren ganzen Kram hinlegen können, ihr Madonnas-Heer, ihren Schmerz.'*

Christmas 1984, the second Christmas Marek spent with me, we went with an Irish girl who was also staying with me to see the house of Dietrich Bonhoeffer, who had lived near me.

The girl was a social worker in a small Irish town and her current project was trying to get a tinker woman from stripping all the clothes-lines in the town.

23 Manor Mount, Forest Hill. It was on a hill looking down on my home. Brown door, peeling bay windows, a line of gnomes' heads across it, dormer windows on top. He used to go back and forth from there to Berlin in the nineteen-thirties.

In Berlin, January 1991, when Marek was in hospital in Swabia, I visited Dietrich Bonhoeffer's house in Berlin, 14 Wangenheimstrasse. A slabbed front yard, a circle of pine trees, snow-berries.

And when I got to the hospital the first time, Marek half-asleep, I told him the story of how Dietrich Bonhoefer as a child during the First World War spent all his pocket money on a hen so he'd have eggs.

'Tell me another story,' Marek would often say when he was in hospital, so I told him about the Jewish lady I knew in Bethnal Green whose son, as a teenager, injured someone in a fight and was sent to Durham jail. When he got out he went to the United States where he worked as a stripper in a bar half-way between Salt Lake City and Las Vegas; he then came back to England, worked in a restaurant, and every Saturday night had Sabbath meal by the light of a menorah with his mother in Bethnal Green; of the Irish boy in Austro-Hungarian-looking squats in New Cross, who lived there with Dublin tinker men. He went off one day and got his hair cut, purchased an old suit and a tie with a yellow mandala in the centre of it and a pattern of two ties coming out of the mandala, one red, one maelstrom white, returned to the squat and was told that he was now sullied – he'd become a Brit.

Stories don't have to be long, they can be very, very short.

And in exchange Marek told me stories about himself and his mother until their lives became part of my mind, of the labyrinth of stories of people whose lives you touch, which are continually flexing and growing so that your mind, when you think of them, becomes like a polychromatic Irish pub, with *verre églomisé* – back-painted mirrors, gilded and flashed glass, and encaustic glass – glass with patterns burned in, or like an Evie Hone stained-glass window in an Irish country church – sloe-blues, dove-greys.

22 March 1992. On Kurfürstendamm an Irish boy with Cherokee black hair walks alongside me. He comes from a part of East Galway where they used to celebrate King James II's birthday, 12 October, until recent times. His house when I visited it was like, for its items, a country auction. A muscular boy in a black polo neck reflected in a curvilinear mirror. What happened to that potential?

But tonight he walks alongside me in the spring evening.

A one-legged man plays with a rubber spider, bouncing him up and down on a string. A boy with a doll sticking out of his rucksack pushes a pram full of electric sockets. A woman with a crocheted cap strides with a staff. A man in cobalt sweeps the street. A woman in a short honey-coloured coat, in black tights, high boots, with a pony tail, walks a muzzled Airedale she calls Nadezhda. A boy wheels two tiers of flowers along, taking puffs from a cigarette. A man at a bus-stop plays Franz Lehar's *'Minne Lippen, Sie Küssen So Heiss'* on a green and mulberry accordion.

On such a spring evening, full of white hawthorn, I first met Eleanor on a train going West in Ireland. On such a spring evening I returned by train, through the former DDR, from seeing Marek in hospital, past argent villages, deer forests, fields of rabbits, station houses with daphne and rows of red tulips outside and men in knee-length trousers and long stockings and two Homburg hats looking at the train.

'Can't go back home again, to the first country, or the second country. Got to move on.'

Brigita's ashes were brought from Munich and placed alongside Marek in the graveyard in Swabia that spring. The black chiffon scarves waved on the headstones in the graveyard, dots on them, hems of black cloth.

In the doctor's house afterwards I sat in a room where there was a photograph of a boy in Third Reich uniform beside a photographic shop, a paper ladybird on the photograph, miniature rondavel houses, a plant surrounded by ceramic geese, the clay stabbed with red polka-dotted mushrooms. These bits and pieces which are a legacy from one of life's rare friendships. Like the aftertouch of someone's hands. When you lose the intimacy, the closeness, the bits and pieces become diffuse, anarchistic, anonymous, a no man's land, a greyness, and you've got to rally them again towards the shape of another friendship, an invitation into a room in a block of flats with its own kitchen witch and peach walls.

Swabia: in such a country is the soul reborn; a village in the mountains, purple rain clouds behind it; a precipitous path through the mountains, over a valley; a wooden cross with a roof on it beside a clump of pignut; a lone ash tree which is tabbed with carved wooden goats on St Vitus' Day, June 15; a soldier's grave: 'George Egger 4.6.1924 – 12.9.1941 *Ist gefallen im Russland.'*

In the Turkish Market in Berlin you see albums and albums of discarded family photographs. People who thought of themselves as families once and then scattered.

My mother in a swimsuit of rhombuses and sea urchins and complicated shells on an island in Mayo on an ethereal blue day in 1968. Deutsche Schlager music coming from the hotel behind her.

So the pattern builds up, a stained-glass window or a poly-chromatic pub, the bits and pieces, the shards of family history, of quest – your own or someone else's. Not just the pictures behind the surface of things, but people who are obsessed with image, images they created, images of themselves, religious images.

When you've kept a distance from Ireland for a while you realize how scarred people are by the history. Maybe not so much Dublin. But you still see it, for all the tinsel of modern Ireland. Like you see victims of the Holocaust in Europe, second- or third-generation victims.

The journeys overlap and you're not sure whether you're seeking forgiveness for yourself, or whether you're seeking forgiveness for someone else. The journeys make a collage. They become like the bits and pieces on an East European wall.

In May 1991, on a day of purple lilac behind rusty railings in East Berlin, I visited a flat near Friedrichstrasse. There was washing hanging up in the sitting-room, tapestries on the wall, paintings, bits of embroidery, many photographs, photographs in oval frames on a dresser, cloth flowers on a biscuit tin which had a goldfish bowl on it.

'It feels like an East European flat,' I told the German man.

'Yes, my wife is Hungarian,' he said and a woman with raven hair in a bun, in a coral-pink blouse, peeped through the washing.

One particular photograph I remember from that day – a woman in a smock-dress, V-opening on a white blouse and ankle socks in a cornfield, speckled by corn poppies, surrounded by beech trees, against a country mansion.

A visit to an uncle who'd run away from his wife, in Shepherds Bush 1970. A black woman whose grey hair was speckled by constellations of white on the street outside the house. Beds in the kitchen and a young bricklayer sitting on one of them, smiling, the afternoon light catching his musculature which was pale despite his profession. A picture of Our Lady with a burning heart behind the boy, a garland of white roses around the heart. A smaller picture of Our Lady of Perpetual Help. There are other pictures trailed in, hugging in, the room – St Bonaventure, St Bernard of Clairvaux, St Joseph of Cupertino, Blessed Bernard Minni – which smelt of bed sheets and old antimacassars and Holland blinds and oatmeal and Spam and Marmite and patent shoes and old British rail tickets and the buddleia and burdock outside. It was like a scene from the Bible.

In the mid-nineteen-forties my grandfather came over from Ireland to London, called because his son was dying of a mysterious illness. He had only been to England once before: he'd gone to a fair in Wakefield where he'd bought his wife a pianola. He came with a little suitcase, in a brown hat and brown suit, the carob colour Turkish men wear in Berlin.

On the bus to South London the bus conductor had told a story in a singsong music-hall voice.

'An Irishman knocked on a door in Scarborough and asked

for a glass of water. "There's no water," the lady said, "The government have turned off the waterworks."

' "Never mind," said the Irishman. "Give me a cup of tea." '

A giant woman in a scarlet scarf vociferously shook hands with a tiny woman in a pillbox hat at the top of the street, like two characters on a cartoon postcard.

In the room was a picture of teddy bears in dinner jackets serving glasses of champagne.

The ginger-blonde English girl stood by the dying boy in mulberry Cuban-heel sandals with bow straps on the front. She'd been the soldier queen in a village in the Home Counties, stood on a wagon drawn by a dray horse, in an oyster satin dress the colour of yellow ivory.

A brother of his had gone on a paddle steamer down the St Lawrence River, many invalids with crutches on board, a priest hearing confessions on the boat, to the basilica of St Anne de Beaupré where people, if their intercessions were heard, had paintings of thanksgiving done on the walls of the cathedral.

The man said he'd have a painting of thanksgiving done in a church somewhere if his son was saved.

His son died.

'Early to go. Ain't it?' said the landlady, who was in the room.

His girlfriend said afterwards, 'Don't know whether he had a premonition or not. Four months ago he said, "I don't want to be buried in England. I want to be buried in Ireland: the Rick, County Westmeath." I don't know why he said that.'

The comment of a woman in County Westmeath became widely known: 'I give credence to reports that he died as a result of sexual indulgence while serving in the British Army.'

Went with my mother to Rick, County Westmeath, once. Two cemeteries, one facing the other. Over my aunt's grave I was reflected in a glass dome which had the Sacred Heart in cellophane inside it. A little boy in a blue coolie-type coat. There was the smell of bog myrtle and nearby was a rusted railway bridge by a clump of lilac bushes, a girl hesitating on the bridge in a dress with a scalloped print and in white barred rubber sandals.

We then went on to Bray, County Wicklow.

My mother with mussed black hair, the glimpse of an earring, a blouse with picot edges, cerise smile against the bay windows of sea houses.

Me in the sea, endomorph father above me.

Then a photograph of my father in a pearl-grey suit, three peaks of a hankie in his breast pocket, sitting on rails, against the sea in Bray, staggeringly handsome, all the beauty of the Wicklow Mountains dipping to one side.

My mother, my father and me, advertisements for Bradmola and Dundyl and Go-Ray behind us.

By the billiard-table-green sea edge my father and I met a priest in a black plastic hat, his gown pulled up in an oyster shape and still a cassock underneath.

Girls who were born around 1918 made their Holy Communion in Moslem-shape white veils, perhaps gathered into white roses at the side or maybe a loop on top, got partial indulgences at the Eucharist Congress summer 1932, were teenagers in the De Valera years, courted during the war, married just after the war – picotees and fern in the buttonholes of their suits – some were not satisfied to leave it just there, marriage, children.

A photograph of my wild aunt beside fool's parsley where the canal ended at Mullingar.

I saw her ghost there as the trains went West from Dublin, lilies on the canal, and she was a Russian woman that evening for me.

When she died six Japanese plates, depicting slender geisha girls and pagodas by autumn streams, came down from her house to us, and a golden gondola with a little cabin on it which had broadcloth curtains on the windows.

Eleanor returned to the United States June 1977. I went to live in Battersea October 1977. The following May I followed her. I got a plane to New York and a Greyhound bus across the United States.

In the Greyhound bus station in Saint Louis a boy with Maureen O'Sullivan and Tarzan on a tree on his T-shirt and an embossment of a clump of bananas on his jeans, came up to me and said, 'I know you.'

He didn't.

There was a dog-rose and tangerine sunset over the arched, lighted Pioneer Bridge.

On the bus was a German boy, a Greyhound bus brooch on his jacket, running away from Germany to San Francisco, who until recently had been sleeping in the porches of the old houses of Kreuzberg.

The America we went through seemed to be one of backways. Small villages: scroll-work houses, white-spired, red-brick churches, general merchandise stores, advertisements for old products – Conté's ice-cream, Nestle's.

In Salt Lake City a group of men got on, all in the same grey suit and schiller tie.

I stayed with acquaintances from Dublin, people who were testing San Francisco, near Russian Hill. Eleanor was living in Northern California.

One evening a boy from Dublin, who was a member of Eleanor's religious group, brought me for a drive in his Barracuda.

On a hill under Gold Gate Bridge, looking to Sausalito, he said, 'By the way, Eleanor Munelly is getting married.'

On our travels in the fall of 1977, when we'd seen Orion over the Pacific and whales going South, we'd met a boy called Beck who looked like a candle which had become molten. He lived in a room which was crimson and damask but for collages of David Bowie photographs.

He and I drove south in his Cadillac. He wore a shirt with swallows on it. I wore a shirt with autumn leaves on it. We were like people who followed a doctrine of shirts. They were talismans, the tales these shirts told.

We walked through towns with Spanish-American alleys over the ultramarine, the comic-book colour of the Pacific. We walked along beaches full of boys with heraldic musculature and faces, with the pores dilated, which looked as if they were suffering from a disease of the epidermis. Boys were surfing on the sea. We walked and walked along beaches which had wild geraniums growing alongside them until the sun was going down behind a little lighthouse, a little yellow sentinel in a golden sky, and the boys were still coming in and there was the smell of barbecue fires and calypso oleander.

Against the blue of the Pacific that day, beside the mosaic of Beck's face, I felt my loss, my hurt, the destruction, but also life as a new collage, a collage reassembled from this destruction. There were lives I could understand now that I'd never been able to understand before and there, against the ocean, in Southern California I saw the workhouse in our town before it was burned down, and a blind man from our town traversing the orange peel at Ballybrit races, led by a little boy with a smock of hair on his forehead.

The light of the Pacific was a nuclear light, the light of an explosion inside me. Everything I'd been had been changed and I'd have to start anew, a new shirt, a grief, a throbbing of pain always there. Part of me gone.

'Once hit by it you are haunted forever.' I felt that from that day on I'd be homosexual rather than heterosexual, Dublin had twisted a part of me and I'd never recover. Near the workhouse once had been green trees and behind those trees the Royal British Legion Club and inside photographs of young men who'd fought in the Somme or Givenchy or Ypres or Passchendaele.

The survivors sang songs of the war just as a little boy at a country fair would sing of 'Spancil Hill' and by song, by story, not just stories of the war but stories of the lady of the manor who had been a London music-hall artiste and who used to go around the streets in a red coat, with grey horses once, we were transported and shared their experiences. By song, we seemed to go back and back until we encountered the first wanderers, those who were first traumatized, in our ancestry.

Beck wore a trinity ring. For friendship. For me from that day on it would be for wandering.

Before the Celts came there was a race in Ireland and the Celts, in turn, treated them as slaves, treated them animalistically, so they wandered the roads of Ireland, tin-smiths, ironmongers.

On the Mexican border, where you could get the smell of sewage pipes and blanched sand of Mexico, Mexican boys in baseball caps wandered through the streets with macaws in cages, stores sold pictures of the Virgen de San Juan and the Virgen de Guadalupe and Thérèse of Lisieux beside conch shells by candlelight, a mariachi band on a bandstand played 'South of the Border' and 'Show Me a Home Where the Buffalo Roam'. I didn't have my passport but I knew I'd come back some day, cross into Central America.

Inside myself, in a room in Shepherds Bush with a collage of Botticellis and Filippo Lippis, I sang 'My Love Is Like a Red Red Rose' before I left for the United States that year; on my return I sang 'The Last Rose of Summer.'

She came Christmas 1976 and stayed until Easter, apart from a few brief journeys, mainly back to Germany.

She arrived on a grey-green train in an anorak with fur edges. The station-master, with his waxed moustache, watched them embrace.

That first time she came she brought in a sailor's bag old magazines in which her photograph appeared – alongside that of Kurt Jurgens and Jacques Sernas and Gina Lollobrigida. A photograph of her in a white dress with black chiffon coming below it and a pair of pink Joyce's shoes she'd gotten from the United States, on top of a Chevy convertible, taken in 1960. She also brought in the sailor's bag a button-down sailor's jersey for him.

There was an effigy of St Nicholas in the local church in a peach burnous, cross around his neck, a basket of gourds and apples and purple grapes on his back and a little white teddy bear peeping out of the top.

Pierina, the woman who looked after him, would come in the mornings with fresh herbs to put in the room where they slept in twin beds. There was a crucifix with dried flowers under it in the room. Pierina would often fry potatoes, mixed with juniper berries, in the mornings.

At midnight mass on Christmas Eve in the church of gold stucco which had a picture of Maria-Einsiedeln in it, she sat in a black dress with a choker of ostrich-egg pearls at her neck.

For Christmas lunch they had rape-seed soup in bowls of Dresden china, tunny fish with leaf parsley and *babas au rhum*.

On the night after Christmas they saw *The Song of Bernadette* in the local cinema. The Movietone News had shown an American nuclear carrier ship. When there was an interval for the reels to be changed the children and the *clociaro* youths stamped their feet on the ground. At the end of the film was a swaying procession, a torchlight procession. The earth around the cinema was dark from the shadow of trees covered in leaves and in summer and autumn you came here to gather truffles, avoiding the little vipers who'd make their home among the leaves.

After the film they had balls of cheese melted on skewers over the fire and Frascati for supper.

In January when the local people got colds they put wax paper with mustard on it on their bellies.

Their first unhurried trip to Rome was to see the Caravaggios in the Galleria Borghese – John the Baptist in a vermilion cloak, David holding the head of Goliath, the Madonna, naked child beside her, stamping on a serpent. Afterwards, they saw a crowd of boys over a brazier as in a Caravaggio or a Georges de la Tour.

It was that day they found a café on Via Merulana which they visited, from them on, every time they went to Rome. They sat over an oil-cloth with patterns of menorahs on it. The proprietress had powder on the front of her hair. There were fly-catchers hanging from the ceiling. On a nickelodeon you could play Puccini. His photograph was on the wall, seated beside Elsa Szamosi who was dressed as Madame Butterfly for the Budapest production and on a little shelf a statue of Madame Butterfly in a pink sarafan, her hair jutting up in two loops.

There Brigita played the humming chorus a lot and 'Ch' ella mi Creda' from 'Girl of the Golden West' and 'Mimi e tanto Malata'.

A red-cheeked Punchinello on the street, in the hand of a little man with a pince-nez, said to her one day, 'Che bel figlio tu ai!'

In February the Judas trees and the wisteria and the lemon trees and the mulberry and the almond started coming into bloom, and the daisies.

Brigita, in a garnet-red coat, went to the Café Leroy on the Cola di Rienzo to have peach ice-cream with film veterans from Germany, people she used to frequent the café-chantants of Hamburg with in the late fifties and early sixties, listening to accordions and pianos and cellos and violins – songs about the sea sung by men in peaked caps.

Marek and she saw pictures on the walls of the catacombs of San Callisto by torchlight, the stricken, beautiful, doomed madonnas, child Jesuses of the first Christians. A mother shielding a child. A lot of red in it, cinnabar red of Eastern Europe. For fear it was like a photograph of a Jewish family, the man with a goatee, the wife and two daughters in pixie hats, being hounded on a cobbled street in Memel by the Nazis.

They went to the Church of San Agostino where there was a diamond in the Virgin's crown in honour of the conversion of the Irish poet Oscar Wilde to Catholicism on his deathbed. A man had given it to a girl but said that she must give it to this madonna when Oscar Wilde was converted.

They walked Rome at night with the Coliseum lighted up, reflections of trattorias in Marek's Arabic eyes.

Old men drank grappa outside the cafés on the Piazza Navona in the afternoons, they and the olive vendors sometimes looking to the water-spouting, naked river gods in the fountain.

Muzio, the tow-headed flower-seller at the foot of the Spanish Steps, sold geraniums, alyssum, violets, marigolds, phlox, white carnations, myrtle wreaths, mimosa.

On February 25, Marek's birthday, they went to Mario's in Trastevere, someone playing 'Addio a Napoli' on an accordian outside.

Come March, azaleas in bloom, they took trains from the San Paolo station to Ostia where boys rode the beach, past the rows of bathing huts, in pale sunshine, on motor-bikes. Boys in vests and cut-downs looked at Brigita and Marek.

As they sat on the beach one fine afternoon they heard a worrisome noise, like the sound of a foghorn, from way out at sea.

Sometimes now there was a Saturday night dance, on a wooden platform under poplar trees, near their house, boys standing around in peach jackets and ties of peacock-green and malachite.

Marek now wore ties for their visits to Rome – a tie with ladybirds on it, a tie with pink elephants in blue dungarees, an orange tie with mushrooms which had sequinned tops.

Both of them holding on to the handrail of a bus which was going along by the Tiber, she in a tangerine velour turban hat, he kissed her, the water low and showing the white river walls.

She left him for a few days to go to Taormina with a German lover and a photograph of her appeared in a movie magazine, buried up to her breasts in sand.

One weekend, excerpts from Puccini were shown on a screen in the open air on the Piazza Farnese – Madame Butterfly, her hair like the inside of a kiwi fruit, giving her son the USA flag and a doll as she blindfolds him; the end of 'Tosca' – the shooting by firing squad of Mario Cavarodossi, and Tosca jumping off the ramparts of the Castle Sant' Angelo with a view of the Vatican in the distance.

Marek wore ribbed vests now and had a GI haircut.

They'd take a *passeggiata* in the evenings under the apricot trees on the Via Calatafimi, she wearing a muslin dress and he always changing for this to an American summer shirt with copper or gold or Rembrandt brown in it.

Come April, there was an ensemble of little boys, who'd just made their Holy Communion, in the woods, in cocoa-coloured suits, turned-up collars, scarlet dicky bows, rosaries on their sleeves.

Then she left, back to Munich for an assignment.

He didn't want to be without her, he was raggedly tall for his age and he followed her, never to return here.

In Munich, twelve years old, he accompanied her to film parties in ties with ringed planets on them and coral-red ties with yellow prisms.

'*Wessen Sohn? Wessen Tochter bist du?*' Dancing under strobe lights, the first marijuana.

His mother saw that he was growing up too early and in the autumn he was sent to a boarding-school in Bavaria where he spent two years before being sent to school in the West of Ireland.

4 October, Feast of St Francis, he started.

In the West of Ireland school, in a composition book, he wrote an essay about a Christmas fair in Bavaria, a carousel of real ponies with faux-ermine-looking fur, a roundabout of ladybirds, Bavarian men in romper suits and fedora hats dancing in a tent robbed by the Nazis from a Dutch seaside resort – a pink baldaquin, *Jugendstil* mirrors at the side – and a flame-thrower throwing up a torch which was reflected in all the mirrors.

Mimi e tanto malata.

Before she died she saw water rising on Atlantis.

She remembered the scene of a terrorist bomb during a Puccini opera.

Her face looked like a Georges de la Tour face, a beautiful face cracking into pieces.

'The glamorous years, the movies, the talk, the drink, the forgetting. A horrible marriage but a beautiful child. Mother and son. Like in a Renaissance painting. But this ikon could not save us, could not protect us. But there was a legend and our love and images will go on, through transference to the people whose elbows we touch, we alarm.'

The skull talked back from a mirror as in a Georges de la Tour painting.

Before he died he returned to Rome, an open-air dance.

The irrevocable arrow in Georges de la Tour's painting of St Sebastian.

Faldinova Triona.

Per il mil Marek, a bunch of geraniums, marigolds, mallow flowers, mimosa, auburn tickseed, purple Michaelmas daisies, poppies, goldenrod, mauve and white delphiniums.

'We're fellow travellers,' a boy at the Greyhound bus station in Saint Louis once said to me.

And I bear his words in mind as I travel by train between Siena and Florence six years later, sticking my head out of the window to look at azure and billowy mountains meeting a surf of evening cloud.

Autumn 1973 I got drunk in a cemetery in Florence, by a block of flats, and then started hitchhiking south through Etruria.

On the coast a row of horse-drawn wagons with grape-kegs on them went over low water in a bay.

One evening I stayed in a youth hostel in a town where all the shutters were green and where young men in high stockings and very brief shorts were playing soccer on a pitch beside a row of parasol pines and plane trees which shaded some salmon-orange ruins.

There was a picture of John XXIII in the hallway, a yellow basin with a tap above it, and an American boy with great deltoids, in shorts, rucksack on his back, walked in, beaming, while I was there.

I was alone in a small dormitory when a boy in a T-shirt with Popeye on it walked in in his underpants. He had Jesuitical black hair, with slight crowsfeet, black stubble on his face. He took off his T-shirt, sat on a bed and looked at me with a suggestion. He sat there like that until I made the first move, going over to him. We started kissing. He had a small, pointed, Italian mouth. There was a mistletoe of hairs around his dark nipples. He held his mouth to the corns of my nipples as if waiting for a sensual land to be awakened – what was being illuminated in me was Grafton Street, the tides of inquisitive shoppers, a picture of an azure Chartres Cathedral above apple blossom at the corner of Westmoreland Street and D'Olier Street – I wanted to deflect some inhibition – the scene changed on Grafton Street and they were nineteen-forties people, a cinema queue outside the Grafton Cinema, a hugely hatted garda directing charcoal-fuelled cars – I touched the boy's hard pectorals as I'd touched the statue of David on the Piazzale Michelangelo in Florence – I called up an image of love-making, boy, boy, girl – his eyes were the turquoise of those Etruscan bays – I wanted to cross some border into sensuality land, and to make this transition I had to forget the country I was from and start again without a country – but country was too logged in me – a group of young people lingered outside the Golden Spoon on Grafton Street, one of the girls in a mahogany fur coat, a flock of gulls making a sea-scene – and the inhibition wouldn't go and there was a noise in the corridor and he flitted away.

I return to Ireland now; I travel by trains, buses and I feel: someone tried to beat me with crowbars here, someone tried to do me in.

I pass landscapes where the bog-cotton is gleaming snow on dark bogs, beds of meringue and I try to put the pieces together, I feel the proximity of the assassin again and I try to determine the motives for the cruelty.

I go into a pub where the mirrors are back-painted, flashed or inscribed with encaustic designs. Carved griffins, lions, basilisks on top of an alcove are silhouetted against streams of blue light like griffins, lions, basilisks in a cathedral. Cerulean cigarette smoke rises against stained-glass windows and the chatter is merry. Young people in denim are reflected in the glass of alcoves which is painted with sprigs of white hawthorn, families of tomtits on twigs, lilies on rivers beside round towers, cornucopias. Cherries are ribboned into the tiles by the wainscot and nude tallow infants gather Indian-red apples on a back-painted mirror. There are rucksacks lying against columns of carved fir cones. Sugar and tea are sold beside the liquor.

In Cork city Our Lady of Fatima stands in the train station, hands outstretched.

In Derry a party of mongoloid women wait for an Ulster bus and one of them shows me her photograph album – holidays in Portsallin, a photograph in cat's-eye glasses, bouffant hair-do against St Columba's Cathedral. She wears ceramic ear-rings with hearts in them.

'Through a glass darkly . . .' What am I looking for? Maybe a face. The face of a boy I knew who committed suicide a long time ago, Cherokee hair, big bones, an elegance of stance.

Once I met him on the street and he said, 'In our school they put penises up backsides. It's lovely.' He went to school in the East of Ireland and I pass that coast by train, water on either side, a field of rape in evening shadow.

It's like peeling layers and layers of plaster off a wound to see what you find at the bottom of it.

It's like putting piece upon piece of a stained-glass window together.

I go into a pub and there's a boy in shadow at the door. Maybe it's him.

Then I go to a seashore with an oblong whitewashed church nearby, electricity windmills on a hill – propellers on huge rods – and I pick up a cuckoo flower and examine the colour as if it's human.

Going to Eastern Europe was like looking through those tubes you got as a child in the stores that sold jelly crocodiles and dolly mixture and tins of peaches, and seeing at the end – an illumination beyond the loneliness, the greyness – coloured constellations.

'And I, the writer, was there twice, always for five consecutive days and saw the wonderful things, not only with the planets but also with the fixed stars.'

When a friend went away to the city when I was ten he sometimes wrote letters to describe the city. Russian logs in Thompsons on the Tivoli. The exotic variety of the mental patients at St Mary's Asylum. Cartoon faces on the borders of the letters. Then I started going to the city, trips to see films in the Astor on Eden Quay. A few weeks before I went to France with the veterinary student and saw the Georges de la Tours in 1972 I went north with her, hitchhiking around.

Orangemen were crossing Craigavon Bridge in Derry, in tartan kilts. We stayed in a house on Lough Swilly and next day on Fahan Strand I went for a swim while the girl and an English boy watched. Afterwards we had a conversation on the beach. I hesitatingly touched him to make a point and he said, in front of the girl, 'Touch me. Don't be afraid to touch me.'

Before I left Ireland in 1977 I sat with a witch who had a Marie Antoinette hair-do in Wexford. 'It's the light. The inner light,' she said. 'If you've got it you'll come through. Some people fake it. It's a continuity. It's going back, been there for a long time.'

Afterwards I walked on Curracloe Strand, wild nasturtiums at the side of it. Nowhere did you see the light going more quickly in some people than in Berlin. Girls with cocker-spaniel red hair who used to smile, beam, before the Wall came down, glared, were horrible-mannered a few years after the Wall was gone.

Nowhere did you see the continuity more either, old people with forever chapped hands selling their bits and pieces on a carpet outside a supermarket, before moving on to a new address.

Berlin 1945, ruined buildings and smoke, a few old people over a stove frying potatoes in a pan, their bits and pieces in bags beside them.

The light breaks through and connects the bits and pieces and makes a glass window in a lonely church.

'We were nonconformists,' Mr Haythornthwaite told me of his childhood.

He came to Ireland looking for his childhood. He would show you blue-eyed Marys and wood sorrel in April, wood garlic and the campion flower in May, purple loosestrife on river banks in June, balsam, woundwort by streams, the bush of St John's wort in the bog, the bogbean flower, white ladies' mantle, yellow mignonette, the deep purple, violet, dun-purple Abraham, Isaac and Jacob. He could tell you how the grass of Parnassus which he saw in the mountains of North Connemara in the twenties also grew in the marshes in Northern Russia. He was forever walking around in a cap and an old manky coat, slightly bent, identifying flowers, looking very serious.

He would cycle to ruined monasteries, Gothic windows outlined against the sky, he in his braces and his honey-brown check shirt stopping to touch hedge woundwort, snapdragon, wild carrot, wild strawberry, storksbill, bilberry.

In the alcove of the guesthouse where he stayed he usually wore herring-bone tweed and mackerel jackets, even on fine days. It was the guesthouse where the American soldier had stayed. It was as if there was still the pubescent, American smell of the soldier from the couch and the armchairs which were the beige colour of a Martin de Porres face.

We were standing at the window of the guesthouse one day when a shadow passed. It was the boy from the country in a shirt and a black polo neck. I went out to greet him but he'd disappeared. His visits to town were rare, as he boarded in the east.

Whereas once there'd been stories, television had come to the alcove by then: Julie Felix singing; a black boy, in woollen cap and donkey jacket, by a moat under a cotton mill in Georgia.

I went to visit him in his room in the Midlands of England in 1974. Women with Barbara Windsor beehive hair-dos went by on the street outside. He played Grieg's 'Solveig's Song' and his 'Gjendine's Lullaby' for me. Nearby was the office-block-looking school of which he was headmaster in his last years as a teacher.

Four years later, on a day of a great rainbow, I came with daffodils for his grave.

'It's a strange world I see now. Life is cheap. Yesterday's death in Coleraine will be a one-day wonder.

Television had killed conversation in bars. Another change is that the town had become car-conscious. I think Mr Cunniffe and I were the only two left who cycled to our fishing. We found a bunch of yellow forget-me-nots one day as we cycled to the bog.

In spite of everything I think of you often, and picture the street. My eyesight lets me down nowadays, but maybe it will improve. They can't take away the days we had.'

Norway in the twenties, staying for consecutive summers in a place called Beverdalen, swimming in a lake during the days and a sauna at nights, open-air dances, the music of the Hardanger fiddle.

In November 1986 I stood at the harbour in Skien with my writer friend's son, mallards on the water, lots of summer yachts in dock.

Mr Haythornthwaite found Ireland after Norway.

For a few decades he taught in Chester. He had a beloved, and used to go to Chester races with her each year. Then he returned to teach in the village he came from. But Ireland had become his continuity and then someone, at the beginning of the Troubles, said something horrible to him in a pub and he never came back.

His bullet head, iron and cream, that bar moustache, fleeced red nose, he in an electric-blue jersey, against the council houses when I went to visit him.

'It's the autumn of my life, and I feel like an autumn narcissus,' he said.

Outside, boys with sculpted crotches stood against mustard, straw, pineapple colours.

When I hitchhiked to his grave I'd moved from Ireland to England. I went to the house of his niece after I left the graveyard. There was a Mediterranean rock rose outside and holographic glass over the door. She and her daughter Dyala let me in. Just inside the door was a coronation picture of George and Mary in 1937. She showed me a photograph of herself and Mr Haythornthwaite in Weston-super-Mare the summer before he died.

In a room with Staffordshire spaniels and miaowing ceramic cats there was a collection of pen and ink sketches I'd done as an adolescent – he in a coat and cap by the bog river, donkeys by the bog river, the grove which hid the bush of St John's wort, turf stacks, a gabled house with a bush of fuschia outside on the edge of the bog.

In the local church was a statue of Our Lady of Walsingham with a three-pronged crown, curled at the ends like Arabian slippers.

I stopped in the Venus Café before hitchhiking back. Baked jam roll and custard.

The Baptists, Quakers, Seekers, Levellers, Ranters still lived in London at that time.

When I got back to my room in Shepherds Bush I was already packing to go to the United States.

'My love is like a red, red rose.'

I met a boy once from his village, by the Thames. A beggar boy. He'd gone back to a wedding in the village, disguised as a soldier, and no one recognized him.

In Derry on Craigavon Bridge I pass a young British soldier with Spartan features. It is a day of rainbows on the Foyle, over the ruin of a huge mill. I smile and he smiles and I wish him safety and I think of Mr Haythornthwaite for no particular reason.

Walking down Gerard Doustraat in late September, a yellow tram pulling up against weeping willows, children, one of them in a white tie-wig, pink lamé horns, pink lamé jabot, I turned around and for the first time in years clearly saw the alcove of the guesthouse with the young American soldier in it. This new city summons him, tie of Indian-red, cornflower blue braces, ears that looped out like Mickey Mouse's.

When lessons were done, you'd go down to Rosie's and Gracie's, pull the key on a brown string through the vertical letter slit, let yourself in, run through the dining-room with a picture of the Lakes of Killarney on the wall as though painted in greasepaint, the work of a passing player, sit in the alcove reeking of turf fire, tobacco gutted from an English fisherman's pipe, the young American soldier maybe there, a tie of downward spilt colour on him, half of it duck-egg blue.

So Amsterdam always became associated with the soldier; when a plane went into a tower block there I thought of him and wondered where he was.

The Broken Tower. The Tarot card of change.

A tram pulls away, with heads lighted against the night.

A girl greets us in her dressing-gown, fur mice on her slippers. We last saw her in North Connemara.

I need you now, soldier. I feel you saw something horrible and came through. I see you, in geranium trunks, looking at me as you sit by the river. Words and phrases help to keep your image before me. Tennessee. Roll Cut tobacco. Image is carried to image. You are handling a marmalade-coloured ten-shilling note, in a nicotine-stain yellow shirt, chinos, canvas shoes, in a grocery-shop-cum-pub, reflected on a mirror back-painted with sunflowers. To get to you I've got to get rid of so much of the horrible education we were given. Like Mr Haythornthwaite, who threw away what he taught at school and was taught by flowers.

Going into a new city, on a street in autumn, it's your face in a tram, lighted up against a window, and the trams in the cities, gold and persimmon and pink ochre, become telegrams to one another, all connecting up a search for a face – a talisman against attack.

A boy from the back-streets of Dublin, stubble on his face, was your face for a while.

A Cockney student in London. Aged sixteen and already married.

A backpainted and gilded mirror in an Irish pub now throws back faces that could be one I'm looking for, a smoke, an explosion of rain outside.

'Aye. Oh aye,' a boy says in the pub lavatory.

A flashed pub mirror – ruby, blue – in a London Irish pub and a song, 'If These Lips Could Only Speak' sung by Bridie Gallagher, brings the journey to its beginning, and it's the soldier's face in a backpainted mirror, Tab Hunter's slightly mosaic face, Venetian blond hair, forever hurt awryness.

Miss Mackassey who taught us at convent school played Mrs Massingham in *Gaslight* in a crimson cord dress and Princess Margaret in *The Student Prince*, sitting with a parasol, in a picture hat, in the Royal Palace of Karlsberg. She got cancer and just after she was told she had it she ordered all of us children to leave the classroom for half an hour. When we returned there was a tableau in chalk on the blackboard, all colours, of the fair – tinkers, horses, caravans, down to the embossments of horses on the caravans – one detail connecting up with another detail, each detail separate in itself, a rung in the journey, the travail, the bravery towards an overall effect.

And so the journey continues. As the train leaves the station Marek slips into a coma. There are cakes freckled with sugar in a booth. The cake boxes have dandelions and orange and blue spider flowers on them. Bottles of lemonade and jars of pickled kohlrabi and beetroot are also sold. A little girl dressed for winter stands on the platform, red hat, coat, trousers, wellingtons. A small boy beside her. Near them a gipsy woman in a flounced red dress, gold bracelets on her wrists. A Red Army man carrying Vecchia Romagna. A boy with an outspread eagle on his belt. A tall boy who looks like Marek.

A bayan playing as we cross a border into Latvia and even now, long before we get to Leningrad – where there will be ghosts in the midsummer light, women in their loveliest dresses, dresses with marigolds on black, bees on bold, doves with outspread wings, red beaks and feet, on green, like the transfers you got in lucky bags as a child and put on white paper – the exhalation of the night-time but still illumined pine forest in the carriage, the dead are resurrected, the boys of the West of Ireland – a teacher from Athlone who killed himself, a student of psychiatry with Cherokee hair who took rat poison, boys who went into the annihilation of England.

Prague, 12 August 1987. An old man in a Homburg hat, a medal of John of Nepomuk on it, crocodile skin shoes on him, feeds doves on his lap on Celetna Street. A boy with a skateboard, marigolds and horseshoes underneath it, on one side of the bench to him and on the other a girl in a blouse with red lips with red roses in them on spring green who looks on. A boy comes out of the building in which there is a vegetarian restaurant. He is very tall, wears shorts, red shower sandals. His hair is the colour of ichor. He is about seventeen. He stands and looks to his right for a moment.

The first day I arrived in Prague there was a poster of Goya's *Miguel de Lardiz-Abal* everywhere, a man with his left hand missing and a letter in his other hand saying *'Expulsis'*, there were plastic tubs of ice-cream with viridian juice running through them in the windows, there were creamy cakes with chocolate papal hats called Budapest. I'd known for a long time I had to get to Prague. I knew that I came from a cruel and hypocritical and unrelenting country. No matter what, they'd be right. I knew that there was an imminent madness, an imminent breakdown in me and I knew I had to get there before it happened. 'You've lost your soul,' a voice on Wenceslas Square whispered. Crossing meadows with cinnabar-red poppies spotted on them, towards the high-rise building in which I was going to stay, I looked around and saw the child I could have had, who would have been my companion now. I could see the child I'd once been. I saw the grief and loneliness of the Irish in Britain. I knew there were bits and pieces I had to gather, to make sense of, not just for myself but for them. I looked towards the country of childhood when I'd had a soul and realized it was possible to get souls back, but only through long journeys, inner and maybe outer.

I could see my own cruelty, hypocrisy. It wasn't a matter of making amends, but of chanelling these things, turning them to good.

I saw another country besides London, the Irish in England, a place where souls were redeemable.

There had been trees once beside the British Legion hut and they'd been cut down. I could shield myself here in Prague. I could be alone here for a while. They wouldn't be able to get me here.

What are you running from? Don't know. But I just run and run, looking for a place of safety.

I keep thinking of my aunt who died, out of place in the family, of a broken heart.

Berlin, 27 March 1992. Sitting in Krzysztof's flat in Kreuzberg in the evening. He wears a blue denim shirt. Turkish boys, in Spanish high heels, with their shirts hanging out, do up their quiffs outside. Turkish men, in brown suits and pebbled ties, stand in clusters. A woman in chador goes by in a temper, holding a bottle of champagne. A boy rides a green stick, red diamonds along it, with a buffalo's head at the top. The lady in Edwardian costume goes by with her hurdy-gurdy drawn by a donkey in socks, daffodils in his ears, the hurdy-gurdy playing Franz Lehar's 'O Signorina. O Signorina'.

Kyzysztof tells me how his father, a teenage Nazi soldier, was captured by a Jewish resistance worker in the forest in Eastern Holland at the very end of the war and let free, allowed to run back into the woods.

Tonight is a night of tranquility, yellow mimosa on the table.

Maybe Krzysztof's face, slightly simpleton and dimpled, is the face of the young American soldier.

You see them all over the world, children of fifties Ireland. People with memories of *Ireland's Own*, who had their knuckles rapped with rulers by Polish-looking piano teachers as trains went through marshy fields outside, who were canvassed for the Boy Scouts. Nervous squirrels. Not really welcome where they go. Pulling back a curtain of rich crimson and entering a pub at the base of a tall building. Eating marzipan cake shaped as a banana on a podium in a frugal Northern café with grill windows on a snowy day. Stealing down cramped medieval streets of steely houses with front gables, each house with a copy of the September bible. These flights into Egypt come from a reason. They saw something which unfits them to live in the society they come from. Sometimes at night, by a canal in a Northern city, a Lutheran clocktower over a lock, they hear it again, *Lives of the Caesars* on the radio and their own screams at night when at the age of twelve they'd go to a window to throw themselves out. On these flights you sometimes meet a kind person, as Nadezhda Mandelstam says. The silhouette of Prague Castle against embers in the sky maybe. As often as not you don't recognize them, because you've become so distrustful of people and of yourself. But you learn that you've got to allow yourself to be humiliated again and again until you discover the kind person, until you make contact with them. In Dublin once a boy gave me a Mexican shirt, oyster white, indigo-blue patterns, oval bone buttons and it became a symbol of the city's possibilities. Each new city was a prospective new shirt, a transcendence, a conquering of the pain, but in each transcendence – a red-haired woman looking at you in London, a candle burning on two embracing Cupids in Paris, a restaurant in Rome with fishnets on the wall which gave bills of yellow with burgundy lines – what was most beautiful about the place you came from: the gabled country houses with their hoards of faience, the eskars crossing the country, the boys with faces subverted by Spanish looks.

France 1968, a Sunday afternoon car journey with a French family in the lashing rain. Suddenly I notice the place name. Avon.

'A le cimitière! A le cimetière!'

There in the Protestant cemetery, in the rain, a small flowerpot on the grave, was Katherine Mansfield's grave. I dislodged the mud on the inscription. A woman in a jaundiced coat looked on.

'But I tell you my lord fool, out of this nettle, danger, we pluck this flower, safety.'

On trips to Dublin with my mother in the sixties we'd always stop at Westland Row Church before getting the train back West from the nearby station, and once for some reason, on the church steps, she looked down the street, in the opposite direction to the station, to 21 Westland Row, the birthplace of Oscar Wilde. She may have been in a crenellated sultan's hat, a sponge hat with tinsel-thin jetties, an ombré fungus hat, a fur hat – cream and grey in turn, a striped woollen hat with a beard around it, a mosaic hat of chocolate-coloured coins – two wings at the back, a coffee trellis hat with rhinestones in it, she may have been in pumps or she may have been in many strapped white sandals, she was carrying two handbags.

For one moment these two Irish lives joined up.

She who'd lost sisters as a child, later on a stepsister and brother, later on again another sister, who'd married and gone West.

He who was jailed, reviled on Clapham Junction for half an hour, who was banished from home and children.

There he is beside Lord Alfred Douglas, he standing, Lord Alfred seated, slightly bowed head, sculpted face – a West of Ireland face – in a school straw, a flash on his delicate high heel, grass at the bottom of the bench like wolf's fur.

With the veterinary student from Dublin I went to Oscar Wilde's grave in Père Lachaise. I revisited it later, the autumn you left me, young people with algal hair strumming guitars among grave lighters by Jim Morrison's grave which was a cloud of graffiti.

And afterwards I walked the city, which smelt of *pissoirs* and wine, and remembered the *Jugendstil* decor of certain Dublin houses – damascened orchids on sofa covers – and ended up somehow in Gare St Lazare where some Irish nuns in madonna blue and stork white had got caught up among the prostitutes who smelt of violets.

What Oscar Wilde did not know when he died was that his *Salome* would be produced with tumultuous success by Max Reinhardt in Berlin in September 1903, in the Neues Theater, with Gertrud Eysoldt.

It is raining in Paris. Today I saw the Ingres in the Louvre, encrusted flowers on the tarboosh of a naked Turkish woman, braids of colour on the snood of a naked woman, a naked woman holding a curtain with fleur-de-lys-on it, jet dashes on ermine, geometric designs on a carpet. I also saw, elsewhere, Rodin's *La Pensée*, a woman's bonneted, fine-featured head in white marble.

There is a sense of lives and lives of exile about this, the first city I have visited after Dublin, the paces of other people's exile, cities, streets of exile.

In Berlin tonight a young boy stood in the rain dressed as a ghost against a mauve light, all white, Ku-Klux-Klan type hood on him, white face, a red rose in his hand.

So it ends, this concordance of Ireland and Eastern Europe. It is my piece of paper under a cairn of stones in the Old Jewish Cemetery in Prague, among the messages on salmon-coloured Munich bus tickets.

The Polish lady stands outside the cinema, primrose hair, in a black suit and a scarf with cornflowers and wild strawberries on it, in solidarity with her people. The black and white stills in the case show beautiful young Polish people among war ruins. In the fair green beside the cinema a girl with a bouffant hair-do, home on holiday from England, sits in the grass with her English husband, who has a crescent of hair over his forehead, and their baby. The girl makes a daisy chain. Two old people are crossing the meandering path through the green. They become a Polish couple before the war – a man with firewood tied to a board on his back, a woman in a scarf with a pitcher in one arm and a basket of fruit in the other hand. The Polish woman has the solemnity about her of Polish women saying the rosary in unison in a church, in Berlin, standing for parts of it, kneeling for parts of it.

Anyone who came to know Berlin in these years will feel what she is remembering – Auschwitz, Birkenau, Treblinka – wounds that opened again when the Schlager music had died down and when the holidays to islands in Yugoslavia had receded, calamities imparted but never really acknowledged, things that old ladies over *poffertjis* in cafés in Amsterdam will tell you about late in the evening, when the street outside is in copper flame, and Leonard Cohen is singing 'Hey That's No Way to Say Goodbye' on the juke-box which is crimson and yellow and sky-blue and mauve.

'Once hit by it you are haunted forever.'

There are other things you are haunted by now, that have slipped between you and the horrible memories, that is a force, a mystery more fixating, the beautiful legacy, the creative travail of lives which are over.

One of the Christmases when Marek was going to school in Bavaria he spent with his mother in Lisbon.

She'd just purchased the house in the Algarve and she met up with him there.

It is the morning of the day after Christmas and they walk the streets of Bairro Alto. Nothing really stops in Lisbon at

Christmas. The boys in singlets had sat early morning on the steps of the cinemas on Avenida da Liberdade, shoes alongside them, their heads on their laps.

She wears black Cossack trousers, he's in a black bomber jacket.

'After the war I had a little bald Dixie doll with a bowed head given to me by a soldier called Buck from Opelika, Alabama, and I always dressed up to hold him, put on long white stockings, a dress with a lace ruff, because he looked so *höflich*.'

'My mother used to put on a snood every morning for her Easter egg factory and people mistook her for a nun and often told her on the street how proud they'd been during Nazi times of Cardinal von Galen – Löwe von Munster.'

A priest in a black cardinal hat, cassock, black coat, patina-thin shoes, carrying an umbrella, passes and bows to them.

Shoe-shining shops are open with men in ripple-flap-fronted shoes on a dais.

A little girl holds a lemon umbrella.

A gipsy girl with gold hoops in her ears, in a flounced red dress and incongruous black canvas shoes with sequinned garlands on them, stands against a wall.

A man in black on a stool holds a baby.

The bakeries on Rua San Pedro de Alcantara are selling *bolo rei* – a barmbrack with crystallized cherries and pineapple and a surprise. The manager in a café with a sign in the window – '*Seja feliz enquanto esta vivo, porque voce vai passar muito tempo morto.*' ('Stay happy while you're alive because you'll be dead long enough.') – tells them that the surprise will be a good hiding. They also have, in this café, to celebrate Christmas, cocktails of fruit slices on custard and chocolate Swiss roll, sequinned on top.

On Rua da Escol Politecnica they can see the whole city, with its yellow trams, and the Sandeman and Brandy Constantino advertisements alight on Praca de Pedro IV although it's daytime.

On the opposite side of the street to the panorama opening,

on a street corner, is a mural of Francesco, Jacintha, Lucia having their vision.

The Mother of God intercepting the world.

When Brigita had been to Fatima she knew it could not have been in the basilica – it was too dull and ugly – but then she found the small church and thought here, it was surely here, it has the feeling.

Perhaps that's what life is all about, we should hold out for the visions. When we have a breakdown just wait, nothing more visionary than another person's compassion.

'He called God compassion,' she says about Buck, who returned to visit them in the nineteen-fifties when he had a wife and children.

The sound of a *fado* comes from the bar, one male voice singing part of it, another male voice answering, accordion music.

In Marek's mind a train of people on a beach north of Lisbon pulling fishing nets from the sea at evening.

The bayan plays on the Leningrad train as Marek goes to sleep forever. A boy-musician, shirt off, beside an urn-like jar of apricot juice. Streams and streams of azure lupins go by the edges of forests. Juniper bushes. Meadows of rape which push back the forest. A little boy, ship with sanguine sails and underneath it a sea-dragon on his dungarees, sleeps on his father's lap while a little girl with black-cherry curls smooths the little boy's hair, chinks in her sandals.

You in trousers like rainfall, sandals with a cross bar, a bar down the middle, chinks on front.

Many of the ladies who peep in while passing the door have tabs of faux leopardskin somewhere on their garments.

A boy on a railway platform in Ireland, petunias on the platform. Maybe it's you. In a white shirt. Maybe it's the boy who killed himself. In a black T-shirt and trousers of dog's-tooth check. The boy becomes a woman and it's your aunt. She had a Sephardic expression and wears a coffee-coloured summer dress. A chorus of girls stand on the railway bridge.

Your aunt smells of old photographs taken in studios in Mullingar and from the canal there's a smell of waterlilies, which look like blowsy madonnas.

Times and people merge now, and fact and fiction cross in the Russian midsummer, become indistinguishable from one another, in one sentinel moment.

It's things, people, coming into a consciousness of themselves, and it's East European and Irish worlds bordering on one another and it's people normally denigrated given a chance, and there's a touching, an abrasion with a consciousness which has just passed out of life.

He knew your country, the West of your country, but now the train goes through the mirror and it passes through the East of your country. Sycamores, horse-chestnuts, copper beeches. Rock in the fields like pearl seed. Walls which are testaments to landlords. Eskars which beckon you on a journey. Gabled houses. Crofters' cottages. A distant friary. Forever lolling piebald horses.

The train stops at a small station and there's a woman in a black silk blouse with lapis lazuli hanging from her neck.

Her son gets off the train. They embrace. It's the boy who committed suicide. He stares at me now from a curvilinear mirror in which the meadow behind him changes into Russian grass with scarlet bellflowers.

The evil is always inside you. What you're running from. You've got to deal with that.

The husbands of those women who were abused in the town I came from; they had their own vulnerability. It was a clash of opposites, those marriages, marriages which destroyed the women.

You brought venom in Dublin on yourself by carelessness with other people's emotions, a clash with sedentary people, people who were content and happy to stay there.

Marek and Brigita, they killed one another.

'Yet each man kills the thing he loves.'

But I know, despite all my contumelies, there's still the child, although the child has become a counter-sign in new cities with new shades of tram.

You used to take the train to Dublin as an adolescent, and when it touched the outskirts of Dublin, Ballyfermot, the council houses, everything, became Russian.

You'd dawdle on winter nights over the Liffey, wanting to be approved by the lights on the water, poppy, lemon, blue-mauve, magenta.

One winter night outside a shop on Eden Quay you saw daffodils, hothouse daffodils, blanched scrolls around their necks, lime in their youthful heads, and you became excited. They made you think of Russia. The Russian spring after the Russian winter. A tram going through Moscow, a man about to die, a woman in a cornflower dress walking alongside the tram. 'He thought of several people whose lives run parallel and close together but at different speeds . . . ' That was the half sentence which had stayed in your head.

You felt at one with people in Eastern Europe whose lives were running parallel to one another like different coloured trams and that killed the loneliness.

The boy in the polka-dot carrot shirt who'd been playing an accordion on O'Connell Bridge became an ikon.

The woman in the shop in the Legion of Mary blue coat, with red cheeks and ebony perm, looked at you as if you were daft.

Bridget was your friend then, though you were forbidden to see her, but you telegrammed emotions telepathically to her and she to you. You told her in this way about what you were looking at.

She'd pushed a note through your door to say goodbye, a print of lilacs on the top of it and the paper slightly perfumed.

That perfume became the whiff of daffodils now.

Daniel was also your friend, but he'd withdrawn from school and was about to go to England in a kerchief.

One Christmas as a child he stood in a blue denim suit on

four tables thrown together as a stage in the National School and sang 'Mary's Boy Child.'

Something about these boys of the West of Ireland was altogether different. It was another country, the West of Ireland. The generosity was so tantamount and the capacity for pain sometimes unendurable – there were many victims. Maybe their romanticism was not compatible with the world.

Each lap of the journey has been like something passed on from one person to another, a message, a secret, an ultimatum – a boy in smoke-blue and a cinnabar-red kerchief going down a road by a melted blue bog in 1967.

It's as though I had to go on this journey to see my own sins. It's as though I had to go on this journey in order to know that the romanticism we grew up with was truthful, that there is a home for it.

In a tailor's shop on Hauptstrasse in Berlin I once saw a poem on the wall by Nelly Sachs about moving. The Berliner who moved to another country and never came back.

'It's not where I thought I'd end up,' Mr Haythornthwaite said. 'On a street of council houses.'

'Yes, but we make lands out of these places.'

The stories come like the sound of a bayan, they come in bits and pieces, you make your own sense out of them.

When I went with my storyteller friend from North Connemara on a pilgrimage to Fatima we were on a wild beach north of Caiscais one day when I said I wanted to go for a swim. I did not have my togs so she removed her prune-purple panties and I went swimming in them, they falling around my loins.

In Berlin I read how during the Second World War Russian soldiers on the front had carried poems by Akhmatova and Pasternak on scraps of paper.

'For now we see through a glass darkly . . .' When I go to Ireland now, on sea-fronts I go into arcades with games machines and snooker tables, where people drink from styrofoam cups, and sometimes there is a room with distorting mirrors. It's as though I'm going through one of those mirrors now and meeting the victims and asking: What happened? Why?

In Leningrad there are games rooms with chandeliers made up of little banana shapes, swans and horses on which children can ride, murals on the walls of pig majorettes.

When you were being washed out to sea in Cornwall it was that landscape which redeemed the sea, East Galway, its Irish dancing green. The boys from that landscape who'd died, been murdered in a way, made me live.

'Child of the fifties, I was very much in love with life. But I failed psychiatry at UCD, and despite the fact that I was very beautiful I didn't have a girlfriend, there was no prospect of a girlfriend, and they made me feel a failure, a eunuch. I did not fit into chauvinism, into categories. It was the pressure on me, like a bombardment.'

For three years Leningrad was bombarded, people queued for twelve hours for food, they ate bread which tasted of kerosene, they burned books for fuel, in summer they ate wild herbs and grass.

I walk along sea-fronts in Ireland on sunny days, promenades on which my parents and I were photographed against Bradmola and Dundyl and Go-Ray advertisements. I always feel on the other side of a glass here.

Two photographs of Mr Haythornthwaite and his beloved on sea-fronts. One on the promenade at Cliftonville, she in a dress with horses and striped riding jackets framed in straps on it. Another on the promenade at Burnham-on-Sea, she in a dress with men in tricorn hats on it and Venetian palaces. Two photographs. Only two or three mentions of her.

A local girl aged forty, walking along Salthill promenade in 1959, with a young actor from the travelling players with whom she was having an affair. She's in black and white penguin shoes and a dress with wine leaves on yellow and he, holding her hand, is in a khaki shirt, chinos, loafers.

In Leningrad pink candyfloss is dispensed in a games arcade. There are holes in the faces of a man gobbling spaghetti and a frumpish waitress in a mini outfit bringing him a fresh supply where you can have your photograph taken. A woman is reading a UFO magazine over a counter display of prizes – a pink pig with white hair playing a bayan, a pig lewdly offering its udders to piglets, bears running a coal train, an ape eating a banana, Michelangelo's David, but he's grinning, a coach drawn by prancing meringue horses, David's Napoleon, a plain-looking fifties type bus, a clock with ears of doves, a whale with big round eyes and its tail in the air.

On a newspaper stall on the street is a jar of anemones and pink roses and gilia with a ruff of cake paper. Above the flowers is a picture of a woman, black-haired with a fringe, lonely-faced, in a floral dress.

A guesthouse with bay windows near the sea in Ireland is called Yorkland House and has gleaming purple rock flowers on the walls.

'Gudgie. Gudgie. Gudgie,' a woman in a dress of red pomegranate flowers bends over the go-cart and starts tickling you.

A woman sits on a bench by the sea now in a dress with gift boxes on it, the lids orbiting around the boxes, telling her rosary on green perspex beads.

The stucco streamers over the houses are painted red now.

Where did the unhappiness begin, mental illness set in?

But Salthill, August 1954, my parents' faces have a loveliness. Those faces don't seem made to be hurt by life. My mother smiles, the camera catches her smiling right on against advertisements for Max Factor of Hollywood and Trebor sweets. Latin, almost out of place hair, cherry bow-lipped smile.

Truth to tell, she is an exile here in the West of Ireland, among a husband and children she mostly does not understand.

Leningrad tugs you back, it is seeing through the glass.

The yellow trams go by under the lime trees and sailors with blue and white striped Vs at their necks dawdle in little parks under the trees. Women in terracotta dresses with chamomiles on them sell kvass from barrels on the street.

In the churches, fluted vases of flowers on the ground, women stand beside ikons of the Mother and Child like Jewish people stand before the Wailing Wall.

Hotel Sancta Maria. Hotel Rio. Hotel Monterey. Beronda House.

In our house when our grandfather came to live a calendar arrived each year, always with the same picture, the basilica of St Anne de Beaupré by the St Lawrence River in Canada.

Down the river on the paddle steamer, a Breton accordion playing, flag with the maple on it flying, confessions on board, hay being turned and Canadian goldenrod growing by the sides of the river, to the cathedral in Montmorency County where we paint our votive pictures – paintings of thanksgiving – on the walls.

The whales going down the coast of Northern California, fall 1976.

On a road in Northern Alabama, faces of home-going football fans being lit by other cars, a woman hums 'May the circle be unbroken by and by Lord, by and by.'

In a room in Louisiana at Thanksgiving a boy in a tartan dicky bow, who'd been in a penitentiary, says grace, and then the Acadian accordion plays, a statue of Our Lady of Montserrat in the room with tiny cactus plants in front of her which have flowers on their heads, the sun going down over the bayous in divers colours.

At the burial of a boy in Swabia a youth plays an accordion, a Southern States song, 'Lord, Didn't He Ramble?'; brief life, AIDS death, but a life of divers colours.

The woman with the sherry-gold wig plays the accordion on Nevsky Prospekt, the V of a dress with sunflowers with red and blue centres through her coat, American flag on her lapel; people in brown alpaca converge on me; there is the smell in the air of the wild grasses people ate during the bombardment.

242

I see the boys of the West of Ireland, heavy-browed, black-haired. 'Many were good heroes, flame-like.'

In the Jazz Club there's a boy in a shirt and polo neck with black hair.

The gilt-edged mirror on the stairway catches the mosaic of a blond boy's face.

The woman sings, 'God, if you can't send me no woman, then send me a sissy man.'

The sun flashes on the mirror and you are walking along a beach in Southern California with Beck on a very blue day, knowing you had to create a new mosaic in yourself, a new country, a new language even.

A gilded and encaustic mirror in an Irish pub, a stag's head over the till, catches your parents August 1954. She's in a yellow blouse with white borders with roses on them, he with orange hair, not the mahogany-orange hair of his brothers. They leave the pub and go on their way in a *nunc dimittis* from the reflection of the sea in the mirror.

There is a bit of stained glass in the pub, and sunlight which has been withholding itself breaks through the opaqueness and the years are thrown into a radiance like a meadow of poppies in Prague after a thunderstorm, and there are cohesions between the bereftitudes and a sediment of totality like a row of orphaned, mainly coffee-coloured, Japanese plates on a wall, or like postcards on the wall which are poultices on a wound on the brain, or like the picture of the Cathedral of St Anne de Beaupré, or like stories which are grafts, lesions – or calls to new countries – on the brain, and the years converge on now.

The gilded and encaustic mirror catches you as you are now, you seem to be in one part of the pub and everybody else in another part.

When you played in *Oklahoma!* at school, Christmas 1966, and the show was over the last night and you were walking home, down the mud laneway, the rest of the actors were singing in the distance 'The Green, Green Grass of Home' and you felt like Berlin feels on 6 January when the Christmas trees are ritualistically dragged out and dumped.

That Christmas, the year your friendship with Bridget was broken up, Dublin became Leningrad, rescuing you, your dreams.

A boy with arctic flaxen hair and cobalt eyes in a rose-scarlet shirt snuggles against the pipes in the urinal under the Irish Life building on Burgh Quay.

On Burgh Quay is a café, with pink walls and a glass pillar of rippling water, which sells cakes with pink icing and fruit cocktail and ice-cream of lavender, and a woman with bobbed henna hair sits alone on one of the vermilion seats, gold knobs in front of her high heels.

In the window of a small maroon-buff-fronted socialist shop on Tara Street is a picture of the youthful Maud Gonne with jackdaw eyes.

'Keep on the right side of the shadows,' her look seems to say.

Beside a hall door is a palmist's sign with the diagram of a palm and there is a diagram of stars in the sky.

The accordion plays 'The Last Rose of Summer'.

I walk through the glass, but first encountering other phantoms by the Liffey – mirrors to your own desolation – and scribble on ghostly foolscap.

'October 1977. These days are recognition that you are gone. National Library, cycling, dinners. Mr Tambourine in the Coffee Inn. Goodbye.'

And there is in passage the screen, the shield, the translucence of another city, Prague – an interim, a meditation, a summons.

Gulls skim the jetties of light of the Liffey in sleek strides and they remember the tang, the narratives, the accordion music of the Liffey in the tremulous and mosaic-making midsummer light over the Fontanka Canal. Gounod's 'Ave Maria' sounds from one of the canal-side houses. The fanlights are those of Cork, of Dublin.

So Dublin would always stay Leningrad a bit, the Liffey, Tara Street flats, the little shop at the corner of Burgh Quay and Tara Street which is there to this day, the detritus of the colour lavender.

Leave something in Leningrad and you'll come back, throw a coin in the Neva or the Fontanka or the Obvodnogo or the Moyka.

In the upper window of a house an ebony-haired woman is looking out, the tattoo of a ladybird on the cup in her hand. She still has an Edwardian poise. She has been spat at. She has been abused like the women in my town were abused long ago. Her bags packed beside her, she is ready to move to another abode, another country even. But like a Georges de la Tour Madeleine at the flame she stares out now at the city whose rags and orphan walls have adhered to her.